Wings of Hope

Brenda Pethtel

Dedicated to my husband Doug; my partner in everything.

I must also express my heartfelt gratitude to my sister, Bug; this would all still be a dream without her.

Chapter 1

Ava ran as fast as her legs would carry her; the wind whipped her hair into a web of tangles. Her lungs ached from the exertion as if as if someone was sitting on her chest, yet she relentlessly pushed herself forward. She pumped her arms back and forth in a vain attempt to propel herself even faster, a slow burn commenced to spread throughout her limbs. This she could feel. This she could control. Running empowered her with the ability to put everything behind her like a road sign in a rearview mirror. It didn't matter how fast she ran or even the distance—focusing her concentration on this one minute task kept her grounded and saved her from oblivion.

She ran until she finally reached the steps of her house, ran in through the back door and shoved it closed behind her. She bent over and placed her hands on her knees trying to get her labored breathing under control. Catching her breath, she slumped down into one of the antique chairs at the kitchen table, the now dull white paint on its surface showing its age with chips and cracks. She looked out the window framed in faded gingham curtains to watch the sun as it slowly made its descent.

Ava had decided long ago that most people were either cruel or artificial. A lesson she was reminded of when school let out that day. As she walked down the front steps of the school, she'd overheard Olivia and her cronies poking fun at who wouldn't be asked to the fall formal. Ava was always ignored, but today for some reason it was different. Apparently, she was at the top of their list of 'losers'. This was unexpected and hearing their harsh comments about her hurt more than she would ever admit.

To avoid complete humiliation, she'd quickly tried to redirect her path so she wouldn't have to encounter the antagonists, but it was too late; they'd spotted her. The look of triumph on Olivia's face cut through Ava's resolve like butter…so she ran.

These unpleasant thoughts were soon interrupted when someone entered the kitchen.

"Why so serious little dove?"

At the sound of the familiar endearment, Ava looked up to see her Uncle Ignacious had entered the kitchen. His face, which was covered in wrinkles and his hair streaked with gray, was so familiar to her. He represented one of the constants in her life—a pillar of strength. She sighed and gave him a small smile.

"Ahhh…a smile—but given to ease the mind of an old man," he wagged his finger at her as if she were a child caught red handed in a fib, "but clearly he sees that it doesn't reach your eyes." He busied himself filling a copper kettle with water. Out of habit he started humming a gentle tune. Ava let the sound infuse her and attempted to relax and clear the day's events from her mind.

Uncle Ignacious placed a steaming cup of tea in front of her, the spicy aroma rising up to surround her and soothe her senses. He seated himself across the table, still humming and stirring his tea with deliberate slowness. Her Uncle never pressured her, but then again he never had to. He seemed to have an uncanny ability of getting what information he needed; he was a very patient man. They sat in comfortable silence for a few minutes savoring their tea and enjoying each other's company. Ava looked over at her Uncle and knew without a doubt that he gave unconditional love and acceptance, asking nothing in return.

She cleared her throat, "Today has been just rotten." She sat forward propping her chin in her hand. "And that's led me to an observation." She fiddled with her cup, unsure of how to proceed. The last thing she wanted to do was upset her Uncle or cause him unnecessary worry.

"Interesting, and what have you observed?" he asked rather amused. For a minute she could have sworn he was trying to contain a smile.

Ava deliberated on exactly how to tell this man, who thought the world of her, that she was like a leper to her peers. No, even worse, she was invisible. Finally, she decided it was best not to sugar coat it…give it to him straight, "I've realized that I don't exactly fit in. Actually, never have; it's kind of like I'm the only apple in an orange grove." She waited a minute before proceeding to gauge his reaction and make sure he wasn't upset. "This isn't news to me…"she stammered, "I've been well aware for quite some time and have made my peace. I've spent the last year basically trying to figure out where it leaves me. I'm suffocating in isolation; is that even rational?" Her words had trailed off and deep in thought, she lost herself for a moment.

Uncle Ignacious emptied his cup and slid it to the side. He reached across the table and enfolded her right hand in both of his capturing her attention. "You are a very special young lady, make no mistake about it. I believe your future holds many adventures filled with true companionship; therefore, there's no need to fret over these trivial matters of today."

Although she appreciated his kind words she didn't see how it changed things. Sometimes when he spoke he sounded ancient. "I can live with transparency." She sighed. "I'm just not into the stuff other people my age are—most of it's foolish drama anyway. What's in store for me? It's not like this town is full of opportunity. I can't be a burden on you and Aunt Irene forever."

"Oh, my little dove, you've never been a burden but rather a blessing." He tenderly patted her hand and stood up. He took their cups to the sink and headed out of the kitchen. As if she knew her name had been mentioned, Aunt Irene appeared in the kitchen doorway. She wore a flowing skirt and a tunic top; very retro. Ava had to admit she was a very hip chic for her age. Her Aunt hugged her Uncle and they shared a sweet kiss. Then she walked up to Ava, gently cupped her cheeks in her hands. "My love," she placed a kiss on Ava's forehead. "How is the most special girl in the whole world, who has never been nor will ever be a burden to us?" Her Aunt's way of letting her know she'd heard her declaration.

"Fine." Ava graced her Uncle with a look to let him know she wanted the rest of their conversation to stay between them. Her Aunt went into the side pantry to retrieve a broom and dust pan. She left the kitchen in a scurry. She was always keeping herself busy doing something. Her Uncle still stood in the kitchen doorway. She looked over at him and was intrigued by his expression.

"Have you ever considered that maybe 'here' isn't where your future lies?" He gave her a moment to consider this. When she didn't speak, he smiled. "I guess not." And with that he was gone.

Ava made her way upstairs. As she changed into something more comfortable her mind wandered. She had lived with her Aunt and Uncle since she was an infant. She'd never had the opportunity to know her parents. She'd been told the strain of childbirth was too much for her mother who was lost on Ava's birthday and she assumed her father wasn't the sort of man to settle down and raise a family. Anything regarding him was circumspect as she had never seen him and no one in the household ever really spoke of him.

Ava counted her blessings each day to have such generous and kind relatives who selflessly accepted the responsibility of raising her from when she was a baby. She had heard rumor that Aunt Irene had lost a child of her own around the same time that Ava was born, but it was never a topic they discussed. Just another reason Ava had a hard time believing in the elusive notion of happiness. Together they all lived about a mile from the town of Elzbeth in a farm house nestled in the woods. The town was small and the house secluded. Rather ironic she thought. Their circumstances weren't necessarily easy, but they made it work.

Ava frequently spent her afternoons in the attic to pass the time. It was where she was most comfortable. She'd turned it into her own little escape with a worn out loveseat and some home-made curtains. She would read from a small collection of books, sketch caricatures of people or animals (her favorite were hung erratically on the walls), or sometimes just sit and stare out of the small attic window. Occasionally on days like today she would snuggle up with a blanket on the sofa to nap. Those were her most favorite days. For when she slept she would dream of the most amazing place. She would fall asleep on the small sofa but when she woke up it was on a soft bed of sweet grass under the most enormous weeping willow tree she'd ever seen. The breeze would shake the branches in a lilting song gently urging her to wake......

Squinting at the soft sunlight that peeked through the leaves and cast shadows that appeared to dance around in sprite like fashion, Ava sat up stretching like a kitten—and yawned the remainder of sleep away. She looked at her strange surroundings. Definitely not the attic she thought rather curiously. Was she dreaming again?

Ava slowly stood and dusted the wrinkles out of her cotton dress. She glanced about her surroundings. The sky was blue with large fluffy clouds. The kind she would spend hours looking out the attic window comparing their shapes to animals or objects; a cherished childhood game. She could hear the gurgling of a stream with what sounded like a small waterfall, but she couldn't actually see it from where she stood. Off in the distance was a dense tree line, but it appeared to be miles away.

As she contemplated what to do next, she noticed there were an abundance of rather large, sparkling flowers sprawled up ahead in a meadow. The contrast of the bright yellow against the green of the grass was breathtaking. As if her feet moved on their own accord, Ava proceeded walking toward the flowers. Along the way she continued to burn the beautiful scenery into her memory. She didn't want to forget any of the details when she woke up. She approached the flowerbed and knelt down for a closer look. The fragrance was fresh and sweet and she inhaled deeply to savor the aroma. With the tip of her index finger she reached out and gently touched a soft golden petal on the flower in front of her. The petals jiggled and she could have sworn she heard a sound like tinkling laughter.

Squinting, she lowered her head to get a closer look. As she exhaled, her warm breath shook the flower. To her surprise the delicate petals started unfolding. Ava leaned back on her heels. As the last petal unfurled, there in the center, stood what appeared to be some sort of miniature person. Make that two. They had a green translucent glow that surrounded them and reminded her of lightning bugs. Wait…that's impossible. She leaned in for a closer look. Simultaneously they looked up at her and grinned.

Most normal people would have been too stunned to speak. Not Ava, she was anything but normal. "Now, this is unexpected." She said a little breathless. She eyed them curiously wondering what on earth they could be and then considered the fact she was most likely dreaming. What else to do but introduce herself, "I'm Ava," she stated, "and just what are you?"

They crossed their right arms over their chests and bowed slightly. In doing so, the one on the right bumped the one on the left with his hip causing him to lose his balance— teetering on one leg and swinging his arms in a valiant effort to prevent the inevitable fall. Down he went and almost rolled off the edge of the petals.

Just then they were startled by the sound of a branch snapping. Ava's head jerked up at the noise and what she saw made her breathing hitch.

A man was leaning against a tree, one foot propped up with his arm crossed over his chest. He looked first at the clowns on the flower and then at Ava. He arched a brow inquisitively. "My guess is you're not from around here." His voice flowed smooth and rich, a deep timbre that was pleasing to her ears.

Just then the tiny man who had disgracefully tumbled on his backside had recovered. Now instead of a lightning bug he looked mad like a hornet. His cheeks were red and his chest was puffed out. He walked up to the other, poked him in the chest and started waving his fists in the air. Before she knew it they were both flinging their arms and making faces. It was like watching mimes argue.

The looks on their little faces was so serious that Ava just couldn't control herself. As she wondered what kind of dream she was having, she was unable to suppress her giggles. Aunt Irene always preached to her that it wasn't polite to laugh at people and she didn't want to insult her new and rather interesting acquaintances, but when those two little people stopped arguing with each other to look at her, simultaneously cocking their heads in opposite directions like she was something strange and unexpected they had encountered—Ava began to giggle. Dream or no dream, the giggles unfortunately turned into a few loud guffaws of very un-lady like laughter. She laughed until her sides ached and tears spilled from her eyes and trailed down her cheeks.

Falcon was quite literally bewildered! His mouth gaped open and he stared at this strange creature before him. He rubbed his eyes just to make sure he wasn't seeing things. He had been travelling for almost three solid days with little sleep. He was on a quest to deliver a message. A message, he had been told, that held the fate of thousands of lives. So, he'd only allowed himself a few short respites. The wariness of travel had finally caught up to him on the third day; he had been too exhausted to continue. He ran onto this meadow and knew it would be a place to rest peacefully…or so he had thought.

The two little spectacles suddenly took off and flew over by the man.   They zoomed in circles around his head.

"What have you done now?" Falcon muttered under his breath.

They looked back at Ava, whose face had turned several different shades of red, almost purple at one point; she seemed to be having difficulty breathing and a few tears were streaming down her face.   What at first he thought was laughter now appeared to be painful.   Falcon hoped his friends hadn't harmed her, on accident of course.   It was never their intent, but they did have a tendency to get into trouble. On more than one occasion Falcon had to rescue his small friends.   Sometimes he wondered if they were worth the trouble.

Things Falcon knew to be true: One, he was an adept warrior who had excelled at every task put before him.   Two, he worked hard and took enjoyment out of all the things he accomplished.   Whether he was risking his life fighting for a cause that he believed in or performing menial tasks such as toiling in the soil to make things grow…these things came naturally to him.   Three, he was well liked and respected, even by those with whom he didn't see eye to eye.

But right now in this particular situation he was at a complete and utter loss.   It had been so long since he had seen anyone so amused.   He scratched his head and took the opportunity to get a better look at this unexpected traveler. She was rather young with auburn hair, a dark shade that hung in waves clear down to her waist.   The sunlight made the tresses shine like fine silk.   Her sparkling violet eyes were hooded with long dark lashes.

Her skin was creamy and smooth; she had a fine chin and high cheekbones. Her clothes were unremarkable—a simple dress with a paisley like design and a sweater that ended above her elbows. Simple slippers covered her feet. She was trim and appeared fit. By the way she was carrying on; she was uninhibited which was also a rare quality.

Then a long sigh interrupted his train of thought.

Chapter 2

As Ava's hysterics subsided she let out a big sigh and caught her breath, she wiped her eyes with the back of her hand. She looked over at the trio standing by the tree and curiously wondered what they were thinking.

"Stunning!" Falcon murmured before he could stop himself. His gut clenched and he felt sick to his stomach; had he just said that out loud? Nothing like a smooth first impression.

Ava blushed slightly, but couldn't help smiling at his remark. No one at Elzbeth besides her aunt and uncle had ever really given her a compliment. Most people thought she was on the thin side and too reserved so no one took the time to get to know her. Really, no one understood her at all. She wondered if she seemed as peculiar to these strangers as they seemed to her.

A scarlet stain was creeping into Falcon's cheeks as Ava's eyes met his. He swore under his breath, it was as if she could see into his very soul. He broke eye contact and looked down at his boots. He couldn't believe he'd just said that...what in the maker was wrong with him? He needed to stay on task and continue on his way. There was entirely too much at stake, but when he peeked back at Ava he had a strange intuition that fate was stacking the deck in this game of cards.

"My name is Falcon," he too crossed his right arm over his chest and bowed. She assumed this must be some sort of tradition here in her dream world. "These are my companions—Everett and Viktor, best known as instigators for causing trouble, or getting into it."

"What are they?" she asked.

"They are fiends, relative of the forest fae."

"I'm Ava," she advised. "Falcon, Viktor, and Everett."
She repeated. "How very unusual!"

"Why are you here? Are you travelling alone or lost
maybe?" Falcon's questions came out all at once and in a
jumbled rush. He silently cursed himself again. Why
couldn't he hold his tongue?

Ava was merely amused by his onslaught of questions.
"I'm from Elzbeth. I live there with my Aunt and Uncle."
Ava stood up and started pacing. She looked back towards
the weeping willow tree. "Why am I here? Hmmm…now
that's a good question. I'm not sure really. Honestly, I
believe I am dreaming and any minute I will wake up. I think
I've had many dreams about this place before. It's unusual.
One minute I'm asleep in my attic and the next I'm lying in the
grass under the willow tree." Ava stopped pacing and looked
at Falcon with her forehead scrunched in concentration. "The
dreams have never seemed to be this real before. I guess I'm
clueless on how I got here or how to get back, unless I wake
up, that is."

Falcon had a keen sense of perception when it came to
reading people and he knew Ava was being honest. Even
though her rambling sounded like that of a mad woman, his
intuition told him if she tried to be dishonest it would be
written all over her face. She thought she was dreaming?
Maybe she fell and hit her head too hard. He also knew the
entire situation was a complication, one he couldn't afford.
Every fiber of his being was drumming a message that she was

special, and this was no chance encounter. Considering his intuition had never steered him wrong before, he was bewildered that it was now telling him their fates would be intertwined. Without a doubt, if he didn't succeed with his journey, all hope would be lost; this indeed posed a dilemma.

Ava watched Falcon out of the corner of her eye. He appeared to be deep in thought as he'd squatted down on one knee and was absently stroking the petals of a flower with his hand. This was so bizarre. She'd dreamed of this place, it was all as familiar to her as her own home town, but this time the dream was different. She'd never before been able to feel the breeze dance across her skin or hear the rustling leaves on the trees. The warmth of the sun's rays heating her skin, the soft grass beneath her feet, and the sweet fragrance of the flowers were all additional indications this wasn't a dream. When she'd been dreaming, she'd never actually seen another person; yet here she was carrying on a conversation with a man and his fiends…unbelievable.

Ava turned her head in order to more closely observe her newest acquaintance. He had a health tan and his skin was covered in what appeared to be intricate tattoos, but they were so faint she wasn't sure if they were real or if her eyes were playing tricks. He was attired in a white cotton shirt under a golden vest and tan breeches that hugged his muscular legs. His brown boots were made of a soft leather and went up to his knees. He was lean and muscular, his hair was thick and muddy blonde with golden highlights…it was unruly and curled behind his ears. He had some sort of golden rope band that curled around his right bicep and a belt that held what appeared to be some type of scabbard that contained the most remarkable sword.

~ 13 ~

Quickly averting her gaze before he caught her staring, Ava took a deep breath. Her Aunt would be disappointed in her. She'd lost all sense of propriety. She couldn't seem to remember her manners. Even with these thoughts running through her head, she couldn't resist another peek. Her earlier inspection was correct about the tattoos. They were not only on his face but seemed to extend from his arms all the way down to his fingertips. They were so very faint at a quick glance you weren't likely to even notice them; very unusual indeed.

Ava didn't really know what to do next. She could go wait by the willow tree. Maybe if she would fall asleep again, this time she would wake up back in the attic; she couldn't help but feel that was highly unlikely. She couldn't shake the feeling that something had lured her here. Out of all of the flowers in the meadow, what are the odds she would pick the one that Everett and Viktor had been in? She knew what she needed to do to prove it to herself. She got up and walked off several yards away from where she started. She knelt down and touched another flower. Nothing happened. She went to another and blew on it. There was still nothing. A few more tries with no surprises. Ava decided there must be more to this than just a dream.

Falcon was so deep in thought he hadn't realized that Ava had left. He couldn't in good conscience let her go off on her own. He lifted his head, "Ava…" but she wasn't there. He stood up and looked over his shoulder to find her kneeling down in front of some flowers randomly poking them. He couldn't suppress a smile. He started walking in her direction.

Everett and Viktor had landed on a nearby tree limb. They sat and dangled their legs over the edge.

~ 14 ~

Falcon quietly approached Ava. "What exactly are you doing?"

Ava looked up at him and simply stated, "Proving a point."

Looking around her somewhat perplexed, "Who are you proving a point to?"

"Myself." She stood up dusting off her hands. "I've decided this isn't a dream. It can't be. I mean...look around. Out of all of these beautiful flowers, I picked the one Viktor and Everett had chosen to sleep in. That's no coincidence. I have this feeling that I'm supposed to be here. Right now I can't fathom why, but since I have no known way of getting home, what else is there for me to do?" She looked at Falcon thoughtfully. "And I have this overpowering sense that you being here is no coincidence." Feeling a little self-conscious for voicing her sensible notions, she tucked her hair behind her ear and gazed out to the trees.

Falcon was surprised that her thoughts were very similar to his own. This was some unexplainable connection. He silently weighed his alternatives and looked her over again. She was staring out in the distance. He briefly closed his eyes and tried to memorize her profile. Closer proximity only enhanced her natural beauty. His mouth went dry and a knot formed in his stomach. As if she felt his gaze she looked over at him. The smile she gave him was genuine and warm and he felt like someone had punched him in the gut.

Falcon swallowed hard, his Adam's apple bobbing with the effort, "Ava," he said, "what is your age?"

She could tell by the tone of his voice and the earnest way he looked into her eyes that this question held great importance to him. She could lie. If he thought she was too young he may not want to be responsible for her. She briefly considered this option, but when she looked into the depths of his warm eyes, she knew she could never lie to him.

"I'm seventeen. I'll be eighteen in a couple of months."

"Seventeen...hmmm." He whispered, shifting his focus off in the distance. Again he looked deep in thought.

"And you...how old are you?" Ava wasn't so sure she needed to know more than she wanted to know.

"One and twenty." He advised, still staring off in the distance.

One and twenty? She thought to herself. A strange way of putting it. "Where is here exactly?" she asked him changing the subject.

"This is Veil Stine," simply stated with no additional details offered. Ava noticed the change in Falcon's composure immediately. He went from the carefree, happy man she had met minutes earlier to one who appeared to be burdened by the weight of the world. His smile faded and the laugh wrinkles around his copper eyes relaxed. He stared off into the distance, an empty and hollow version of himself with his shoulders slumped. She could have sworn his tattoo's changed color, like a glimmer on a lake. It was a heartbreaking sight and she felt an intense and overwhelming urge to soothe him but no idea how to go about doing that. Even more peculiar was the intense connection that she felt toward him…it was stronger than anything she'd shared with anyone else, ever.

Falcon lost in his own thoughts missed the look of understanding and compassion that crossed Ava's face. If he had seen, it would just be something else that left him conflicted on what to do. His journey would be tedious and long with the certainty of great danger. It was a risky undertaking for someone familiar with the area, but perilous to someone foreign. Leaving her here alone wasn't an option as it was entirely too unsafe. Besides, his conscious would never allow it. So, he racked his brain to come up with a suitable alternative.

Ava realized Falcon was considering their predicament. She was mulling things over herself. She started walking back toward the weeping willow with her thoughts in a jumble. Stopping halfway between the tree and where she had left Falcon she closed her eyes. Tilting her head back she let the rays of sunlight bathe her from head to toe and infuse her with strength. It was obvious that Falcon was a man of strong convictions and was already considering her his responsibility. It was no fault of his own that he was unaware of the fact that she was very resourceful. Her Aunt and Uncle were older so she'd learned to be independent quite early on. Being completely honest with herself, she would have to admit she did tend to keep people at a distance. That way the risk of heartbreak was minimal, making it even more bizarre that in a very brief amount of time she was already thinking in terms of 'we' instead of 'me' when it came to her new companion.

Ava couldn't begin to fathom how all of this was possible. She knew she wasn't dreaming but went ahead and pinched herself for good measure. She increased the pressure until she had to bite her lip to keep from letting out a squeal.

Okay, time to stop wondering about the hows and whys she decided. She needed to deal with the here and now. She had already considered the possibility of trying to fall back to sleep under the willow tree and ruled that option out. This was unfamiliar territory so she didn't think it would be wise to remain here alone. One thing she knew for certain is not all people were trustworthy or kind. She didn't prefer to sit around and wait to have an unpleasant encounter.

Then there was Falcon. She glanced back at where she had left him and he hadn't moved. She didn't want to burden him. Her presence was completely unexpected. He and his fiends had been headed somewhere before their paths crossed. She thought that was probably his dilemma where she was concerned, a sense of duty versus his chivalrous nature. Standing in this meadow filled her with an amazing sense of peace. She had no explanation and didn't think logic applied anyway. This surreal place made her feel complete...not something she'd been able to say too many times during her lifetime. She wasn't afraid or necessarily anxious to return home. Her Aunt and Uncle would be worried and that was the only thing she had left behind that even necessitated any consideration. With that realization, she decided even if Falcon was unable to have her accompany them, she would proceed on her own. She took a deep breath and exhaled slowly trying to alleviate the feeling of unease the latter option brought with it.

Chapter 3

With her mind made up, Ava approached the branch that Everett and Viktor had turned into their personal recliner. They looked so relaxed it was hard to believe they had been fighting moments before. Then again a few hours ago it would have been hard to believe she was looking at fiends on a limb.

She felt more than heard Falcon approach from behind. She peered over her shoulder at him. His presence was like a warm balm, soothing yet disconcerting at the same time. At this proximity she was able to see the breadth of his chest. From a distance you couldn't see how the muscles bunched beneath his shirt. Ava was fairly tall and figured his height to be near six foot. She could also see how the faint filigree tattoo outlined his eyes, the set of his square jaw, and lips that looked very appealing. She turned to face him.

"We've been travelling for three days and this is the first time we've stopped to rest. We started in Songston Proper. You see, there is great unrest in the kingdom. I bear a message that must be delivered to the palace. The matter is urgent and requires us to travel at a relentless pace." He glanced around them. "It isn't safe for you to stay here. But if you were to accompany us I would not want you to have preconceptions that the travel will be anything but difficult." He started pacing before her. "There is a village about 20 miles from here. We can escort you there for safekeeping and then we can continue on our way."

Ava considered these options. She knew it would be safer to travel with them, but she wasn't exactly attired for what he was describing. She was positive she would hinder their progress. "I understand. Thanks for the offer, but I'll pass." She stated. "If you could just point me in the direction of the...village," she waved her hand as she repeated his choice of words, "I should be able to make it there on my own so you can continue to your own destination."

Falcon wasn't expecting this response. "Either you are very brave or very foolish!" he barked, throwing his hands up in the air clearly agitated. He already felt a responsibility to her and he wasn't about to leave her behind.

"Neither," Ava replied a little perplexed at his outburst. She crossed her arms and raised her chin in defiance. She didn't particularly like the tone he had taken. It was obvious he underestimated her. "I'm not dressed for that type of travel. And since it is of the 'utmost importance' that you deliver your message, I can't in good conscious slow you down. But I also can't promise that I would be able to keep up."

Falcon regarded her attire. He'd not thought of that. "And you've no other clothes?"

"Only what you see. I wasn't exactly expecting to come here."

This is when Everett came buzzing around Falcon's head. He was so worked up he reminded her of a sparkler on the fourth of July.

"What's the matter with him?"

"He's lecturing me. 'Leaving her isn't an option, it would be dishonorable' and so on and so on." Now Viktor follows and they're both buzzing around his head. She didn't know how Falcon restrained from swatting at them like mosquitos. "There are many dangers that linger in the darkness. They advise I've wasted enough time squabbling. We've never failed a mission yet and we won't fail this one. We'll just make up for lost time once you are safe."

Ava was a little bewildered. All she could hear was buzzing sounds, but Falcon appeared to be carrying on a conversation. "You can understand them?" Could that explain the laughter she thought she'd heard when she'd discovered them in the flower?

"Unfortunately…Fiends are only heard by those they choose to have hear them. Their trust must be earned and it is an honor they must bestow."

Falcon quirked a brow at his little friends and wondered what had come over them. They were the ones always having to be bailed out of trouble, one shenanigan after another. Now they were the voice of reason. What other possible surprises could this day hold?

Ava was chewing on her bottom lip. "I'll try my best to keep up. I won't intentionally slow you down."

"No, they're right." Falcon consented. "We can make up for lost time after we get you to Ash Knoll." He could see she didn't seem completely convinced. "I must apologize for my behavior; it appears this journey has made me weary and short tempered."

Ava felt guilty that he was apologizing. She just nodded her head in acceptance.

"Alright—that settles it. Both canteens are filled and I found some berries by the riverbank." He was looping the canteen straps across his shoulder as he spoke.

Falcon picked up a sack and slung it over his free shoulder. "Shall we?" he said to Ava gesturing the way they should start walking with his free hand.

They headed east towards the dense tree line she had seen earlier in the distance. There appeared to be several hours of daylight left. Falcon set a determined pace and thought they walked briskly the ground was fairly level and she managed to keep up. They walked in companionable silence, but Ava had to admit she was grateful for the company.

Falcon estimated they must have been walking for a good three hours and Ava was gradually starting to fall behind. He'd been inconspicuously checking her condition over his shoulder. He'd not heard one complaint from her which surprised him, but it was obvious she wasn't stepping quite as lively. Viktor and Everett had disappeared again. Typical Falcon thought.

Falcon stopped and turned around. It took Ava a minute to catch up to him. He dropped his bag on the ground and opened one of the canteens. He took a long swig of the water and then another. He held out the canteen to Ava who graciously accepted. She did the same, practically inhaling long drinks of the cool, refreshing water. She smacked her lips as she handed it back to Falcon still breathing fairly hard.

'Would you like to sit and rest awhile?" Falcon asked.

"Is there time?"

"We have a few minutes. I'd like to make it into the woods before dark. There's a spot about an hour in that serves as a good camp."

Falcon sat down on the ground with one leg propped up which he rested his elbow on. Ava sat down tucking her legs up under her. Smoothing her dress down around her knees she looked at the trees that were much clearer at this closer distance. She was beginning to realize just how dense they were. She wondered how she would manage her way through all of the brush. With that thought, she had to admit to herself that she was weary. The day had taken quite an unexpected turn and just as she anticipated it was proving difficult to keep pace with Falcon. But continue she must…it would be just a few more hours before they could make camp, and she wouldn't hinder their progress if it could be avoided.

Falcon was thinking much the same thoughts as Ava. What was the best method to maneuver through the woods with a female in tow? In the past his companions had always been other men. If you fell behind, you were showered with derogatory remarks and sometimes even threats. No man wants to show weakness, so all it takes is a few rebuffs to get motivated. He looked over at Ava and thought that definitely wouldn't work in this case. At least the brush was only dense for a mile or so…the dense tree cover opened up some after that. He looked up to gauge the position of the sun. They really should be on their way, but he couldn't force himself to give the command—he could give her just a few more minutes to rest.

Sensing his anticipation to continue, Ava stood up and arched her back to loosen the muscles that had stiffened from sitting. She knew his reluctance to proceed was for her benefit and her stubborn pride demanded she prove her resilience. She pasted a smile on her face, "Ready," she asked. She didn't wait for a response—just continued walking in the direction they were headed.

Falcon watched her for a moment with her head held high, back straight—so full of pride. Her manner reminded him of royalty and something else he couldn't quite put his finger on—or could he? Stubborn, he thought. He hopped to his feet and grabbed his bag; throwing it over his shoulder he followed after the unusual female who seemed to be full of surprises.

Chapter 4

Falcon had spent the past hour filling Ava in on some of the more interesting adventures he'd been on. The constant chatter was a welcome distraction from the blisters that had formed on her heels and the aching muscles in her calves. She'd heard about Harold the peddler who had tried to steal from them while they were camped on the outskirts of a small town. Of course Harold was unsuccessful and Falcon had taught him a lesson by making him carry their supplies around for an entire week. Falcon informed Ava that they wouldn't have ran into Harold if they hadn't deviated from their original course because Everett and Viktor just had to have a certain pie made by a certain bakery that was nowhere near their destination.

Then there was Joretta, a nasty old hag that owned an inn where they had tried to spend the night. She wouldn't hear of having fiends stay in her establishment. Might as well be infested with rodents she had informed him. Even when he offered to pay more, she still refused. Said they could sleep in the barn with the animals and wouldn't even offer them a meal. Falcon hadn't left his companions alone for the comfort of a bed. He had chosen to bunk down in the barn with them instead. Later that night, they were awakened by shouting. Bandits had broken in to the inn and were trying to rob Joretta. Lucky for her Falcon was there and made short work of the intruders. The hateful inn keeper, although reluctantly, offered to pay him for his intervention, but he advised her that he had a better idea. He'd made her prepare a meal for them and deliver it to their room where they enjoyed a good rest and full bellies after all.

Ava was beginning to realize what a genuine individual Falcon really was...her Aunt had always told her actions spoke louder than words. Her reverie was interrupted by the beginning of his next story.

"Funniest by far was Gunther." He continued. "A very large man indeed, probably two heads taller than me and twice as wide. He had the whitest beard I've ever seen." He held his hands up to his face cupped in an O. "His nose was round and bulbous and always bright red. He always looked like he had a terrible cold…he was deep in his cups this night—spinning tall tales of his supposed heroic adventures to a bunch of strangers. But you see I already knew him to be the biggest coward in six districts and the only thing bigger than the nose on his face was his ego."

Ava smiled at Falcon's antics. The more stories he told the more animated he became. Ava noticed he would occasionally smile or roll his eyes as he spoke, reliving the memories.

"Well, we'd been back in the corner of the inn, inconspicuous you see. It's better to have a wall to your back that way you don't have to worry about someone sneaking up on you. Anyway…it all happened when we got up to leave. We were making our way to the door when he spotted me. He barreled his way over to me and started shouting all sorts of obscenities and gibberish that made no sense. He wasn't very steady on his feet. All of the shouting brought Everett and Viktor out with fists flying. They don't like feeling threatened you see. They took off after him and he didn't know what to do. He was swinging his arms trying to swat them away and yelling for me to call them off which I couldn't do for laughing so hard. He tried to run but ended up tripping over his own feet. He staggered around begging for me to make them stop." He paused shaking his head. "He refuted his own story of bravery by running and squealing from two little fiends."

Ava giggled thinking of what a sight it must have been. The way the two had buzzed around Falcon when they weren't mad, she could only imagine what it would be like if they truly had a reason to be worked up.

They had reached the edge of the woods and decided to take another short rest. Falcon had told her they would have to set up camp in about an hour and there wasn't much further to go. Their pace slowed down as the dense brush became thicker and much harder to navigate. There were several times they had to back track in order to get around briar patches or thorn bushes. It was warm, but shade from the trees provided a comfortable temperature. And speaking of trees—when she'd first seen them in the distance she never imagined they would be so massive. Their enormous trunks and height meant they must have grown undisturbed for hundreds of years. She had to crane her neck completely backward to even attempt to see the tops which were obscured by leaves. Trees surrounding her home were puny in comparison. This colossal forest gave a new appreciation to how an ant must feel.

Their conversation died down since they were both tired and had all of their focus on navigating the brush. They had just topped another slope and Ava honestly didn't think she could take another stop when Falcon pointed and said, "This is it." There was a deep curvature in the embankment. "We will be able to have a small fire since the enclosure will block most of the light from anyone above or outside. It will be easier for us to keep watch also."

Ava sat down on a log and started rubbing her legs—they felt like Jell-O. It crossed her mind to ask what they were keeping watch for, but the thought vanished as she watched Falcon busily prepare a pit for a fire. He didn't even have to think about what he was doing and she noticed he didn't ask for her to do anything. Before she knew it he had a small blaze burning. She moved closer to the flames. The ground was covered in soft pine needles and moss. Falcon handed her a canteen and a bowl full of berries then disappeared mumbling something about checking the perimeter. She ate every last berry and washed them down with several drinks of water.

Leaning back, she gingerly started to peel off her shoes. Even though they were comfortable, they weren't intended for recreational purposes. They had rubbed and her heels were now spotted with a cluster of blisters. The left foot was worse and she cringed at the idea of ever having to put her shoes back on. She decided it would have to wait until morning.

When Falcon returned he found Ava leaning back against a log, her legs stretched out with her feet crossed at the ankles. Her head was leaning back and her eyes were closed. He couldn't tell if she was asleep. He hated to disturb her but he knew her feet needed to be tended or they would make no distance the next day. He kneeled down to observe the damage and then fished in his bag for a jar of salve. He returned to her left foot and started applying the poultice. She jerked up pulling her foot out of his hands—eyes wide with shock.

"It's just something for the blisters…it will help." He saw her focus and she reached out her hand to take the medicine from him. "Just rub it anywhere it hurts and it will hopefully be bearable tomorrow."

He went around to the other side of the fire and got comfortable. He watched her apply the medicine and couldn't help but think he'd never found this particular activity so fascinating to watch. When she'd finished she lay down on her side and curled up in a ball. "You'd best get some rest." He told her. "Everett andViktor will keep the first watch. We need to get an early start tomorrow." He wasn't sure she had even heard his comments—her breathing already steady in the rhythm of sleep.

Ava heard sizzling and it reminded her of Sunday morning breakfast with her Aunt and Uncle. She could smell familiar aromas but just couldn't quite wrap her head around it. Everything hurt—from the hair on her scalp, everything in between, clear down to her toes. Groggily she blinked— trying to force her eyes to stay open. Above her were trees, their leaves rustling in the wind and scattered sunlight peeking through. She looked to the side and realized that she was lying on the ground. Through all of the protesting muscles, groaning with the effort, she inched her way into a sitting position. Looking to her left she saw the fire pit…still glowing. Her stomach rumbled as she saw eggs cooking on top of a scrap of metal. She groaned as it all came rushing back to her—she hadn't been dreaming after all.

Ava ran her fingers through her long locks trying to loosen up some of the tangles. She didn't have much success so she twisted it in a knot and secured it with a band from her wrist. She became aware that her feet didn't hurt nearly as bad as they had the day before and looked down to inspect the blisters. Pleasantly surprised to see they weren't as bad as she'd anticipated, they day's travels might be bearable after all.

Falcon scooped them each up an egg and distributed berries evenly in their bowl. He went and sat down next to Ava handing her a plate which she happily accepted. "It's not much I'm afraid." Falcon started eating his food.

"It's fine." Ava dived right into eating. After swallowing several bites she observed Falcon. He had meticulously cut his egg in several pieces with his fork. He ate each bit of egg, chewing with great relish; he then moved on to the berries. He took his time and thoroughly enjoyed each bite.

"If you don't eat your food it will get cold." Falcon said slightly amused at the fact she was observing him so closely.

She resumed eating and had her plate cleaned in a matter of minutes. Falcon handed her the canteen so she could wash down her breakfast.

"So, you've told me a lot about the frequent trouble you and the fiends find yourself in, but nothing specific about yourself."

He found it oddly pleasing that she was interested enough to be curious, "What would you like to know?"

"Umm, let's see. Do you have any family? Where do you live? What do you do to pass the time…that is when you aren't on some daring mission?"

He grinned and contemplated which question to answer first. "I have a sister Penley. She's a few years older than me. She lives back in Songston Proper with her husband, Owen. They run the local inn. They have a daughter, my niece, Gracie. A little she-devil that one."

Ava laughed at his description. Even with his description his fondness of Gracie was evident. "She devil, huh? How old?"

"Four."

"Serious, you're going to tell me she's only four years old and you have already labeled her 'she devil'?"

"You haven't met her. She terrorizes the cat—it hardly has any hair left on its tail. She is always conspiring something and you have to be on guard at all times. If not, something unexpected and usually unfortunate will happen."

Ava giggled again at his nervous expression. "She sounds like a genuine little monster. I believe she's got you bluffed." He gave her a slight look of disbelief. "So, do you live there as well? In Songston Proper?"

"Me? No, I still have a bunk at the Palace. The First Commander keeps it for me. But I have places I can stay just about everywhere and there's always the forest. There's always room out here." Falcon took the empty plate from Ava. He cleaned them up and packed them away.

"Do you ever get lonely?" she wondered.

He mulled over this question. "Not really. Everett and Viktor are always popping in."

"Are you ever frightened?"

He threw his hand up against his chest and his jaw dropped open in mock outrage. "I'm deeply wounded. Do I appear to be the type of man who is easily frightened?"

"I don't know," Ava said, teasing, "...you do appear to have an unusual fear of four year old little girls."

He shook his head in disbelief. "Seriously, you haven't met her."

They both laughed and Falcon couldn't help but stare. He considered her earlier question about being lonely. He'd never thought so before, but he knew now after spending this brief time with Ava, that he would certainly miss her company once they parted ways. He shoved the thought aside. "We should probably get started pretty soon."

Ava nodded agreement and slipped her shoes on. Given the circumstances she had to admit she was actually quite pleased to wake up where she was. She had no idea what events would take place, but for the first time in a very long time she was genuinely looking forward to it, whatever it may be.

Falcon had just finished kicking dirt on the remaining cinders of the fire when she heard the first kerthunk. The rest was a blur it happened so fast—Falcon's head shot up, his eyes darting in all directions, senses keen on the impending threat. In a flash he was crouching at Ava's side gripping her by the shoulders, "I see at least six." He was hovering over her using his body as a shield. Ker-think, thump, swoosh. Thump, they were surrounded—one arrow hit not two feet to Ava's left. Arrows—someone was shooting arrows at them!! "We have to find better cover," he said urgently scanning the landscape. "Over there by those trees." Pulling her to her feet, they ran, weaving back and forth in an attempt to make themselves less likely targets.

When they got to the first tree Falcon pulled her down to the ground. "Not good odds," he mumbled as he peeked through a fork in the tree. "There, there and two there—the others will try to flank us." Sitting on her knees she stretched her neck to see where he was pointing and flinched when an arrow hit not two inches from her cheek. With lightning quick reflexes Falcon wrapped his arm around her waist dragging her tightly to his chest, out of harm's way. Ava gasped at the intense pressure of his grip and looked down at his arm and realized she was practically sitting on his lap.

The strangest thing happened—everything around her ceased. She could still hear arrows whizzing by and common sense told her she should be frightened, but apparently all common sense had abandoned her, pushed out of the way by raging teenage hormones. She was intimately embraced by a man who smelled of mint and fresh air, whose warm breath was gently fanning her cheek. She could feel the strength in his arms as they circled her waist in a vise like grip, the muscles in his thigh and the steady beat of his heart against her breast. He was solid and warm—her only coherent thought was how very safe she felt.

A little flustered, she lifted her head up to look at him. Like being drenched by a pail of ice water thrown in her face, reality came crashing down. Falcon was intensely focused on their assailants. Ava disentangled her hands from his shirt and eased back whispering, "Who are they?"

When Ava spoke, Falcon glanced down…his eyebrows shot up as recognized their rather compromising position. He removed his arm from around her waist and scooted her to the side so she wasn't in such close proximity.

"My guess would be the Krypts, but I haven't been able to get a good look at them." Another arrow whizzed by. "I can't encounter them at this distance, not with their bows. I'll have to wait until they close in." He frantically scanned the area trying to think of a better plan. He wished there was a way they could make a run for it. He dreaded an encounter with Ava nearby—it was entirely too dangerous, but he wasn't certain they could outrun them even if they tried. He wasn't one to sit around and wait but he couldn't leave her to go thrashing through the woods to tackle them head on. He turned back to Ava—she wasn't in hysterics—her face a blank slate. He grabbed her hands in his.

"Listen very carefully." Although his tone was calm there was no mistaking the underlying urgency in what he was about to say. "In a few minutes they will be here. Krypts are ruthless scavengers—mercenaries of the vilest sort. If they get through me, you need to run. Go the same way we were heading and do not stop until you reach Ash Knoll—it's a good ten miles. Don't stop running. Don't look back. Death is the only blessing you could pray for if you're captured." Reaching down into the side of his boot he pulled out a small dagger and placed it in her hands.

Ava swallowed hard but was unable to speak. She just nodded to let him know she understood. He got down in a crouch and withdrew his sword in preparation; he was poised and prepared. It was clear he'd done this sort of thing before. She looked down at the dagger she held loosely in her hands. It looked foreign—heavy and cold. She didn't know how to use a dagger. Was this really happening? The arrows had stopped and she could now hear the thrashing in the brush; it must be the Krypts as Falcon called them making their approach. She felt like a fox waiting for the hounds to descend.

When the first Krypt reached the clearing Falcon lunged forward. The Krypt raised his bow but Falcon swung and snapped the bow in two. He jumped back and the Krypt retrieved a dagger from his belt and started forward swinging. Ava watched completely fascinated by the scene before her—it was surreal. Falcon's entire demeanor had changed—he was a fierce warrior, determined and confident. He was graceful and swift—each motion fluid with the next. The Krypt was vaguely human but mutilated beyond recognition with piercings and raised scars. He looked fierce and dangerous and her heartbeat accelerated. What was transpiring before her was like a dance. One would lunge, the other would block. It was all happening so fast but she was seeing it in slow motion. Behind Falcon, Ava saw another Krypt approaching.

"FALCON!!" she screamed. But it was too late. By the time he turned the Krypt had already released an arrow. Falcon lunged to the right but couldn't evade the full impact the arrow grazed his shoulder. He fell to the ground and rolled over. Ava could see the tear in his shirt and watched in horror as a crimson stain appeared and began to spread along the fabric. He immediately jumped to his feet to block the next assault from the first Krypt he'd been battling with. Fear gripped her as she saw the second Krypt join the fray. They were circling him like buzzards. Ava gripped the dagger tightly in her hands remembering what he had told her.

To her amazement it didn't faze Falcon when the second Krypt joined, instead he took a deep breath and crouched low, holding his sword with both hands angled out before him—his hands started glowing subtly at first and then gradually brighter. It went from the hilt of his sword to his hands—creeping its way up his arms. Absolutely amazing—Ava could tell she wasn't the only one surprised by this. The Krypts paused long enough to look at each other and reconsider their attack. It was too late. Falcon was all over them. One ran straight toward Falcon with his blade raised which he blocked with his left hand and ran him through with deadly precision. He immediately started in on the other but there were two more Krypts rapidly approaching. Falcon circled as they closed in on him calculating the odds against him. He looked over to where Ava stood and although she couldn't hear him from that distance, she could see he'd spoke only one word. "Run."

And that's exactly what she did. She gripped the dagger fiercely and sprinted in the direction he had told her to run. She glanced back to see that he had engaged the four Krypts and was miraculously holding his own. Something caught her attention out of the corner of her eye. It was a Krypt running directly toward her. She took one last look at Falcon and threw up a silent prayer he would be ok. She urged herself to run faster through the ache in her muscles and the blisters on her feet. The hairs on the back of her neck stood on end as the Krypt running behind her reduced the distance between them.

Terror seized her and she lost her footing on the slick leaves—stumbling to the ground. Her arms barely prevented her face from eating dirt, but she could feel the tearing scrapes on her bare knees. Ava didn't lie there to assess her injuries. Instead she scrambled to her feet as and took off again. Unfortunately the fall had cost her a great deal as the Krypt had narrowed the gap even more. She was fast, but given the circumstances, she wasn't going to be able to outrun him. The tears she was trying so desperately to hold back were starting to blur her vision.

Her lungs were on fire—she knew she hadn't covered much distance and realized she wouldn't be able to go much further no matter how much willpower she had because the hunter almost had its prey. She was grateful for all of the times she ran home from school. At least it had given her enough wind to run as far as she had. Distracted by all of the thoughts running through her mind, she failed to pay attention to where she was headed. She scanned ahead and skidded to a complete stop. Twenty yards up the trail stood a hooded Krypt—bow drawn back, arrow pointed directly at her.

Ava just stood and stared. Falcon had said the rest of the Krypts would flank them and they had certainly done just that. This was it—this was how it would end. Although she couldn't see the face of her soon to be assassin she could still present a brave façade. So she lifted the hand that held the dagger, held her head high, and looked straight at him. That's when she heard the release of the arrow—the whistle as it spiraled through the air—the sickening sound of impact.

Ava held her breath, her ears roaring, and felt her already damaged knees buckle. She landed on the ground barely catching herself with her arms. She looked up to see the hooded figure sprinting towards her cocking another arrow to finish the job. She braced herself and couldn't prevent closing her eyes this time. She had no other alternative but to wait as each stride brought him closer. A strange calm settled over her. This was something out of her control so she could only wait for the inevitable. Under no circumstances had she expected him to run right past her, never slowing down.

That's when Ava finally dared to glance down and patter her chest with her hands. To her surprise there was no arrow protruding from her chest and she was obviously still breathing. Standing, she turned around to see the Krypt that had been chasing her had an arrow protruding through his neck; blood was bubbling out and there were gurgling sounds with each futile attempt he made to draw breath.

The hooded man had saved her life.

Chapter 5

Falcon watched just long enough to make sure Ava followed his command to run. When he saw her take off, he returned his focus to the task at hand. There were four Krypts surrounding him now; they multiplied like the fleas he was certain they were infested with. The odds were not stacked in his favor, but he always looked forward to a good challenge. The Krypts were covered in so much filth and grime it was unimaginable to think they ever bathed. Their tattered clothes were stained with dirt and food debris—soaked with sweat. Their appearance alone was enough to frighten a person.

It didn't take long before the Krypt with the protruding teeth and nasty scar across his cheek engaged, but Falcon successfully blocked his onslaught. Another came at him from behind and he deftly deflected the blow forcibly shoving the Krypt who then lost his balance and fell to the ground.

Providing absolutely no time for recovery, the third Krypt was on him before he had a chance to react. He was only armed with a bow and managed to land one solid punch square across Falcon's jaw. The blow resonated through Falcon's temple but he recovered by pivoting on his heel. He swung, slicing the Krypts chest open in one effortless strike. The Krypt grabbed his torso wrapping his arms around his wound and fell to his knees with a look of shock on his face.

A wave of intense dizziness hit Falcon, blurring his vision, and he barely shook it off before he was again bombarded by the brave Krypt who initially engaged him, now back for more. Falcon's arm was beginning to throb and he was grateful that the injury wasn't inflicted on his sword arm. He centered himself, closed his eyes, and summoned all of his energy which slightly intensified the glow. The Krypts again hesitated upon seeing this strange occurrence, but only momentarily. The last two charged toward him at the same time. Falcon was on the defensive, trying to prevent their blows from actually hitting their target. They were pressing their advantage and inch by inch Falcon was starting to lose ground.

Out of nowhere he heard another arrow being released. Frightened there were more adversaries, he glanced over his shoulder just in time to see the third Krypt who had been sneaking up behind him, fall to the ground. In the distance he saw a hooded figure running in his direction. He had no time to decide friend or foe as he already had his hands full. He'd had just about enough of these filthy monsters. Turning back around he pressed forward and took the offensive, putting all of his battle honed skills into action.

One Krypt fell back and Falcon pushed his advantage on the other. It was obvious this Krypt was not skilled with a blade and Falcon bid his time until he saw the opening he'd waited for, which didn't take long. The clumsy Krypt drew his arm back like he was wielding an axe and Falcon charged forward impaling him. He started to slump to the ground, but instead of falling backward the Krypt made one final dive that ended up toppling Falcon over—his mutilated body partially pinning Falcon to the ground. The fall had caught him off guard and he was unable to dislodge his weapon. The final assailant made his approach with deliberate leisure; triumph shone in his eyes at the simplicity of his victory. He had a revolting smile displaying a mouth full of rotten, decaying teeth.

Falcon struggled to push the heavy body of the dead Krypt off of him but knew he would never get him moved in time. Survival instinct made him reach for his boot to pull out his dagger but he came up empty handed and remembered he had given it to Ava. He stopped his futile struggles and looked at the Krypt who now stood above him. He wasn't afraid to die, but if he had ideas of grandeur it certainly didn't involve being impaled by a filthy Krypt in such a ridiculous manner. The Krypt raised his sword above his head and with one last sardonic laugh he went to sink the blade into Falcon's chest, but the blade hadn't descended more than six inches when an arrow lodged straight into the Krypt's ugly heart. A momentary look of disbelief fluttered across his disfigured face before he fell over—dead before ever hitting the ground.

Falcon exhaled a sigh of relief and returned to his struggle to free himself from the odious monster sprawled across him. Then there before him appeared an outstretched hand. Falcon looked up and couldn't believe his eyes. Griffon Gray—his closest childhood friend, well, that was until Manford Gray, Griffon's father's scandal not only tarnished his reputation but their friendship as well, stood above him.

The lineage for the Reeds and the Grays had always been that of guardian to the High Deacon and Deaconess. The High Deacon had great respect for both boys' fathers and trusted their judgment above all others. And so it had been for their fathers and their fathers before them.

Long ago, Falcon's father, Gideon Reed, was to attend the Deacon and Deaconess from the palace, a routine travel escort. The Royals had arranged a meeting for negotiations for the Regionals, who were the leaders of each smaller district. Gideon had prepared the regiment that would serve as escort, with him at point. Everyone was prepared to depart within the hour when Gideon received a message that Manford needed to see him on an urgent matter at an offsite location before his departure. Only Gideon and his First

Commander knew that he even received a message and who it was from.

Since Manford was one of his closest friends, he departed immediately, but when Gideon arrived at the destination, Manford wasn't there. He waited around for a few minutes but knowing Manford was always punctual he realized something was amiss. By the time he had made his way back to the keep the First Commander informed him the regiment along with the High Deacon and Deaconess had received a message from 'him' advising they should head out and he would meet them at the first forks. That's when Gideon knew something was terribly wrong. The travelling party had a good ten minute head start. Gideon mounted his steed and charged out after them, but by the time he arrived at the forks there was chaos. Most of the soldiers were already dead. The others seriously wounded but still trying to fight off the attackers. They were gravely outnumbered.

The Deacon's carriage was on its side, partially engulfed in flames, arrows embedded throughout. He climbed up and tore open the door to find the High Deacon sitting at the bottom cradling the Deaconess in his arms. He had a handkerchief over his mouth trying to breathe through the smoke, tears filling his eyes. Gideon could see the Deaconess already appeared to be lost. He reached in and pulled her from the carriage. When he went back for the High Deacon he could see the man was gravely injured. When he was finally able to get him to the ground besides the soot and grime that covered his face, Gideon could only see a long gash across the man's forehead, but his lips were blue and his skin pasty white. His injuries must be internal for each breath he managed to take rattled in his chest and his struggle to breathe became increasingly more difficult.

The High Deacon gingerly held his wife's hand and placed his other upon her stomach. The Deaconess had been expecting their first child in a mere matter of weeks. As his last breath was spent he slowly closed his eyes never speaking a single solitary word.

Gideon was engulfed with rage at himself for failing as their protector, for not realizing sooner that something was wrong, and at the misguided villains who had ended an era of peace with this ignorant show of force. His sense of loss was so great that he had temporarily forgotten about the ensuing battle. Leaning over the bodies to tenderly close the eyes of the Deaconess, Gideon was struck down from behind. Arching forward he sprawled his body across their lifeless forms as his last protective gesture. That is how they were discovered—the two most admired leaders in ages and their loyal guardian. The Kingdoms would mourn for many years to come.

Falcon and Griffon, relatively close in age, were small children when all of this transpired and totally oblivious to the implications. Falcon had lost his father and Griffon's had disappeared. Falcon's mother had died when he was two and Griffon's mother was said to be a renowned healer that travelled far and wide. Not long after the attack on the Royals, she too disappeared without a trace. So, now the boys were orphaned, their care fell into the hands of the First Commander. He became their surrogate parent and the two grew up joined at the hip—the very best of friends.

They were ornery and always scheming something mischievous, but bravely faced the consequences of their actions as a united front. The First Commander was very fond of both boys and trained them extensively on how to survive. He paid special attention to each boy figuring out their individual strengths. Falcon was swift on his feet and had an eye for not only seeing but taking advantage of an opponent's weakness. He was proficient with a sword—confident in his abilities. Griffon was a good sparring partner for Falcon, but his expertise was with bow and arrow. He was light on his feet giving him the uncanny ability to sneak around unnoticed. He was dexterous—his aim constant and true. Each wielded their weapon with deadly grace.

It wasn't until they were in their early teens that they became aware of their history. Boys will be boys you see. Other children overheard stories from their parents talking or idle gossip amongst the villagers. Although there was no proof, most people assumed Manford Gray had been a traitor who sacrificed the Royals for monetary gain and disappeared with his newfound wealth, abandoning his only child. Even though Manford had served the Deacon with loyalty and honor—he was still depicted as unscrupulous and corrupt. Even though Griffon had been but a small boy when the events occurred, like an infected wound the rumors festered making Griffon the new target of ridicule and shame—a constant reminder of the past. Although he barely remembered his father he just couldn't comprehend his relation to someone who committed such an evil deed. If he accepted what was being said that knowingly made him a traitor's son—no better than the dirt you would scrape off of the bottom of your shoe.

At first Griffon and Falcon faced the adversity together. Tempers would flare and when the confrontations turned physical they fought together back to back. They were often outnumbered and each suffered several split lips and black eyes defending Griffon's honor. The longer this went on the more introverted Griffon became. He secluded himself spending more time alone wallowing in self-pity and doubt.

Falcon was his friend, but he knew Griffon thought he was suffering at his expense. Though it broke his heart, Griffon started pushing him away as well as if all of his will to fight had vanished.

Falcon didn't take this very well and made numerous attempts to draw Griffon out of his despair. For over a decade they had been inseparable. Now Griffon was treating him with cold indifference. He not only ignored but also avoided his best friend. Both of their actions could be blamed on youth and ignorance. Griffon continued to disregard Falcon and Falcon became so infuriated with Griffon for pushing him away in order to protect him that they both just stopped trying. If they would pass each other, eye contact was avoided and they never spoke. As if the past never existed, they treated each other as strangers passing on the street.

The First Commander was sorely disappointed in both of them. He did everything in his power to reunite them and make them reconcile their differences. He was heartbroken to see them so miserable and alone but all of his attempts proved unsuccessful.

One day while training in the yard Falcon saw Griffon approach the First Commander. He was not dressed for practice but rather for travel, wearing a long hooded cape and he carried his bow. Falcon watched the two as they conversed for a few moments, but he was unable to hear their conversation. He tried to appear like he wasn't watching them but his curiosity was beyond piqued. The First Commander placed his hands on Griffon's shoulders and looked at him. He quickly pulled him into an embrace that ended almost as soon as it began and they each headed in opposite directions. The First Commander, head hung, headed into the keep. Griffon with his shoulders squared headed out of the bailey and down the road. He never even spared a glance in Falcon's direction; that fact didn't bother him nearly as much as the tremendous sense of loss he felt as he watched the retreating figure walk out of his life.

Later he learned from the First Commander that Griffon had decided to begin a journey of self-discovery. He didn't know his father but knew he needed to find out the truth for his own reasons. He felt he couldn't move forward without learning the past—hoping the truth would set him free. Falcon was furious with the First Commander for letting him leave, but never openly expressed his feelings because in doing so would be admitting he cared, something he hadn't conveyed in a very long time. And so that's how it had been—one bitter and alone; the other angry and alone.

Chapter 6

Reluctantly, Falcon reached up his hand and let Griffon assist him to his feet. The two stood facing each other—at a complete loss for words and no idea how to react. There were so many things unsaid between them and they had no clue how to breach that gap. But Falcon's anger swiftly resurfaced; all of the past hurt replacing his momentary shock.

As Griffon watched, Falcon extricated his sword from the dispatched Krypt and he himself recovered some arrows. They warily regarded each other with skeptical glances; neither knowing exactly how to engage in a conversation or even if they wanted to. Griffon was stunned by this new development. He'd been headed in the direction of Ash Knoll when two fiends came barreling down on him in a frenzy. He couldn't make heads or tails out of what they were saying. At first he had ignored them and continued on his way, but they were very persistent in their persuasion; he came to the conclusion that they were not going to stop pestering him until he saw what was about. He had started walking in the direction the fiends had flown, but they soon returned flying in frantic circles around his head until he was dizzy so needless to say he picked up the pace.

It wasn't long until he could hear the sound of metal against metal and pure warrior adrenaline kicked in. Two figures came into view—a girl clearly running for her life from a Krypt who was just about to overtake her. Griffon stopped and swiftly readied his bow. The girl lost her footing and fell to the ground. Taking advantage of her mishap, Griffon drew back aiming his sights on the Krypt, but just as soon as she went down the girl recovered her footing and started running again—she was directly in his line of sight. That's when she glanced up and saw him. She stopped dead in her tracks;

pure terror registered across her face and it occurred to him that she thought he was one of the bad guys.

Griffon held his stance, bow drawn back, his breathing slow and steady. Distracted by a slight glow emitting from his hands, he shook his head to focus. This would be tricky and he had to wait for just the right moment; no margin for error here. He heard the Krypt's cynical laugh as he ran toward the girl with grimy hands outstretched to lay claim to his bounty, but he made one fatal mistake; as he lunged, he barely veered to the left. Griffon didn't hesitate, not for a split second; his arrow pierced exactly where he aimed. Wasting no time, he prepared another arrow and ran towards the clearing and the sounds of battle.

Now here he was looking at the brother who he never imagined seeing again. Falcon had always been home to him—an inseparable duo. In all of his endeavors, Griffon's only regret was leaving Falcon behind without any explanation. And even though they were estranged when he departed, he knew Falcon all too well—he would have either insisted to accompany him or tried to convince him not to leave. With all of the suffering that Griffon had caused him he didn't have the heart to face him. It had been torture saying good-bye to the First Commander so he knew he'd made the right decision where Falcon was concerned.

Griffon cleared his throat. "It's been a long time, Brother." Falcon whirled around and glared at him with a look of pure contempt. Giving a derisive snort Falcon shoved past Griffon and headed up the trail. Griffon lowered his head and smiled—same old Falcon.

Unperturbed by Falcon's dismissal, Griffon followed slightly behind him and curiously asked, "Are you looking for the girl?"

Again Falcon turned, pinning him with a venomous look. He looked away briefly and although Griffon could see it aggravated him, he finally spoke. "Well, did you see her or not?"

"Matter of fact I did. She was being pursued by a very determined Krypt..."

Before Griffon could finish his sentence Falcon was in his face—nose to nose. "You stupid fool!! Why didn't you help her? Have you lost all of your senses not to recognize when someone needs help?"

Bewildered, Griffon just quirked an eyebrow. This provoked a curse from Falcon who spun on his heel and headed down the trail at a run.

"...which I quickly dispatched." Griffon finished to himself since Falcon was now out of earshot.

Griffon realized he was at a crossroad, but it didn't take long for him to know what he was going to do. He never realized how much he'd missed his friend or maybe he'd just never let himself dwell on it. Regardless of the reception, he still had an overwhelming sense of fulfillment and before he knew it he had started jogging down the trail after his long lost family.

Falcon ran up the trail. He scouted left and right in an attempt to catch sight of Ava. Panic started to creep in on him when he finally caught a glimpse of her. As he got closer he saw she was kneeling on the ground. She heard his footsteps and whirled with a sharp intake of breath and scrambled backwards. He realized she was frightened.

"Shhh, it's okay Ava, you're safe." his voice firm but calm. He waited as her dazed expression dissipated. He approached her with arms extended, palms up in a submissive gesture you would you use to approach a wounded animal. When he reached her, he knelt beside her. "Are you injured?"

She looked down. She was filthy and tired, but she was alive. She shook her head. "Scrapes and bruises." She shivered and looked at the ground to her right. Falcon glanced over and saw the dead Krypt with the arrow protruding from its neck. Falcon grimaced, but it wasn't the dead Krypt that made him groan, but rather the fact he'd just berated Griffon for not aiding Ava when in fact he'd obviously done just that.

Falcon relieved Ava of the dagger she still held in her hand and slipped it back in his boot before helping her to her feet. She was dusting herself off when the hooded figure returned. He stopped a few feet away from Falcon who appeared to be intentionally ignoring him, bracing his long bow on the ground. Ava innocently stared in shock for lack of anything better to do.

Falcon knew he couldn't ignore Griffon forever. So he turned to face him. "I see your aim is still accurate."

Griffon nodded and tried not to smile. He would take the compliment even if it was laced with sarcasm.

Ava inched her way toward Falcon. "Ava, this is Griffon, a former acquaintance." There was more than a little bitterness attached to his choice of words.

It wounded Griffon to hear the obvious hurt in Falcon's tone, but it didn't deter his resolve. He made no sudden movements, but just looked at Ava. It appeared the two were travelling together and he didn't want to startle her any more than she already was. He slowly raised his arm and pushed his hood back.

For the second time in twenty-four hours Ava couldn't breathe. Seriously, she had to be creaming. Standing before her was yet another epitome of the perfect male. His hair was raven black; it was fairly short and somewhat choppy. He was exceptionally tall; at least a head taller than she. He was lean and muscular—this was evident by the way his shirt clung to his torso and his pants sat low on his hips—both outlining every nook and crevice of the underlying muscles. He had a five o'clock shadow, probably been on the road awhile.

The cape he wore was an unusual mix of charcoal and blue—almost like smoke—and fell close to the ground. His shirt appeared to be a silvery charcoal and reminded her of chain mail. She could see a dagger secured at his hip that looked very similar to the one that Falcon had given to her earlier.

It wasn't as if Ava had been so sheltered she'd never seen an attractive male before; there was just something so unusual about these two. What they had was more of an overwhelming presence that literally submerged those around them with acute awareness.   But there was also obvious tension that radiated between them.

Griffon stood motionless while the girl scrutinized him. He was more than a little unsettled by the agonizing silence so he looked at Falcon who was now wiping blood from his blade.   In a flurry the fiends appear before Griffon circling him several times.   Then they made their way over to Falcon and were fussing over his injury.   "These pesky fiends are with you?"

Ava was shocked by the soothing tone of his voice and let herself relax.   She saw Falcon's back stiffen and realized it had the opposite effect on him.   As the uncomfortable silence stretched she assumed that Falcon had no intention of providing an answer to the question—no excuse for poor manners.

"Everett and Viktor are their names."   Ava supplied shyly.   She felt a little out of sorts.   It's not like she was a social butterfly and only moments ago she did think this hooded man was trying to kill her.   As if beckoned, the fiends darted forth in front of Griffon, crossed their arms over their chests and bowed in greeting.   Taking courage from their display Ava tentatively stepped forward and held out her hand, "I'm Ava."

Griffon eyed her warily but stepped forward and clasped her hand in his; he was stunned when an incredible, almost electric sensation shot all the way up his arm and spread through his chest.   Ava gasped and looked up at him. She'd obviously experienced the same and for a moment they awkwardly stared at each other.   She was transfixed by his piercing sapphire blue eyes and he was lost in her violet orbs.

Everett and Viktor exchanged an amused glance.

Gathering his wits he cleared his throat, "Griffon." He informed her.

Falcon approached them and Griffon released her hand as if she had burned him and took an awkward step backwards.

Falcon avoided looking at Griffon and spoke directly to Ava. "There's a stream about a half mile ahead. We can get your wounds cleaned and tended. Do you think you can make it that far?" He took her hands in his and examined the scrapes on her palms.

"Yes, but what if there are more of them?" she asked glancing around them nervously.

"There's no way to be sure. We'll just have to be more careful. Everett and Viktor will scout ahead." Falcon shouldered their supplies and placed his hand on Ava's lower back to usher her in the direction they were headed, but the fiends, in a not so subtle gesture, blocked his path.

"And Griffon?" Ava asked. Falcon closed his eyes in frustration.

Through clenched teeth he ground out, "What about him?"

"He saved me...and you for that matter. Safety in numbers—wouldn't it be wise if we traveled together?"

It took Falcon a moment to rein in his anger. Ava was unaware of their history and didn't deserve to have the past taken out on her. "I'm sure Griffon isn't travelling in the same direction. He has somewhere else to be."

Ava placed her hand on Falcon's arm. She could feel the rage emanating from him and knew at some point in time Griffon must have wounded him deeply.

Falcon glanced down at her hand and then looked up at her—he could be content just standing in her presence, but couldn't put himself back in a position to be disappointed. He barked, in a tone that was harsher than he intended, "I travel alone and will continue alone once I escort you to Ash Knoll." He wrenched his arm fee harder than her light touch would warrant and stormed down the trail. Everett and Viktor expressed their evident anger at his decision by buzzing him, but he merely swatted them away.

Ava sighed in exasperation. She knew he was upset but he was also being stubborn. She heard Griffon approach from behind. They stood side by side and watched in silence as an angry Falcon stormed away.

Griffon was the one to break the silence, "It's not you, it's me."

She peeked through her lashes at him with just a hint of a smile, "Well, you wouldn't have to be a genius to figure that one out." Her smile was contagious and he couldn't help but chuckle.

Again he caught himself staring at this stranger. Who was she he wondered. Her presence felt like a gentle breeze that cooled the inferno of his tortured soul and infused him with a sense of peace he hadn't felt in a very long while. He had an urge to grab her and crush her in his embrace which was not only utter lunacy since they'd just met, but a feeling he'd never experienced before.

Shaking his head to clear the random thoughts he looked to see how much progress Falcon had made. He had stopped at the top of the first rise and was now watching them. Griffon wasn't exactly sure of the relationship between Falcon and Ava, but they did appear familiar to each other. "You're headed to Ash Knoll?" he asked.

Ava nodded. "Yes, a rather long and unusual story, but that is where Falcon is taking me. And you? Before you became a knight in shining armor?"

Her choice of words made his heart do a little flip flop in his chest and he felt himself blush which rarely happened. He looked away in an attempt to hide his unease. "I was also headed to Ash Knoll, but we both know that he,' Griffon inclined his head towards Falcon, "would never be convinced." Twisting his head and quirking a brow he informed her, "That too is another long story."

They shared a moment of mutual understanding. "So, what now?" she asked.

"Well, you are going to walk up the hill to meet the clearly impatient Falcon—if those daggers he's shooting my way are any indication of his mood."

"And you?" she inquired somewhat hesitant.

"I'm going to travel to Ash Knoll as well, but given the circumstances I think it's best to keep some distance between us…give Falcon time to absorb the day's revelations."

Ava understood the logic in his plan, but couldn't help feeling anxious. She had a suspicion there were more Krypts lurking about.

Griffon sensed her anxiety, as if his hand moved on its own accord he tucked a stray lock of hair behind her ear. "Don't worry, Ava, I'll keep one eye on you at all times." His thumb stroked her cheek and his hand quivered from the ripple of electricity that passed between them. This time it wasn't such a surprise and they both smiled shyly.

"Go on, before he storms down here in a temper or worse, sends those pesky fiends to fetch you."

Ava turned and started walking up the hill.

"Ava."

She turned around to look at him.

"Stay safe." He said. She nodded and continued up the path toward Falcon—the whole time wondering exactly how to bring him out of his black mood.

Chapter 7

Of course it took longer than expected, but the stream was now in front of them. Ava sat on a rock at the bank soaking her feet in the water. Falcon had been in no mood for conversation and she hadn't pressed the matter during their walk.

Now, he watched her leaning back on her arms, head tilted back and eyes closed, soaking up the rays of the sun that cascaded down through the leaves on the trees. She appeared to be enjoying the moment which he found miraculous considering everything she had been through.

He'd left her for a few minutes while he prepared a paste from different herbs to apply to their injuries. After he finished with his arm he found a strip of clean cloth in his sack to wrap it up. Then he moved to apply the medicine to Ava's injuries. She had moved one knee up and was examining it.

"I've made a salve." He said kneeling down beside her and was rewarded with a smile.

"You're just full of surprises." She said swinging her leg around so he could see the damage to her knee.

Remembering her distress when he'd tried to administer the blisters on her feet, the fact she trusted him to address her injuries now oddly pleased him. He gently pulled her leg across his lap. Ava had already washed the dirt away, but closed her eyes and held her breath in preparation.

"What are you doing?" he questioned.

"Being prepared—in case it stings." She never opened her eyes when she spoke.

Shaking his head Falcon dabbed the medicine on the lacerations. She released the breath she'd been holding in obvious relief. "What's in it?"

"Aloe, comfrey root, and calendula." He finished with one leg and she then moved the other where he could reach it.

"Smells funny." She said scrunching her nose.

"I probably should have warned you before—it can take weeks for the smell to wear off, but don't worry. I'm sure no one will notice." His tone was joking and he tried incredibly hard to keep a serious expression.

Shoving hard against his shoulder she said, "Real funny." She unconsciously glanced down the grail. True to his word Griffon was watching them. He was obscured by dense brush, but still just barely visible. She'd looked back on several occasions. At times she couldn't see him but then he'd appear as if he sensed she was looking for him so he would make himself momentarily visible. She barely knew him and it was unfathomable to her why his presence was so comforting. It again made her thoughts stray to the conflict between the two men. She felt like an interloper sticking her nose where it didn't belong.

"Falcon," she said nervously, "you are aware Griffon is behind us… aren't you?" He didn't cringe this time, but he didn't respond right away.

"Of course." He replied frankly.

"I'm not sure what's going on and it's entirely none of my business but I can't help but wonder the reason you are trying to ignore him."

He sighed as he deliberated her question. "I'm not ignoring him. That would be impossible." His latter statement was dripping with cynicism. "I'm just trying to wrap my head around this unexpected situation." His tone was sincere, his eyes were expressionless as he gazed straight ahead trying to see reason. "Griffon was my brother—not by blood but by everything else that mattered. Let's just say unfortunate events transpired when we were very young which we were unaware of until we were much older—every single day I wish that fact were still so."

Falcon moved her legs and stood. Ava was surprised when he quietly continued. "Our decisions mold us; they shape us in to whom and what we become, but not just you, they inadvertently affect others as well. An intricate web spun by encounters and relationships. So very fragile that damage to one thread can make the entire structure unstable." With that he walked away, giving her no opportunity to pose more questions.

Chapter 8

After they'd finished dressing their wounds, they'd pressed on for another mile or so. With the initial shock of the attack worn off the full impact of what had transpired started to sink in on Ava. Mental and physical fatigue started to take their toll. To put it simply, she hurt. Her muscles ached, her scrapes were burning and she didn't know if her feet would ever be the same. Now that her focus was centered on all of her ailments she also realized that she was absolutely starved.

Falcon recognized she was beat. "Why don't you sit down and rest a while. I'm going to scout ahead a bit and see the best way for us to travel."

Ava looked skeptical, but knew her limits. "Okay but don't go far." She watched him leave. He was also injured, but clearly it had little to no effect on him and she was irritated with herself for being so pathetic. She hated to admit how disappointed she was in herself. She typically had much more stamina and it irritated her to think she was coming off as weak. She found a stump and dropped down. She took off her shoes and wiggled her toes—stretched her arms up in the air and arched her back trying to loosen some of the stiffness. What she wouldn't give for a good meal and a nice hot bubble bath.

"Are you hungry?" Ava nearly jumped out of her skin she was so startled. She whipped around to see Griffon standing behind her. She placed her hand on her chest to try and calm her now frantic pulse.

"What is wrong with you?" she snapped. She gestured in the direction they'd just travelled from, "Do you not remember the monsters back there? Are you purposefully trying to give me a heart attack?"

He looked quite amused. "It wasn't my intention to frighten you. I noticed that you haven't had anything to eat for some time." He held out his hand offering a gift in the form of jerky.

"Thank you." She said surprised at his kindness. He had no reason what so ever to share this with her, yet he offered it freely. She sat back down and started nibbling on the jerky. Griffon rested his hip on the other side of the log.

"How did you do that?" Ava said around a mouthful of food.

"Do what?"

Ava swallowed, "Sneak around like that. I never heard a sound—it was like stealth or something. With these leaves and branches it should be impossible not to make a noise."

Entertained by her flustered state, Griffon advised, "If I had the intent to sneak I wouldn't have walked straight up to you. If I was trying to be evasive, you never would have known I was here.

"Are you arrogant or conceited?" she asked incredulously.

"Neither." He said. "Just stating the facts."

She had to laugh. "Well, I certainly can't argue." She finished her last bite of jerky. Griffon offered her a canteen and she took a long draw of water. She handed it back to him.

He also took a long drink. She was captivated by his adam's apple as it moved up and down when he swallowed. A drop of water escaped and started to drip down his chin. She reacted before she even had time to think—she wiped away the drop of water with her fingertips. Griffon paused—canteen still to his lips. She looked up to see him watching her. He unhurriedly lowered the canteen and she pulled her hand back hastily a little embarrassed.

He swallowed the mouthful of water and cleared his throat. He put the canteen away. He was at a loss. He didn't know what to think and he didn't really comprehend what he was feeling. He looked over at Ava to see her closely observing him—he couldn't look away. He had only just met her and he was already smitten.

In Griffon's presence Ava was very aware of her femininity. She'd always considered herself ordinary and unattractive at Elzbeth. She was a little self-conscious sitting this close to him. Beyond a slight sheen of perspiration on his brow, he looked perfectly put together. She not only felt filthy, but she could only imagine what a tangled mess her hair was in. All ridiculous thoughts considering their lives could be in danger. She tried to banish the vain thoughts running through her head. Guys rarely paid her any mind back home and Falcon and Griffon were in another league entirely.

"What are you thinking right now?" he whispered never looking away.

She wanted to remember this moment--sitting so close to such an attractive man and not fidgeting. "I was thinking I'm a wreck."

"Completely inaccurate, what else?" he prompted her to continue like he knew that wasn't the only thing on her mind.

"I was thinking," she hesitated a moment, "there's some girl who should consider herself very lucky to possess the heart of a man like you." She couldn't believe her own ears. Did she really just say that? His expression never changed, but he slowly leaned closer to her and just when it looked like he was about to say something...

"What's he doing here?" Ava was startled to see Falcon had returned.

"He brought me something to eat and drink." Ava replied. She looked back to Griffon who'd not moved a muscle and was still looking directly at her. He seemed slightly disappointed for the interruption.

"I think it best we make camp early." Falcon continued. "That way we can set up a good perimeter. Everett and Viktor will be back soon. I sent them out to do one last canvas." Falcon stood with his arms crossed and a scowl on his face. "We should probably get moving. I'm afraid the temperature will be much cooler than it was last night."

Ava nodded her consent and bent down to get her shoes. Griffon quickly scooped them up and placed them on her feet. "You really need to do something about these shoes." He said.

"Let's just say I didn't exactly plan on this trip, so it's not like I had a bag packed. I'll make do." She said light heartedly. He offered her his hand and helped her to her feet.

"Thank you." She knew saying those words would never be able to truly convey her gratitude for all of his kindness.

Falcon grabbed their supplies. "Ready?"

Again Ava felt the substantial tension between the two men. "Ready." She said. It felt rather ridiculous to separate, but with one last look at Griffon who inclined his head they headed off and all she could think was it felt incredibly wrong.

Chapter 9

The sun had descended past the tree tops and it didn't take long for the surrounding woods to become dark and spooky; Ava could imagine the temperature on the thermometer plunging. Falcon found a suitable place to make camp and informed Ava they should reach Ash Knoll by the next evening and she was relieved. Maybe they could do something about her clothes or at least she could freshen up. He had built a small fire advising they couldn't risk anything bigger as it could be a beacon for any nearby Krypts. She was surprised to learn they had an acute sense of smell which she found rather amusing considering their own personal state of hygiene.

Everett and Viktor zoomed in only momentarily to check on things. She was coming to think of them as little body guards. They always seemed to be concerned for everyone else's welfare; a monumental task for them to undertake considering their size. Her Aunt always told her that great things came in small packages and now she could certainly see the truth in that.

Falcon redressed his shoulder; Ava worried that it was bothering him more than he let on. She offered to help him but he politely declined. It was clear he preferred not to be fussed over—probably something he learned during all of his combat training. Or maybe he just wasn't used to having travelling companions. She thought herself a pretty good judge of character and had had already developed a great amount of respect for this interesting man.

The air started to cool and a misty fog shrouded the woods like a cloak. A damp mist carried by the breeze left a trail of goose bumps all over Ava's exposed flesh and she couldn't suppress the shivers that followed. She'd seated herself as close to the fire as possible and rubbed her arms vigorously in an attempt to warm herself.

"You're freezing."

She said through chattering teeth, "Aren't you?"

"No, but I'm used to the climate. You've not had enough time to acclimate and your clothes don't provide much protection." He sighed. "I wish I had something more to offer." He sounded disappointed.

Falcon had nothing besides the shirt off of his back which he would willingly give if he thought it would improve her situation. But it was damp from his earlier exertion and wouldn't provide much additional warmth to her. His only other option was body heat and the very idea of being so intimately close to Ava made his blood pressure sky rocket, his palms sweaty, and his pulse race. It was not a rational reaction for him and that made him very uncomfortable.

Yet he couldn't stand to watch her suffer. He placed another branch on the fire. "I'm going to gather more firewood. We have to get you warmed up so we'll just have to take the risk." As he walked away Everett and Viktor met him. "You stay with her. Find me if there's any trouble. I won't be far." And with that he disappeared into darkness.

Everett zipped over to Ava and examined her. He went back to Viktor and they did the opposite of what Falcon requested. So much for following orders...they were off in a flash.

Ava had her knees up to her chest and her arms crossed over them. She rested her head against her knees and tried to think about anything except the shivers that racked her body. The sun. The desert. Raging fire. Nothing provided relief to the paralyzing cold. She was concentrating so hard she didn't realize someone had joined her until they were directly behind her. Awareness kicked in only when strong arms enveloped her and pulled backwards. She was embraced against a broad chest radiating pure warmth. She opened her eyes and saw long legs stretched out on each side of her. She looked over her shoulder to discover it was Griffon. He unfastened his cloak and wrapped it around her. They shared a momentary look where she could tell he was giving her an opportunity to protest. A doze couldn't have made her budge. Like a moth to a flame she turned into him and laid her head on his shoulder. She closed her eyes and absorbed his heat. The last thing she remembered was thinking he smelled of open woods and fresh air.

Ava groggily stirred to the sound of hushed voices. Falcon? Yes, that was him. He didn't sound very pleased.

"It just doesn't matter. Don't you see it has been too long? I really don't want to have this conversation." Falcon said irritably.

Ava was aware her shivers had dissipated, but she was so exhausted she couldn't get her eyes to pry open. She could feel Griffon sigh beneath her cheek with the steady rhythm of his breathing.

"Falcon, you are being unreasonable. Not that I'm surprised, but you need to consider this from my point of view. We were young and I was confused. I felt like a sinking ship and I just couldn't see dragging you under with me." His baritone voice rumbled in his chest against her ear. "I've travelled so very far and have little to show for it. Just when I 'think' I have learned a clue about the past—about my father—I run into a wall." Although his words were solemn she recognized the underlying frustration.

"I gotta tell ya man…you are barking up the wrong tree if you think I remotely care. Don't you get it? Don't you understand the day you took it upon yourself to decide what was in my best interest—you broke our trust. You excluded me from your plans, basically exiled me from your life." His words trailed off and just when she thought he wasn't going to say anything else she heard, "You left me behind." Those words were infused with raw grief.

She felt Griffon's sharp intake of breath and heard his heart accelerate. Raspy with emotion all he managed to croak was, "I'm sorry."

Unable to fight off the pull of unconsciousness Ava slipped back into the black abyss of deep sleep. Unfortunately, it wasn't peaceful sleep. It was lunchtime. Everything in the cafeteria was sterile and cold. Like always, she sat at a table in the corner with a book opened in front of her…head propped up on one hand as if she were studying. In reality, she was silently observing the predictable routine of her class mates. First, she'd watched Olivia walk past, the girl considered to be the most popular in school. Her father owned several businesses in town so she had that notoriety. At first glance you would immediately notice her appearance. She was a classic beauty; almost like a flawless diamond. The problem was if you remained in her company for more than a couple of minutes you'd realize that her beauty barely scratched the surface. The person on the inside wasn't nearly as pretty. This particular diamond had plenty of internal flaws and imperfections.

Olivia was followed by the mysterious guy that all the girls secretly drool over…even those high class girls that will roll their eyes when his name gets mentioned, but secretly they want find him just as appealing. He was an attractive rebel that no parent ever wants to see their daughter bring home. What was his name? Trent, maybe. He personified the 'come what may attitude'--didn't really seem to care what anyone thought. Maybe that's why everyone envied him. They simply wished to be more carefree. Trent smoothly sat down at his usual spot by the windows that everyone else reserved just for him.

To the left of Trent's table, sat a table of athletes. Basketball, football, and swimming are the only sports the school has to offer, but it's just enough for this group to share a common bond. She watched a cocky boy from the swim team make a snide remark to someone at the next table where the students who take their studies very seriously were seated. They were nerds--a few of their own accord, the rest due to their parent's high ambitions.

Straight across from her were a few tables full of unremarkable people. Some purposefully trying to stay under radar and others were there because they had no choice. She knew all of their names and their faces, but she couldn't recall the last time she'd had a conversation with any of them. She preferred being out of the spotlight, it was her comfort zone.

All around her was excited chatter about the upcoming black tie fall formal. There was speculation from the girls regarding who would ask who and whether or not they'd accept. Of course, all of the guys were dreading the prospect of not only getting up the nerve to solicit a date, but actually having to attend the black tie affair. Ava knew she would not be going so all of the talk was meaningless babble to her; not as if anyone would think to include her in their conversation anyway. She was practically invisible. And for some reason today the sights, the sounds, the heat pressed in on her; she felt like she would suffocate.

Ava felt totally disconnected as if she were watching a film of her life instead of living it. Olivia tossed her perfect gold mane over her shoulder then turned around to look right at Ava. Her eyes were cruel—something was wrong with her eyes. They were black as pitch. Ava gasped.

Everything got blurry. Faces started to melt like wax and her surroundings started to fade and darken. There was darkness. It was calling to her, beckoning for her to "Come now to us." A hauntingly, rhythmic chant--it was confusing at first because all she could see were shadows. She was completely alone in the dark with the chanting—her mind screamed for it to stop. Just when she thought she couldn't take anymore…the shadows moved. They bent and weaved around the contours of the walls. They slithered ever closer bringing with them emptiness, a despair. Unable to move or breathe she simply stood--watching and waiting. She could see more clearly now. There were many shadows, not just one; although, they moved almost as a single unit. She could differentiate where one ended and the next began. Closer and closer; they reached out for her extending their arms like tentacles they wrapped around her arms, her legs, her neck and started to pull her…she struggled to resist, but they wouldn't release her…pulling her into the oblivion she always feared.

Ava jerked awake. Her breathing labored and fear evident on her face. She frantically looked around to locate the shadows. She was completely disoriented. Falcon rushed over to her, "It's okay, Ava. It's okay." He kneeled down beside her. "It was just a dream." He finally got her attention and awareness dawned on her face. With a cry of despair she dived into his chest and wrapped her arms around him. She couldn't prevent the tide of tears that spilled down her face or the sobs that wracked her body. It was the intuition that one day soon her nightmare would turn into reality putting her face to face with the menacing darkness and the emptiness that it possessed.

Chapter 10

Falcon was so unprepared for this. Soothing a distraught female was definitely not included in the First Commander's curriculum. Each sob that wracked her body broke his heart. Finally, he wrapped his arms around her and whispered soothing words against her ear. This always worked with his niece when she would fall down and get injured, maybe it would work in this situation too. After several minutes passed, Ava appeared to be calming down but he continued to gently rock back and forth.

Finally, getting herself under control Ava looked up at Falcon. She swiped the remaining tears from her cheeks. "I'm sorry. It was just sooo real. I could feel them—all over me, pulling me towards them. They were so hollow, so empty. I felt like they were ripping out my very soul." Ava shuddered as the recalled the disturbing images.

Falcon pushed her hair back from her temple. "What was it?"

Another shudder wracked her body and another tear slipped down her cheek. Falcon was afraid the water works would start again. "Shadows, I think." She whispered.

Falcon couldn't mask the look of astonishment that crossed his face or the way his body tensed at the word she had just spoken. Being the perceptive person she was, Ava picked up on it immediately. "This was just a nightmare." She watched him closely. "I dreamed of this place, like, all the time. Now, here I am." With pleading eyes and a catch in her voice she asked, "Tell me, Falcon. Tell me this isn't real." He only continued to stare at her which confirmed her suspicions. A single tear trickled down her cheek. She laid her forehead on his shoulder. "What kind of place is this?"

They remained the way they were for several more minutes until Ava gathered her wits. She realized hiding her head in a hole like an ostrich wouldn't make this disappear. She leaned back and Falcon released his hold. She pulled herself back and looked at him. "I'm not usually this emotional." She looked down to see she was still covered by Griffon's cape. She was flooded with memories of a warm chest and strong arms holding her while she slept. She cleared her throat. "Where did Griffon go?"

Falcon was relieved that Ava's tears had subsided. He'd felt like he had no control over the situation which put him out of his element. "He went scouting to make sure there were no Krypts in the nearby vicinity. We had the fire stoked a little higher than we would have liked." He couldn't hide the annoyance in his tone. He hated to admit he was a little more than irritated with the man and didn't care to see him anytime soon. He'd left the camp to find some more fire wood; when he returned what did he find? Ava cocooned in Griffon's arms. The man had no respect for boundaries as far as Falcon was concerned. He'd made it very clear he had no desire to travel with him. If Ava hadn't appeared so warm and completely sound asleep he would have physically removed Griffon and taken great pleasure in doing so. It might have provided an outlet for some of the frustration and anger he had pent up inside him. But, he just couldn't do that to Ava. So he'd sat in miserable silence cursing the day he had ever set eyes on Griffon Gray.

What was even worse, he'd had the gall to try and take advantage of the situation and have a heart to hear about their past. Even though Falcon had shut that notion down he was still forced to watch Ava sleep cradled in Griffon's arms as the night wore on. He couldn't deny that it tormented him and he was even a little jealous. What should it matter so long as she didn't freeze? That's the question he'd been trying to answer logically all night, but no matter how hard he tied to be rational, it appeared to matter a great deal. Over and over he couldn't keep from thinking if he hadn't been emotionally handicapped he could have been the one holding Ava instead of running away scared at the prospect of being in such close proximity to her.

There were much more urgent matters that required his attention so he forced his irrational jealousy aside. "Could you tell where you were in the dream? Is there anything else you can remember?"

Although the prospect didn't appeal to her, she closed her eyes trying to retrieve details from the nightmare she only wanted to forget. She couldn't see anything but darkness that felt alive. Wait…the walls. "The walls…were some kind of stone. Everything else was just," Ava paused trying to articulate, "oblivion." She shuddered. It wasn't the first time she'd felt oblivion on her heels.

"It's the Reach."

They both turned to see Griffon leaning against a tree.

"You don't know that Griffon! There's no way to be sure." Falcon said quietly. There was no tension between them, just a shared concern.

Obviously the only one who had no ideas what they were talking about, Ava asked, "What's the reach?"

A guarded look passed between the two men, but neither took the initiative to explain. The ominous dread that hung in the air was more than she could bear. Ava stood and looked both Falcon and Griffon in the eye. "I need to take a few minutes. I realize that you don't know me very well. But I've been an open book, so I would appreciate honest answers when I get back." She walked by Griffon and held out his cape. Griffon reached out to take it from her placing one hand on each of hers. "Thank you," was all she said as she continued on her way.

Griffon watched her until she was no longer visible. He shook out his cape and fastened it around his shoulders. He looked over at Falcon who hadn't moved from his sitting position. "Tell me you have a better explanation, Brother, 'cause this is one scenario I would prefer to be wrong about."

Falcon looked up at him and said, in a way that sounded more like he was trying to convince himself rather than Griffon, "It just can't be, it's impossible. You and I both know that the Deacon and Deaconess were both killed years ago. There's been no other Deacon—the blood line is extinct."

Griffon nodded in agreement. "True. That's what we've been told, but this mysterious girl appears out of nowhere, dreams about the Reach, and gave more detail in their regard than any person could in the last century." He rubbed his temples with his fingers. This was all too much to process. "And there's something else," he continued, "during the encounter with the Krypts—I noticed your marks glowing. So did mine. Tell me, has that happened to you before yesterday?"

Falcon looked perplexed and muttered, "I thought I imagined that."

"My marks glowed—for the first time in all my 21 years." Griffon inspected his arms in bewilderment and looked at Falcon to see how he absorbed this information. "My father told me stories when I was little, about my markings. Did your father speak of it?"

Falcon was confused. This couldn't be happening. He got up from the ground and started pacing back and forth. He didn't want to try and remember things from his past that he had worked so hard to leave behind. Besides he had somewhere he had to be. "I vaguely remember—his markings would change in the presence of the Deacon or Deaconess. I thought it was magic or trickery of some sort. No one else seemed to pay any attention so I guess I just forgot."

Griffon was a little uneasy. Ava's arrival and the unexplained connection they all seemed to share, her nightmare—presumably about the Reach, it just couldn't be coincidence. They were in over their heads. "We need to take Ava to see the First Commander. He has much more knowledge on this than either one of us. Maybe he could fill in some missing pieces."

Falcon considered this proposal. He hated to admit Griffon was probably right. His message was intended for the First Commander after all; he'd just planned on leaving Ava at Ash Knoll where she would be safe before moving on. "We still need to go to Ash Knoll. We'll need to prepare, see if we can get Ava some better travelling clothes and pick up a few supplies. It couldn't hurt to rest a day before heading out." So, that was decided. Now they just needed to convince Ava. Falcon started packing up their supplies. "Oh, and Griffon, one more thing—she has to agree to this—I won't force her."

Griffon nodded his consent. He took a seat on the ground and anxiously awaited Ava's return. He chuckled while thinking that she most definitely wasn't the type of person that would be forced into anything. They had no back-up plan and he was certain these occurrences were not coincidental so he hoped Ava would see reason and agree to take this journey with them. Having the opportunity to spend more time with her was also incentive for him to make sure she was convinced.

Chapter 11

Ava considered herself extremely fortunate. She'd found a small brook not far from where they'd camped. She washed as much filth as possible from her arms and legs. She splashed cool water on her face and cupped her hands to take a drink. She swished the water around in her mouth and then spit it out. She even took the time to undo her hair and comb her fingers through it. Once she felt like she'd gotten most of the tangles out, she pulled it forward and braided it. She was trying not to think about anything. She was bumfuzzled. A myriad of questions were running laps in her brain. Why was she here? What on earth was happening? She knew Falcon and Griffon had some answers and she fully intended to have them when she returned. She was reluctant to do so because she also couldn't help thinking she may not want to know the truth once it was revealed.

"Coward." Ava muttered under her breath. What else was there for her to do? She turned around and headed back to the two Adonis's waiting for her at camp—how absurd.

As she entered the camp she saw Falcon pacing—not a good sign. Griffon was seated on the ground but scrambled to his feet when he saw her approach. Looks like they were more than ready to talk which worried her a little. "Alright, I want the whole truth no matter what. Don't leave anything out in some macho attempt to shield me."

Falcon went first. "We can tell you what we know Ava, but there are so many details that are missing. All we have is a theory."

"Your nightmare—about the shadows, we believe it was what they used to call the Reach. Exactly what that means we couldn't tell you.   There were stories from when we were children about the dominance of the Reach, but we thought they were just that—stories—intended to frighten children."   Griffon supplied this information with a shrug of his shoulders.

Falcon sighed as he watched Ava quietly evaluating this information, "There's more."   He advised.   "Something Griffon noticed during our encounter with the Krypts.   Our markings, they are inherited from generation to generation.   They are marks of pledglings.   Our grandfathers and our fathers carried the markers; therefore, so do we."

"That's all they were, until yesterday.   It's like something activated inside us.   They radiated some sort of light.   It was empowering.   I don't know exactly what it was, but I know it has never happened before."   Griffon's voice trailed off as he himself was still in disbelief.

They took turns filling Ava in on the details they knew to be true.   They explained about the Deacon and Deaconess and how they were renowned for their kindness and generosity.   Their actions were transforming the kingdom until something happened.   A battle in which they were both lost.   There was talk of betrayal and sabotage, but no one could really prove anything because turmoil and unrest overcame the land.   Complete chaos.   It took several years for things to settle down and just when it looked like the kingdom was back on track, Prime Sovereign Ezekiel—a tyrannical king in the West, decided he preferred the chaos.   He was responsible for attacks on innocent villages all across the land. People couldn't trade because travel was unsafe.   There was also evidence that he was somehow connected to the Krypts who were certainly not to be trifled with.   It was almost like they were programmed to destroy whatever they encountered.

They explained about the First Commander and how he was there the day of the battle. And that's when it got tense. Ava could tell neither of them wanted to continue, so she remained silent and tried to be patient.

Falcon took over, "My father Gideon, and Griffon's father, Manford, were guardians to the Deacon and Deaconess. On the day they died, my father was to serve as escort to the Deacon, but for some reason he was summoned by a messenger and by the time he returned the travelling party had already departed. He caught up to them, but there was nothing he could do." Falcon's voice trailed off and a look of sadness settled over him. "The party was attacked. By the time my father reached them he couldn't save them. He too died that day."

Ava moved forward without thinking and grabbed Falcon's hand in both of hers. "Oh, Falcon, I'm so sorry. It must have been awful." She squeezed his hand and wished she could take away all of the terrible memories. He tenderly squeezed her hand back, but avoided eye contact. She could tell that his eyes were getting watery.

"Didn't you forget the most important detail?" Griffon asked bitterly.

Ava turned to look at Griffon—his face a blank slate until he looked at Falcon with a look of such utter despair. She couldn't imagine what else possibly could have happened to these two. She looked back to Falcon. He continued to stare at the ground. "Griffon...don't..."his voice gravelly with emotion.

Griffon looked at Ava, "The whole truth, right Ava? That's what you said."

The manner in which he asked her that question seriously made her reconsider her earlier statement.

"The summons that Gideon received, it just so happened to be from my father; he'd requested an audience with Gideon before they all departed, but when Gideon arrived at the requested meeting place, my father was nowhere to be found. Gideon realized something was wrong but it was too late." Griffon paused. He squinted his brow and gritted his teeth—it was bad enough to think these terrible thoughts but it was even more difficult trying to articulate them. "My father hasn't been seen since. Rumor has it that he was bribed to betray the Deacon and that he left to live off of his newfound wealth." Griffon stumbled through his next words and couldn't hide the bitterness in his voice, "leaving his only son behind."

So there it is Ava thought to herself, the reason for the enormous rift between them.

"There's no proof of any of that Griffon. It's speculation." Falcon interjected.

Griffon gave a derisive snort. "And you are the only fool that believes that.

"Our fathers, they were more than comrades. They were like brothers. Manford never would have done anything to cause my father harm or the Royals for that matter." Falcon spoke truthfully without thinking and then realized what he had just said. What right did he have to school Griffon on brotherhood? He hadn't exactly been living up to the description. He shook his head agitated at the unexpected turn his thoughts had taken.

The three stood in silence, one way or another, each a broken soul that needed to mend, and all completely unaware that in order to do so they would have to learn to trust one another.

What better to interrupt an extremely tense moment than Everett zooming by at the speed of light? All three of their heads whipped in the direction from which he came— defense mechanisms kicking in, but all they saw was Viktor covered in brown mud from head to foot. He looked none too happy as he also zipped by them hot on Everett's heels. Ava didn't envy Everett once Viktor caught up to him.

Falcon realized he was still holding Ava's hand which he released. He went and started gathering his supplies. Griffon was still staring in the direction the fiends had flown. She approached him. "Tell me the rest."

"The First Commander, the man who took us both in, we believe he can provide us with some explanation as to what has happened. That was Falcon's destination when you met him. He was going to take you to Ash Knoll and continue on his way from there." He paused. Ava could tell it was to consider the best way to propose whatever they had discussed. "Instead of leaving you at Ash Knoll, we want you to consider travelling on with us to see the First Commander— maybe he can help rationalize some of this."

Ava's heart hurt as she gauged the depth of Griffon's pain and if there was anything within her power that would provide any amount of comfort, knew she wouldn't hesitate. She took his elbow and stood in front of him. She didn't speak until he dared to look at her. "I'm not sure exactly how I can help, but I will go with you…and try." She paused to look at Falcon. "On one condition."

That statement caught their attention and both men looked up. Griffon was the first to gather his wits, "Okay, let's hear it."

"We stick together, no matter what, which means we also travel together."

"That sounds reasonable enough." Griffon agreed, but Falcon's immediate reaction was one of pure outrage. He glared at Ava in disbelief, dropped his pack and stormed off toward the tree line muttering curses under his breath. Several yards away he stopped, put his hands on his hips, and shook his head in obvious agitation.

Falcon was well aware that something unusual was happening and this was probably the most logical solution. It would mean more protection for Ava if they stuck together, but to hell and back with logic. He didn't know if it was his ego or his pride that made him react so; regardless, he knew what he had to do. Taking a deep, cleansing breath to regain control of his temper he stalked back to the two figures staring at him with slightly amused expressions. He picked up his pack and slung it over his shoulder. "Agreed." That was all he said as he walked by them and headed down the trail.

Ava and Griffon released a simultaneous sigh of relief. "This isn't going to be easy." Griffon told her gathering his own things.

Ava nodded agreement, "Nothing worthwhile ever is." And they both trailed along after their comrade.

Chapter 12

They travelled several more miles with minimal conversation which Ava was grateful for. She was afraid that her request would cause more friction between the two men, but couldn't see the point in continuing separated. Each of them was involved in one way or another and it was dangerous to travel so this was the only rational conclusion. She didn't look forward to any more encounters with the bloody Krypts. It wouldn't hurt her feelings at all if she never saw one again, but she knew that was highly unlikely.

The terrain leveled out and became much easier to navigate so they were able to keep a steady pace. Unsure of just how much time had transpired Ava was thankful when Griffon tapped her on the shoulder and pointed out toward his left. The sun was shining through the trees which obscured her vision. Ava squinted and shielded her eyes with her hand in an attempt to see what he was pointing at. In the distance she was finally able to distinguish the outline of several buildings and could see movement as people milled about. She immediately became energized and started rambling questions one after the other which rather amused both Griffon and Falcon who couldn't help but chuckle at her excitement.

"Do you know anyone here?" Ava asked. "What will we do first?"

Falcon glanced over at Ava and was amused by her antics. He thought this was the first time since the day they'd met he'd seen her so uninhibited. It was something he'd certainly like to see more often. But it made him realize something else also. She was so very young to be faced with everything that had been thrown her way over the last couple of days. She had not only been brave but steadfast. She hadn't complained about anything. Not about their meager fare, the cold, or the numerous blisters on her feet. She was truly incredible.

"I have several friends in town. I think we should get cleaned up first and then get something to eat. Then you can rest while Griffon and I gather some supplies." Falcon advised and was surprised at the excitement he himself now felt.

The idea of a eating something other than jerky and berries made Ava's mouth water and the notion of soaking in a hot bath made her very anxious to get to town. She looked down at her dress and cringed. She'd be surprised if she could ever find herself under all of the dirt. Suddenly she stopped. She couldn't go into town like this. She looked up as Falcon and Griffon continued walking and examined their clothes. She would clearly stand out and that would raise unwanted questions. "Guys, we have a problem."

Both men quickly turned around. Of course their protective instincts had them on high alert. Falcon had his hand on his sword and Griffon had already reached back to withdraw an arrow. As they ascertained there was no danger they relaxed. Griffon gave her a quizzical look. "What's wrong?"

"My clothes—I think they will draw attention? I'm not sure how different they are from what girls here would normally wear?"

Both Falcon and Griffon's eyes got big as they finally absorbed what she was telling them. "It's much shorter than what we are accustomed to; and the shoes, they will definitely get attention." Falcon noted.

"We'll have to find her some new travelling clothes, but for now," Griffon removed his cape, and walking back to where Ava stood, wrapped it around her shoulders. He pulled the two sides together to clasp them. "That should do it."

Ava looked down to see the cape covered everything. It just drug the ground which only exposed the toes of her shoes when she took a step. Satisfied that she wouldn't attract unwanted attention they made their way into Ash Knoll. It was a quaint town. The buildings were wooden and rustic, but the greenery surrounding the town gave it a vibrant and homey feel. There were street vendors scattered here and there selling their goods. Ava could smell fresh baked bread and it made her mouth water. The whole atmosphere was so different from Elzbeth. Things seemed so simple here and moved slower. It was a welcome change for Ava from the hustle and bustle of life at home. All of this just seemed to suit her she felt like she actually fit.

As they made their way through several dusty streets they were greeted with mixed reactions. Some of the town's people seemed shocked to see the two men together and didn't do a very good job of hiding their disbelief. Others smiled and greeted them with a wave. And there were a few bad apples that threw derogatory slurs toward Griffon. Although he ignored the remarks she didn't miss the way his jaw clenched.

They guided Ava toward a building that appeared to be built right in one of the trees. It was amazing. The interior was warm and well lit and she immediately felt right at home.

A tiny old woman with a slightly hunched back and missing teeth eyed them warily.

"I'll not be having any trouble in my establishment. I'll tell you that right now. Don't you think I won't take a broom to the both of you, and I'll do it too."

Both men looked down and attempted to hide their smiles at the little old woman's rants.

Falcon was the first to recover. "We'll not cause you any trouble. We need rooms for the night and hot baths if possible."

The woman continued to eyeball them. She perused each one of them from head to toe. Sizing them up and trying to determine if she would let them be patrons. "Well then, I suppose that will be three separate rooms, and there's no discount. It will be the full price for each room. And I'm an old woman, so you'll have to carry your own water for the baths." She headed towards the counter. "Name's Ghunta. Rooms are up the stairs and on the right. First three doors will be yours." She turned around and pinned them with another piercing look. "And I mean no funny business. I may be old, but don't think I can't kick the lot of you out on your rumps."

The three followed Ghunta up the stairs to their rooms. Griffon and Falcon took turns carrying buckets of water up to Ava's room for her bath. Then they parted ways. Ava lowered herself into the warm water that filled the wooden tub. She lathered herself from head to toe and took her time scrubbing all of the filth away. Then she leaned back and relaxed. She was aware of Ghunta briefly entering her room with a package and laying it on her bed muttering something about new clothes from the boys who had brought her there and reiterated her earlier statement of not wanting any trouble from those two, but they both looked like dormant volcanoes about to explode and she didn't want to be anywhere around when that happened.

Ava felt like a newly hatched spring chick and could only marvel at the enormous influence a hot bath and clean clothes could have on her mood. She felt invigorated, refreshed, like she could take on the world and come out on top. She was even pleased with the attire that Griffon and Falcon had picked up for her. She made a mental note to thank them later. The pants were made of dark brown leather. More than a little skeptical when she'd first seen them, she couldn't imagine she would be able to squeeze her way into them and still be able to breathe. As she slipped them on, she was pleasantly surprised to find the material soft and flexible, basically fitting to her contours like a glove. The blouse was a light violet that almost matched her eyes with dark purple trim. The sleeves were long and the hem fell even with her fingertips. The neckline was draped in layers that flattered her shoulders. There was a wide belt and sturdy boots that almost reached her knees. They were adorned with the most unusual buckles. There was also a coat made of some sturdy material, maybe wool, which complimented the ensemble quite well. It had the same buckles as the boots which she found rather interesting. She had to give them credit, they had good taste.

She braided the sides of her hair and secured it at the back of her head and decided to let the rest hang loosely down her back. Given the circumstances, she was surprised to find herself so concerned about her looks, but she had to admit she actually felt attractive. With one last glance at herself in the mirror, she was ready to go. Falcon had told her to meet them at the tavern called Knoll's Cavern when she was finished. It was two streets up and two streets over—should be easy enough to find. There they would get something to eat and discuss their upcoming journey to the Palace. She made her way down the stairs and out the door. She must have spent more time than she realized soaking in the tub. The way the sun's rays were lazily casting shadows on the town, it appeared to be late afternoon. She felt a slight twinge of guilt and hoped Griffon and Falcon hadn't been waiting on her too long.

Once outside, she turned left down the street and smiled to several passers-by as they greeted her. She walked by a dark alley and had a strange creeping sensation all over her skin. She tried to shake it off but it wouldn't go away. She considered where she was and thought maybe this was some sort of sixth sense and shouldn't be ignored. She made the first turn and decided to pick up her pace. She turned her head to look over her shoulder. She couldn't see anyone following her but she wasn't going to take any chances. She broke into a run and closed the distance to the second turn. When she rounded the corner she realized that the woods lined the left hand of the street. She quickly examined her surroundings for anything she could use to protect herself. Her effort was rewarded when she spied a large sturdy branch on the ground.

Never slowing up she altered her course and bent down to grab it as she ran by. She secured herself in the shadows of the next small alley she came across. Plastering herself against the wall she gripped the branch in both hands so tightly her fingers were turning white. Running had made her breathing raspy so she held her breath. Her heart pounded furiously: unbridled adrenaline coursed through her veins.

A minute passed. She started breathing. Then two minutes. Maybe she'd been mistaken—then she heard the footsteps. She readied herself. Closer, closer they edged toward her. In the back of her mind she thought that for someone trying to sneak, they were making an awful racket. Again she held her breath. Finally she saw a figure start to cross in front of her hiding place. With every ounce of strength in her possession, she swung the branch like a baseball player would swing a bat trying to get a home run, but her swing never made impact.

Falcon heard the whoosh of something being swung toward his head before he actually saw what it was. Acting on pure instinct with his lightning reflexes he spun and was able to duck the blow grabbing the assailant around the waist to keep them both from falling. Finally regaining his footing, Falcon wrenched the branch from the swinger's hands and roughly swung them around to inquire why they were trying to pummel him with a stick. Just when he opened his mouth, he looked down to find Ava in his arms, which was certainly not what he expected. His jaw still open, he slightly relaxed his hold. "Ava? What are you doing? Why are you taking a swing at me?" Falcon asked a little more than perplexed.

As realization dawned on Ava her eyes got big as saucers and her hand flew up to cover her mouth. "YOU! Why are you following me?"

"I wasn't following you. It's late and we were getting worried so I went to the inn to fetch you but you were already gone, I was just headed back to the tavern to see if you were there."

Ava's mouth opened and closed in an effort to speak, but no sounds were forthcoming. Her brows scrunched as she recalled the last several minutes. Her gut told her that someone was following her. If it wasn't Falcon, then who had it been?

Again Falcon thought. Seriously, how is it possible for them to end up intertwined like this? He couldn't resist the urge to bend his head down and inhale the intoxicating fruity smell of whatever soap she must have bathed in. It reminded him of berries and he wondered if it would taste as delicious as it smelled. Whoa!! Pull yourself together Falcon. Your thoughts are straying down a very dangerous path.

"Falcon, did you hear me?"

He looked down at Ava's questioning expression and realized that she must have said something. "Huh?"

"You can let me go; now, I'm not going to fall."

Finally gathering his wits, he slowly started to slide his hands from around her waist, but took his time in doing so--he could feel the outline of her slender hips and let his hands linger. She placed her hands over his and looked up at him, violet eyes full of questions that he had no answers to. Honestly he couldn't form a rational thought; he was swept away by her simple presence. He squeezed her hips and pulled her closer. She didn't resist and took a step forward until there were mere inches left between them. He could feel her breath gently fan his neck which made goose bumps tip toe up his arms. It felt like they were in sync—one heartbeat, one breath, one unit. He dipped his head never breaking eye contact. Her hands moved up to grab the collar of his shirt. He stopped breathing and slowly inclined his head he was going to kiss Ava.

Chapter 13

Time stood still and Ava held her breath. *Was he going to kiss her? Surely not. There was no other logical explanation. She had no previous experience to compare it to since she'd never truly been kissed before, she didn't count the sloppy peck on the cheek from Joshua when she was eleven. She realized in this moment that she'd never wanted to be kissed before. But this was different. She didn't try to rationalize it. She just watched as his lips inched closer to hers.*

A mere second before their lips touched Falcon's head jerked up. "Did you hear that?"

Ava completely swept up in the moment still had her lips pursed and her eyes closed. Finally, she opened her eyes to again see Falcon's entire demeanor had changed. The smoldering look in his eyes had vanished and his attention was completely focused on something else. Feeling foolish she disengaged herself from his arms. Did she just imagine that or was he really going to kiss her?

Falcon was now reconsidering Ava's earlier statement about someone following her. At first he'd thought it was just her imagination getting the best of her being in a strange place after dark. But now he knew she'd been correct. No doubt about it. Holding his breath and closing his eyes he concentrated with all of his senses. Whoever it was they were very skilled. Could it be trackers? Why would they be following Ava? Or was it just coincidence and she just happened into their path?

After several more minutes of hiding in the alley Falcon determined that whoever it was had not continued their pursuit. It was best to get Ava to the Tavern where he and

Griffon could at least stand a better chance in protecting her. Falcon glanced around the wall in both directions. He grabbed Ava's hand and pulled her along behind him. He hugged the shadows along the walls just for precaution.

Finally, they entered the busy tavern and a huge weight lifted from Falcon's chest. He scanned the crowd until he located Griffon seated at a corner table with his back against the wall. Their eyes locked momentarily and somehow this must have communicated the danger to Griffon as he immediately sat forward and examined the crowd for trouble. Falcon led Ava to the table and scooted her on the bench by Griffon and seated himself on her other side.

"What happened?"

"I found Ava in an alley; she thought someone was following her."

"Did you see anyone?"

"No, but I think she may have been right."

Ava couldn't look at Falcon without vivid memories of their close encounter in the alley, so when a man brought over three bowls and wooden mugs filled to the brim with a frothy liquid her grumbling stomach forced her to focus all of her attention on the steaming vegetables and savory broth. Regardless of everything that had happened, Ava picked up her spoon and started eating. Falcon and Griffon followed suit, but they never really relaxed. Their eyes were continuously scanning the crowded tavern for any sign of a threat.

Ava cleaned her bowl and picked up her mug. She took a big gulp of the brown liquid and swallowed. Before it could even hit her stomach she started coughing and sputtering. Griffon gave Falcon a knowing grin and started pounding her lightly on the back.

"Are you alright?"

"What is that stuff?" She asked setting down her cup.

"The Cavern's finest ale, I'd say a bit on the strong side."

Ava had never had any type of alcohol before and wasn't prepared for the burning sensation that lingered. She sucked air in through her mouth in an attempt to cool the inferno dancing down her throat. She tried to ignore the obvious amusement her companions were having over her reaction. It was beyond her how they were more than halfway through with their mugs as if it had no affect what so ever on them. It would take a large quantity to build up such a tolerance. "No-good lushes" She muttered under her breath. With the sting finally subsiding she became aware that her two gentleman companions had become still as stone. She glanced at each of them and saw their gazes were fixed on something across the room which was so crowded and busy it was hard to concentrate on one certain person. She glanced back and forth several times until she spotted what had riveted their attention.

Two people had entered the tavern—a man and a woman. They appeared Asian. Their clothing was pitch black, but shiny like the scales on a fish. They both wore baggy britches and had on high collared chogas. They each had a red sash wrapped several times and then tied around their waists. At first the sashes also appeared black, but they were in fact a deep dark maroon. Their faces were light brown with golden under tones; their almond shaped eyes were not only unusual, but trained directly on her. She swallowed the lump that formed in her throat. Not only did they appear exotic, they looked lethal.

So, someone had been following her after all. *Who can they be? I just got here? Maybe it's a case of mistaken identity.*

She held her breath as they weaved their way through the crowded tavern and approached their table. She waited for some sort of signal from the men beside her. Did they flee or fight? But the two men continued to stare as if transfixed. Since she couldn't get around them on the bench she was a sitting duck.

It wasn't long before the exotic duo had weaved their way through the crowd and were standing before her on the other side of their table. For what seemed like an eternity no one said a word or moved an inch. They sized each other up and all Ava could do was hold her breath and wait. She certainly didn't expect what happened next.

Simultaneously, both men jumped up with mile wide smiles plastered on their faces. They made their way around the table and greeted the two newcomers with an obvious familiarity. She released the breath she had been holding. Everyone was happy—all taking turns slapping each other on the back. Griffon even picked up the young woman and spun her around in circles. When he put her feet back on the ground, she simply smiled up at him with genuine fondness. Their greetings died down and Falcon invited the two to join them at their table. Once they were all finally seated, Falcon introduced her.

"Ava, this is Cricket and Slye. They were in training with us under the First Commander. We haven't seen them in years." She could tell he was sincerely pleased at their arrival.

Now that they were seated across from her, she could see that Cricket was beautiful. Her hair was black as coal-- shiny and smooth. It was twisted and twined in an elaborate up do adorned with some type of bone. She seemed to be a little shy and didn't hold eye contact for very long, but kept glancing around the room. Slye was a ruggedly handsome man. He had several scars on his face and hands. From the way he had his arm wrapped around Cricket's shoulders he was clearly protective of her. Rather sweet Ava thought. Her first assessment of them being lethal was still accurate. There was no doubt if they were threatened in any way they would most certainly hold their own.

"Nice to meet you," Ava said reaching across the table. She shook each of their hands and was surprised at the underlying strength in Cricket's grip. Looks could be very deceiving.

"How did you end up with these two miscreants?" Slye asked Ava.

"That's a rather long story."

"It always is with these two, believe me. But aside from Cricket, there are no two men I would rather have at my side if there was trouble. That's a fact. We didn't mean to alarm you earlier. We noticed who you arrived with and were curious so we followed you from the inn. Once we saw Falcon with you we realized you were in good hands."

Subtle, Ava thought. *Was it possible that anyone missed his underlying suggestion? They couldn't have possibly seen them in the alley, it was too dark.* Wasn't it? She started squirming in her seat clearly uncomfortable by Slye's comments so he graciously changed the subject. He looked at Falcon, "What have you been up to?"

Falcon proceeded to fill the two in on some of the escapades that had transpired over the last few days. Ava took the opportunity to look at each of them and for the first time since her arrival she felt a little out of place. As if he sensed her discomfort, Griffon leaned over to her and whispered in her ear, "*Ava, banish the thought.*"

She found it rather odd that a few whispered words of comfort from a man she barely knew could erase any doubts she possibly had. She smiled at him with gratitude and took another large gulp of the amber liquid from her mug and was pleased that it didn't burn quite as bad the second time around. Falcon ordered more food and drink for all and she found herself engrossed in tales of their past.

All four of her companions had been trained under the First Commander. She learned that he always focused on a person's genuine talent--with Falcon it was his sword and Griffon his bow. She learned that Cricket was skilled with Shuriken blades. It made Ava curious as to where she kept them in her present ensemble. Slye on the other hand was a pyromancer and his skill with martial arts far surpassed all others.

They'd all been thick as thieves during their training. Of course as they got older their lives took them in different directions, but they clearly shared a unique bond of camaraderie that time and distance couldn't dissipate. This made Ava think of her Aunt and Uncle and she shot up a silent plea that they wouldn't worry about her too much.

Slye filled them in on some of their recent travels. They had been on the outskirts of Melbirch. They'd encountered several groups of Krypts. Two they were able to dispatch of but there were at least three with numbers so great that they had no other choice but to slip around them. It clearly caused them all discomfort that the Krypts were in such close proximity to the districts. Cricket and Slye were on their way to deliver this news to the First Commander and get new orders.

Griffon told them of their Krypt encounter and suggested that they all travel together since they were going in the same direction. It was decided they would head out the next morning. Then their conversation took a lighter tone with stories of their youthful escapades. They laughed and talked for several hours.

Ava lost track of time. All she could remember thinking was Cricket was so quiet. She occasionally leaned over to whisper in Slye's ear. She smiled and laughed, but Ava couldn't recall her saying even three words. How very strange.

Chapter 14

The pounding was so loud it echoed in the room with relentless precision. Her head felt like a tree being splintered by a bolt of savage lightning. Ava rolled over and covered her head with her pillow. There it was again. She moaned and tried to sit up but immediately became nauseated and laid back down. *Heaven help her, what on Earth was wrong?* The pounding at the door became more persistent and she realized someone was shouting from the other side. She rolled onto her side and took slow deep breaths. Just when she was going to attempt to sit up for the second time, the door crashed open and Griffon barreled in. Ava was so startled that she fell off the edge of the bed onto the floor. Her sore knees caught most of the impact, but she felt like a limp noodle and couldn't catch the weight of her torso with her hands and ended up bumping her right temple on the floor. Her vision was completely clouded with bright white stars swimming all around.

Griffon cursed and reached down to help her up. She shook her head no and put her hand up to stop him. It was obvious she was in no shape to move just yet. He stood up to wet a towel with water from a basin. He bent down by Ava and placed it on the back of her neck. After a few minutes he used it to wipe her brow and gingerly cover the small goose egg at her temple. Finally Ava scooted around to a sitting position and leaned back against the bed, but didn't open her eyes.

"Why did you break the door?"

Griffon looked at the door that was now swinging by only one hinge. The entire closure had been ripped out of the wall. A little sheepish because of the damage he'd caused, he replied, "I thought you were in trouble."

Ava squinted at him and realized she didn't recall how she even made it to her room. "What exactly happened last night? How did I get back to my room?"

"I carried you."

Ava looked at him to see if he was serious. Clearly he was. She groaned and closed her eyes again. How many drinks had she had? They were having such a good time and she'd been so caught up in their tales of adventure she had obviously lost count. *Who's the lush now* she thought.

Ava groaned as a new wave of nausea hit her. She felt like she'd been run over by a bus. Once it passed she decided to try and stand. Griffon steadied her as she stood up and navigated her to the foot of the bed. She sat down and put her head between her knees. Griffon knelt down beside her and began to rub small circles on her back. He worked his way up to her neck and worked out some of the kinks. She didn't know how long they sat there, but the stars slowly seemed to vanish.

"I'm going to have Falcon bring you something that will make you feel better," and with that Griffon exited through the now mangled door frame.

Ava hadn't moved when Falcon entered the room carrying a steaming mug. He looked down at her with a mixture of amusement and pity and wrapped her hands around the mug. "Drink up, this will help." He sat down beside her. She looked at the contents of the mug and her stomach did a flip flop. It was thick and almost black.

"What is it?" she croaked through dry lips.

"All you need to know is it will make your head stop spinning and settle your stomach."

That was good enough for her. She took a small sip. It didn't taste nearly as bad as it looked and before she had drained the contents. In a matter of minutes she had a warm and fuzzy feeling; her stomach was completely settled.

"That's amazing! How do you know this kind of stuff?"

"I'm brilliant of course." That earned him a sour look from Ava. "Honestly, after being in your shoes once or twice myself, I figured it out real fast.

"Now that was much more logical she thought.

"What happened to the door?" Falcon queried.

"Apparently Griffon broke it." She said a little bewildered. "I didn't answer fast enough and he thought something was wrong."

Falcon nodded as if that made perfect sense and he would have done the exact same thing. "I don't remember the doors having locks."

Falcon looked at her and then back at the door. "I don't think they do." They both laughed and she was grateful that it didn't cause her discomfort.

As if he appeared out of thin air Griffon was in the doorway. "Feeling better?"

"Very much so."

He gave her one of his sideways grins, almost a smile, but not quite. "That's good. Everything's prepared and we're ready to head to the palace."

Ava nodded and stood up, this time with no difficulties. "Give me just a few minutes and I'll be ready. Meet you downstairs."

After the men left Ava folded up her sweater and dress and placed them along with her slippers in the traveling bag the men had picked up for her. She also packed the hair brush and pins thinking how very thoughtful they were to pick up something so girlie. She stopped at the door to take one last look around the homey room and spent an extra minute staring longingly at the bed as it would be a while before she saw another.

Ava didn't make it halfway down the stairs when she heard raised voices. She quickened her pace to see what was happening. She made it to the bottom step and stopped dead in her tracks. Guntha, wielding a broom, had Griffon and Falcon pinned up against the wall. "No funny business that's what I told ya. Just couldn't leave without causing me some trouble. Now I'm gonna teach ya a lesson."

Falcon had his hands up in a defensive manor. Griffon was just looking at the floor shaking his head. Guntha took a step forward to swing at them when Cricket entered through the front door. Guntha, in mid swing, paused in awe at the exotic creature that had just entered her establishment. Cricket walked over to Guntha and gently removed the broom from her hands. Guntha just continued to stare slack-jawed. Cricket smiled sweetly at the woman and leaned over and whispered something in her ear. Guntha bobbed her head up and down. Cricket stepped towards Griffon, whispered something to him, and she left as quickly as she came. Griffon walked over to Guntha, placed some money in her hand, and apologized again for the damage to her door then he and Falcon also left the inn.

Ava walked towards the door. As she passed Guntha she looked down in the old woman's still bumfuzzled face. What on earth had Cricket said to her? Ava smiled and extended her gratitude to Guntha even though she probably never heard a word. With this unexpected excitement behind them, the rest of the day would have to be smooth sailing.

Chapter 15

Wrong again.

The words repeatedly ran through Ava's mind like a record player with a stuck needle. It hadn't even been an hour since they departed Ash Knoll and more than anything she wanted to turn around and start the whole day over again.

She practically skipped out of the Inn with a smile on her face excited about all of the possibilities of the day just to come to a screeching halt at the scene before her. They were all there—Falcon, Griffon, Cricket, and Slye. Mounted. On horses; horses the size of elephants. Okay maybe that was exaggerating, but they were really large and very intimidating. For several minutes she continued to stare at them. She saw a horse with an empty saddle. It was a dapple gray—beautiful animal. From a distance, that is.

Realizing something must be wrong since Ava was standing as if in quick sand, Falcon dismounted and walked over to her.

"Something wrong?"

"Is something wrong? Hmm. Let's see. I'm guessing you want me to ride that elephant I would say that's the first something that's wrong."

Falcon laughed. "That's Cecil. He's a good mount—faithful and strong—there's none better."

Ava looked at the monster named Cecil and swore he was laughing at her. He's probably thinking I'm a chicken standing over here. Well, he would be correct. He has to weigh at least a ton—could snap me like a twig, crush me like a bug. What other option do I have? Clearly this is the intended mode of transportation. Ugh. Now would be a good time to wake up.

Ava looked pleadingly at Falcon. "I can walk."

He didn't do a very good job at hiding his amusement. "Well, you could, but I'm afraid you'd never be able to keep up. It's imperative we travel swiftly with all of the Krypts around." Not giving her any more time to consider, Falcon tugged on her hand, pulling her closer to the beast. He grabbed the reins and pulled Cecil's head down. He rubbed his muzzle and spoke words of soothing intent. Ava was awestruck at the way Falcon interacted with the animal. There was an explicit understanding between man and beast. 'Now Cecil, this is Ava. She's a little uneasy so I need you to take extra care with her.' He looked at Ava. "Ava this is Cecil. There's nothing to be afraid of here." He took her hand and placed it on the monstrous muzzle.

Ava was stunned at the velvety smoothness beneath her hand and slowly moved her fingers around. The beast leaned down further and nudged her shoulder with his massive head. Ava sighed, sent up a silent plea, and left Falcon assist her on top of the beast. When she got settled in the saddle she looked at the ground. It seemed well over twenty feet below her. *How many bones could you break from a fall at this height?* Better not to think about such things.

Now here she was clinging precariously to the beasts back. Each broad stride he took jarred every inch of her. Surely she would be shattered from the inside out before they made it to their destination. What other choice did she have but to hold on for dear life and try to remain seated?

It took not only all of Ava's concentration but also her strength to ride the beast over the next several hours. They always made it look so easy in the movies. She'd missed most of the conversation that occurred between the others. She realized a good while back that she wasn't really steering Cecil; he was basically following the horse in front of him, which was perfectly fine with her since she didn't really know how to maneuver him anyway. Just then, Cecil stopped so abruptly she had to grab a handful of his dark mane to keep from flying over his head. His ears were perked forward and he snorted. He pawed at the ground with his massive hoof and danced around clearly perplexed.

"Easy horse what's wrong?" Ava glanced all around and didn't see anything, but she knew animals had much keener senses than humans. The road they were travelling had a downward slope on the left and an incline on the right obscuring what was on the other side. With each second that passed Cecil became more agitated. Ava was just about to call out to the others when a huge cat bounded to the top of the rise. It looked like a bobcat but much, much bigger. Cecil clearly wanted to bolt. Ava held onto the reins as tightly as she could. The horse did a circle dance and when she finally got him back to the direction in which she saw the cat, there were now two others exactly like it. *Oh no.*

Simultaneously all three of the cats sprang into action, their sleek design with the sole purpose of overtaking whatever their primal instincts targeted, in this case—her. Cecil took over matters by bolting over the hill. If she thought she was being jarred while he was walking, galloping was an entirely other matter. Every leap caused her behind to come off of the saddle and she'd be airborne for a splinter in time. When she came back down the impact would knock the breath from her which prevented her from screaming out warning to her companions. She dared a look behind her which was a huge mistake. The cats had just hit the road and started to barrel over the hill. When Ava turned back around Cecil made a sharp left. She lost her hold and flew through the air. She hit the ground with such force she thought her arms would break. She rolled several times before coming to a stop.

Ava was disoriented and her vision slightly blurred. She shook her head to try and clear the ringing in her ears. She rolled onto her back and winced as a terrible pain shot through her side. In a matter of seconds what had just transpired came flooding back. She rose to her feet as quickly as possible looking in all directions. The cats were still running towards her at a break neck speed. What could she do? Run? No good they were too fast. She turned around to face them. Too far back she saw Falcon and Griffon were now in pursuit. They wouldn't make it in time.

When the cats got within ten yards they stopped running and started stalking. Five yards. She was toast and then the ground vibrated. Cecil bounded in placing himself between the cats and Ava. He reared back on his hind legs thrashing them in the air and stomping the ground with his massive hooves, leaving indentures in the earth. He snorted and whinnied clearly making his intent known—warming them to come no closer.

Of course the cats outnumbered the horse and this made them foolishly brave. One stalked closer to Cecil and he stood up on his hind legs thrashing the air with his sharp claws visible and shrieking his own form of battle cry. Cecil would not be intimidated and bravely advanced on the creature. The other two cats took the opportunity to go around the ensuing test of wills and continue to stalk their prey. Ava had backed up as far as she could--her back was against a tree which she already assessed had no limbs within reach for her to grab hold of. They would just climb up after her anyway. She looked one more time to see Falcon and Griffon still riding in her direction with the look of sheer determination. Ava looked from one cat and then to the other. Which would strike first? She would never find out.

First one cat fell and then the other. Ava blinked several times to make sure she hadn't just imagined what she saw. They were both twitching on the ground with their life blood oozing out of gashes on their neck. Something had severed their jugulars. Cecil had stomped the third cat beyond recognition. If the beast hadn't intervened on her behalf then it could have been her laying there. She walked over to him and grabbed his reins pulling his head down. His nostrils still flared and his large eyes were still wild from fear. Ava smoothed his muzzle and leaned her forehead against his.

Falcon was the first to reach them. He practically jumped from his mount in mid gallop, drew his sword, and was by Ava in a heartbeat. Griffon was next, bow at the ready. They remained that way for several tense minutes until Cricket and Slye came into view.

"That's all of them, for now." Slye informed them.

Only then did they relax their guard and sheathe their weapons.

"Are you hurt?" Falcon grabbed the reins and gave Ava a quick inspection. He saw she had one arm wrapped around her side. He moved her hand and ran his broad hand down her ribcage. She winced. "Just bruised, nothing's broken."

Ava shook her head. She knew she couldn't speak or she would start to cry and she didn't know if she would ever stop.

Griffon had inspected Cecil for injuries, "Only a few minor scratches, he'll be fine."

The look of concern that passed between the two men didn't go unnoticed by Ava, but it was more than she was able to handle at the moment so she just continued to rub Cecil's neck. She watched Slye dismount and approach each cat carcass to retrieve a small metal blade from the animals. He wiped them clean and carried them over to Cricket who placed them in a belt concealed within a fold of her sash. Griffon gave Ava a leg up onto Cecil's back and again they headed in the direction of the palace, only this time at a much faster pace.

Chapter 16

Over four hours later, they crossed a bridge and rode under a large metal portcullis into the palace courtyard currently bustling with activity. There were groups of men practicing with different types of weapons-- long swords, spears, hammers, axes, and archers high and low trying to hit different targets. There were men wrestling and sparring against one another. It was constructive chaos.

Their arrival didn't go unnoticed for very long. It got very quiet as the activity ceased and everyone's eyes were suddenly trained on them. They all dismounted except for Ava who sat and stared trying to soak up these new surroundings. It was only a matter of minutes for the silence to cease once people realized exactly who had just ridden through the gates. Greetings spewed forth in abundance until out of nowhere a booming voice coated with command roared, "SILENCE."

All heads immediately turned at the bailey entrance where a man stood with his hands on his hips, clearly displeased. His biceps looked like tree limbs. The crowd slowly parted as he advanced forward toward the travelers. Griffon and Falcon stood side by side and the man stopped directly before them. He had on a loose blue sleeveless tunic with gray pants. He had dark hair with salt and pepper along the temples; cut very short compared to the other men. The silence was thick as this man looked back and forth between Falcon and Griffon which was making Ava very uncomfortable, so she was more than a little shocked when he reached out and grabbed each of them with a massive arm and pulled them up against his chest in a hard embrace. Ava was certain she saw tears forming in his eyes beneath his bushy eyebrows.

The man finally let go and stood back to look at them one more time. "I honestly never thought I would see you together again" his voice caught with emotion and it took a moment for him to regain his composure. He released both men and stepped back to turn towards Cricket and Slye whose hands he shook in greeting. Turning back to Falcon he said, "Your fiends arrived yesterday, I figured you wouldn't be too far behind, but I never imagined you'd have so many in tow. To be true, I am grateful to have you all back safely."

Griffon turned around and helped Ava dismount. She never released Cecil's reins.

"Ava, this is the First Commander." Griffon informed her.

Ava looked into the grayest eyes she'd ever seen and could immediately comprehend why this man was so well respected. He placed a kiss on the back of her hand and squeezed it gently. "The pleasure is all mine—come, let us have refreshments and you can fill me in on all that has transpired." The First Commander gave several orders to the men standing around. Ava reluctantly surrendered Cecil's reins to a young squire only after he promised to take good care of him.

They entered a Great Hall where women of various ages were in the process of putting away trestle tables. The first thing that caught Ava's attention was a great stone fireplace at the front of the hall. It took up almost the entire wall and still maintained a low burning blaze. They were seated at a table that had benches on either side. The First Commander grabbed a chair and got comfortable at the head of the table so he could see everyone.

A very young girl who couldn't have been more than eight years old, dressed in weathered green with her hair in pig tails placed cups on the table. A woman followed filling each glass from a large metal pitcher she carried. On the principle of good manners Ava was able to mutter thank you to both of them but she dreaded the thought of consuming any more ale. She was pretty sure she'd learned a life lesson the night before. Closing her eyes she tilted the glass back and was so grateful that sweet water was all that touched her tongue. In fact it was so delicious she quickly drained the entire mug. The woman smiled and refilled it for her. Trays laden with bread and cheese were placed on the table. As Ava nibbled on a roll and sipped the sweet water she began to feel more like herself again.

Later, after they'd all finished their meal and the hall was cleared of everyone except the First Commander and the newly arrived travelers, Falcon tried to explain all that had happened. He started with the discovery of Ava, their close call with the Krypts, crossing paths with Griffon, and picking up Cricket and Slye at Ash Knoll. The First Commander listened intently never interrupting with questions until he was certain he was up to speed. "Clearly you have some theory or you wouldn't be here together of that I am certain."

Griffon nodded, "This will likely sound insane, but these marks that we both have in our encounter with the Krypts, they seemed to glow."

"Impossible." The First Commander's face was pale and by his expression was that of disbelief.

"Falcon would agree with you, but that doesn't change the fact that it happened. And there's more."

Griffon looked at Falcon prompting him to speak which he did although reluctantly. "Ava also had a dream about shadows. We think it may have been something to do with the Reach."

You could have heard a pin drop. The silence stretched for several minutes as the First Commander absorbed everything he'd just been told. "I need time to think on this. I'm sure you are all exhausted. Let's call it a night and we'll talk more in the morning."

They all said goodnight and the young girl escorted Ava upstairs to a small apartment. Along the way she noticed embroidered tapestries adorned the walls, the rich colors drew her attention and she realized that each separate piece gave a small glimpse of the past, history of the Royal families that had called this place their home. It was almost like a story book. When they arrived at what would serve as her room, the only furniture was a small table that held a pitcher and basin of water, a three prong candle sconce on the wall, and a bed in the corner. There was no window and she couldn't help but feel claustrophobic. She washed her hands and face and hastily brushed her hair. She removed her coat and boots and lay on the bed. Forcing everything from her mind she willed herself to sleep.

Surrounded by a suffocating darkness she couldn't escape, she knew she wasn't alone. 'Come to us hurry'. The rhythmic chant repeated over and over. No, not this again and then she saw them.

The shadows weaving their way towards her, slithering like serpents. She wanted to run, but she couldn't move. 'Hurry to us Ava'

She jerked straight up in the bed. Perspiration beaded her brow and silent tears streamed down her face. It was just a dream, but the sound of the voices calling her name would haunt her.

Ava knew there was no chance of falling back to sleep. She was frightened to the core and felt cold and vulnerable. The one thing that popped in her head was the fire place in the Great Hall which had seemed so comforting when they'd first entered, so she headed there as quickly as her legs would carry her.

She sat cross legged in front of the fire poking at the embers. She wasn't sure how much time had elapsed when she heard someone behind her. Clearly jumpy from her earlier nightmare she scrambled to her feet wielding the fire poke.

"Easy girl. It's just an old man unable to sleep."

Ava sighed and sat back down.

"We didn't get to talk much earlier. How do you feel about everything that has happened?"

Ava considered this carefully before replying. "I'm still not sure this isn't a dream."

This made the older man chuckle. He sat down on the opposite side of the fire place. "What has you up this time of night anyway?"

"Unfortunately, bad dreams."

"Do you want to talk about it?"

Ava didn't immediately say anything. A long silence ensued. "It's dark, cold. I'm alone, at first, and then I hear them, calling for me--over and over. There are so many of them. It's overwhelming, but at the same time, it's empty." She paused momentarily. "This time they knew my name. Is that even possible? You probably think I'm insane."

"On the contrary my dear, you don't live as long as I do without being witness to some very unusual things. Would you mind telling me about life before Falcon found you? Only if you want to that is. It may take your mind off things."

"I live in a small town called Elzbeth with my Aunt Irene and Uncle Ignacious."

"Ignacious? That's a very unusual name."

"Yes, it suits my uncle well. They raised me since I was little. My mother died during child birth."

"I see, and you don't have any idea how you arrived here in our world?" he inquired.

"I went to sleep at home and I woke up here. Every night since, I continue to wake up here. Honestly, I thought I was dreaming. Now I'm not so sure."

"No matter what the circumstance, I am forever grateful for your arrival. I was certain I would go to my grave never seeing my two sons together again. Now, when it's my time, I can go at peace."

"They've both saved my life. Did they tell you that?"

"We spoke briefly. It is obvious they have both come to care about you a great deal."

"When I first arrived, I've never felt more at home than I did sun bathing in that meadow. Then I met Falcon, there was almost an immediate connection and the same thing happened with Griffon too. It's almost like we're kindred spirits in some way, but since yesterday I'm beginning to feel out of place."

"What a shock it must be, thrown into a strange land in complete chaos. It's been this way since the Deacon and Deaconess were lost. They were kind and generous people and I held them in the highest regard." His tone changed as if he was aggravated with what he was about to say, "Prime Sovereign Ezekiel has been the most aggressive for power to rule. Implicit fear would be the foundation. This alone has him opposed by many as well as the fact it is believed that he was involved with the death of the Royals, but it couldn't be proven. He's no leader, of that you can be sure."

The mention of Ezekiel clearly upset the First Commander and as he continued to speak he sounded tired. "You've already become acquainted with the Krypts, ghastly creatures. From the reports I've heard, their numbers are tremendous and they continue to spread like a plague. I receive new reports daily that they have been spotted somewhere new. My soldiers are spread so thin the way it is, I just don't know how much longer we can maintain control."

"What do you think will happen if he does gain power?"

"I'm afraid we won't be here to find out. They are slaughtering everything in their paths. No one is being spared."

Ava was now ashamed with her self-pity. She was aware that things were grim but didn't realize how bad they were until now. The First Commander stood up to leave but paused to look down at Ava. "Try and get some rest girl. The morning sun brings with it a blank slate." When he reached the door to the Great Hall he turned around to ask, "What did you say your Uncle's name was again?"

"Ignacious."

He shook his head and disappeared through the doorway.

Chapter 17

Griffon was up and about before the crack of dawn. It had been years since he had been in the Palace and wanted to look around unobserved. He took a walk down memory lane and visited places he used to play as a boy. He took care to be quiet and not wake any of the others. He'd made his way into the Great Hall and went to the center of the room. Kneeling down he searched the stone tiles one by one until he found the crack that ran corner to corner; exactly what he was looking for, he ran his fingers across it.

The First Commander had showed him and Falcon this crack when they were very young. He told them that night with tear filled eyes that neither of their fathers would return. Giving no additional detail he proceeded to assure them they would be well cared for and not to worry over anything. That's when he showed them the crack. He had said that even something as hard as stone could be damaged. But because of all of the other surrounding stones providing support, the crack causes no weakness.

At the time, Griffon thought it was a line of jibberish. It wasn't until long after he'd departed the keep that he realized it wasn't jibberish after all. It was a soldier's way of telling two little boys that they weren't alone. It was ok for them to be heartbroken because they were surrounded by people who cared for them and would look out for them no matter what.

Griffon wished he had realized all of this before he'd left Falcon. He now knew there may have been a better way to handle the situation. He got to his feet and headed for the door. He glanced over at the dwindling fire and stopped. Ava lay curled up on her side in front of the fireplace. The light danced across her features only enhancing her natural beauty.

He had to wonder what made her leave the comfort of her bed to sleep on the floor. Walking over to her he sat down beside her and soaked her in like a sponge. Why was it he felt entirely different in her presence. He felt bold and empowered. He moved a straying strand of auburn hair away from her face and she stirred.

She blinked her eyes open and took in her surroundings. Griffon was sitting quietly by her and she automatically smiled. "Hi."

"Morning." Once Ava sat up he noticed the dark circles under her eyes. "Didn't get much sleep?"

She shook her head no. "More dreams of shadows."

"I thought maybe it was the sappacks . You should have woken me. I would have sat with you."

"Sappacks?"

"The big striped cats those were sappacks. It's not unusual to find them when Krypts are around."

"Oh, I see."

"I was worried, seems you haven't been quite yourself since."

Ava nervously rolled her hands in her lap. "I was so helpless," she whispered. "I could see you and Falcon coming towards me, but I knew in my heart you wouldn't make it in time. I've never been more afraid." She looked over at him and couldn't prevent her bottom lip from trembling.

That sign of vulnerability sent Griffon over the edge. He wrapped his arms around Ava and hugged her tightly to his chest. He'd almost let her down and he couldn't, no wouldn't, let that happen again.

When Ava laid her head on his shoulder and wrapped her arms around his waist, a small crack opened in his heart and a sliver of hope escaped. He couldn't comprehend how he'd become so protective over someone he'd just met. He never stuck around one place for very long so he'd not had a lot of opportunity to actually get to know someone beyond the physical sense. For now, he didn't want to think about anything other than lovely Ava and how it felt to hold her like this; only described as Heaven on Earth.

They remained that way until the kitchen staff came in to prepare the tables for the morning meal. Reluctantly, Ava leaned back. She took Griffon's hand and held it up to her cheek. He then took her hand and placed a kiss against her inner wrist and secretly wished it were her lips.

That's how they were when Falcon saw them. He'd entered the hall just in time to see the intimate exchange and he felt like he'd swallowed hot coals. Bile rose up in his throat and he thought he would be sick. Just when he was about to charge across the room and thrash the hall with Griffon, a strong hand gripped his shoulder.

"Falcon, I need you to gather your companions and meet me in the bailey, quickly." The First Commander didn't release his shoulder until he saw the rage dissipate. Falcon turned back to the fireplace, but there was no one there. He stalked out of the room but didn't immediately look for his companions. He headed through the kitchen and into the gardens. He had to get his emotions under control before they exploded like a cannon. He had no claim to Ava; therefore, he had no right to get so emotional, but it didn't keep him from punching the scarecrow in the face when he walked by.

Simmering rage dissipated into a consuming sadness as he followed the Commander's orders and went in search of his companions.

A short while later they had all gathered in the bailey. Everyone's curiosity was genuinely piqued. The First Commander ambled into the center of the yard. "Falcon, Griffon, please step forward."

The two men walked over to stand before the First Commander. "Also, Ava, I need you to join us." He extended his arm and held out his hand.

Ava looked around the circle and hesitantly stepped forward to take his hand. The First Commander placed her in between the two men.

"I've things to explain to you. Some of which you may not want to hear. Some you may take to heart. The single most important thing I want you to understand is freedom; freedom of choice, freedom of heart, freedom of soul. Your lives are your own. Do you understand?"

In unison the three nodded their understanding and the First Commander continued. "I will start by telling you what I know to be true. Long ago, before the first Deacon was crowned, there was terrible unrest in the land—no safe haven to turn to. Death was the one certainty for everyone and typically much sooner than desired. People couldn't settle down—start a life, raise a family, die of old age. These were fruitless dreams--they were all hopeless, doomed to certain fate. Then one day out of nowhere a man appeared. Some say he was a saint sent by the maker himself. Others say he was a wizard of a most powerful magic." The First Commander paused to collect his thoughts.

"Did he stop it? The fighting I mean?" Ava's curiosity got the best of her and she couldn't stop the thought from blurting out of her big mouth. The First Commander walked over to her and smiled a sad smile.

"No, I'm afraid not. Mostly he wandered from place to place just watching people live and people die. He was always a bystander until one day he happened across two very brave men in a gruesome battle where they were vastly outnumbered. He watched as these two men fought relentlessly back to back. They never surrendered. Their desire to live was greater than their fear and their loyalty to one another immeasurable. When the battle was over the two men lay bloodied and battered surely to die. But astonishingly, one of the men gradually made it to his feet. His companion wouldn't walk away as his injuries were far too grave. And even though the man who stood was grievously injured himself, he stooped and somehow managed to pick up his companion. He didn't make it very far before he stumbled down to his knee.

That is when he met the mysterious stranger that had arrived. On his knee still struggling to stand the stranger appeared before him and asked him 'Tell me the reason you try to carry this man? You will both certainly perish, but if you go alone, there is at least hope for you to live.' The man, heaving not only from his injuries but from the exertion of extra weight he carried, looked up at the stranger for a long moment before he replied, "My spirit and my heart would be broken if I were to leave him. If my last breath is spent in honor, then it will not be in vain.'

This surprised the stranger and he smiled at the man, 'Rare you are, if only there were more like you, things could be different.' He told the man to lay his companion down and he would help them. He told them of baby that would be born in a small cabin in the woods. He told them that this baby boy would be their charge. They would need to protect the child and ensure it would live to adulthood. This child would be the start of a new world. Then he spoke strange words they'd never heard before and his hands were glowing with a strange light. The stranger then placed one hand on each of their chests and a bolt of energy shot through them. That was the last thing they remembered. They woke up whole and hearty, their injuries were healed and their bodies were now covered in faint tattoos. The stranger was never seen again.

The two men knew they'd been given a second chance and did as the stranger advised. They found the baby boy and they protected him so he could grow. The baby boy turned out to be very special and as a man he became the very first Deacon. He changed everything and many years of peace ensued."

The First Commander turned to the two men. "Do you know who those two men were?" They gave no immediate reply but a dawning look of understanding was written on their faces.

"One was a Reed, the other was a Gray. They were your long lost ancestors. So you see that is why you carry these markings. It was your relatives that so long ago had the courage to stand together bravely when there was no hope left. And so that is what is passed to a male heir from generation to generation. Some thought it was a blessing while others swore it was a curse. Through time, as a new child was born with your namesake, they also became pledglings, and this is where your freedom is important. Every pledgling could decide whether or not to give their oath to the Royals. It is not something that can be forced or coerced. Once a pledge was given they would become a Sentinel—a keeper of the Royals."

Both men were now curiously eyeing their markings trying to comprehend the magnitude of everything they had just been told.

Falcon found his voice first, "But why did they just start glowing after all of this time?"

The First Commander started pacing considering how to explain this. "This is speculation of course, but pledglings and sentinels would only glow in the presence of a Royal and not necessarily all of the time. It usually occurred if the Royal was threatened or in harm's way."

Falcon closed his hands into fists, "What happened if a pledgling decided not to give his oath."

"The effects would still occur, nowhere near as obvious, and it would dissipate with distance but it never goes away entirely. This is something inborn—you have sharper instincts, quicker reflexes, and greater will. There are very strong emotions between Royals and their protectors. They share an unexplainable connection—an indestructible bond."

It was Griffon who finally put two and two together. He asked, "But the Royal bloodline has ceased, so how is this possible?"

The First Commander rested his gaze on Ava. "We have all thought that to be the truth, but what if we were wrong? Ava, I'd like to try something if you would let me."

Ava looked surprised and confused. "Of course."

He took her hand and led her toward the other end of the bailey. He walked back towards the two men. "It's obvious you both have a connection with Ava. Do you trust me?" Both men conceded.

"Good. Follow me." He placed them in the middle of the bailey, one on each side. "Falcon, Griffon, as your First Commander I order you to stay in these positions, no matter what occurs." He returned to the center of the bailey. "Mace, come forward."

An enormous, battle-scarred man made his way through the crowd and approached the First Commander, who quietly gave him instructions. Ava just kept thinking his presence alone on a battlefield would be intimidating enough to cause foes to turn tail and run.

Ava tried to be patient, but it was wearing thin. She hoped the First Commander would make his point already. Mace had turned in her direction and was stalking toward her. There was no other way to describe it. She wasn't sure what was going on and was genuinely shocked when the burly man grabbed her roughly around the shoulders and jerked her up against him. Falcon and Griffon both visibly tensed, but maintained their positions.

Mace held Ava for a moment longer as if waiting for something and then shoved her forward. She stumbled but was able to maintain her balance. She threw him a scathing

~ 126 ~

look but he roughly pushed her again. This time Falcon took a step forward about to protest.

"Hold your position!!" The First Commander yelled and Falcon grudgingly stepped back into place.

Two pushes was just about all Ava could take from Mace. When he approached her again with the same intent, she stepped around him. Mace lunged forward and grabbed her, this time he slung her several feet. She was unable to keep her footing and rolled numerous times. She landed past the point where Griffon and Falcon were standing, both visibly seething with anger.

Mace paused momentarily and looked at the First Commander who after a brief moment gave a nod of consent. Mace withdrew a dagger from his waist and started forward toward Ava. "Mace!" Falcon shouted out a warning. Mace persisted slowly forward toward Ava who was just recovering from her spill and had made it to her hands and knees. When she looked up and saw the man approaching her with dagger in hand, all she could do was back away in a crab like fashion. She looked back and forth between Falcon and Griffon waiting for them to do something.

"Commander?" Falcon yelled, but his plea was ignored.

That was more than Griffon could stand. He drew his dagger and propelled himself forward placing his body as a barricade in front of Ava's. Falcon sprinted to Griffon's side, but Mace was not deterred and continued forward.

Griffon was now so enraged he felt like he was on fire. Seething from the inside out, he shouted a warning to Mace, "Cease your advance, if you value your life." Mace was undeterred. A look passed between Falcon and Griffon. They didn't need to speak in order to communicate their thoughts-- they both took a fighting stance. Mace was easily twice their size and could crush them if he chose to do so.

With blatant disregard to their threats, Mace purposefully continued stalking forward with dagger in hand. That was the final straw for Griffon as he could no longer contain the poisonous rage that had seeped through his veins like venom. He lunged forward to tackle Mace. He grabbed the arm holding the dagger and both men hit the ground rolling. Somehow Griffon managed to wrestle himself on top of Mace. He hit Mace's wrist with the hilt of his dagger several times finally causing him to release his weapon; Mace recovered quickly and brought the same hand up to smash his fist into Griffon's mouth. They rolled several more times causing dust to rise that stung Ava's eyes and made her cough.

Griffon was holding his own with this much larger foe, when he landed a solid punch to Mace's cheek several of the man's comrades angrily started to come forward. Falcon immediately interceded. One man would try to pass and Falcon would push him back. There were several punches thrown and a deafening roar echoed against the walls as all of the men started to shout at once. Just before complete chaos ensued the First Commander shouted his command.

"HALT!!"

The two men on the ground were covered in dust and Griffon had blood oozing from his bottom lip. Mace stood, collected his dagger and sheathed it. Falcon helped Griffon to his feet.

The First Commander approached them. "Look," he told them and pointed to their arms. From where their hands gripped their daggers to the top of their arms they were bathed in a soft glow.

Everyone was silent as all of the bystanders were awestruck by this strange phenomenon. And then murmurs of excitement started to spread.

"What does it mean?" Griffon asked unable to mask his confusion.

Falcon looked over at his friend, "From everything he's told us, I think he means the Royal bloodline may not be extinct." Then all eyes rested on Ava.

Mace stepped forward and was immediately grabbed by both arms—Falcon on one side, Griffon on the other.

"I mean her no harm." Mace advised them gruffly and Falcon released his hold.

Griffon who still had potent adrenaline pumping through him stood nose to nose with the giant and told him, "I have warned you once. Hell would be a sanctuary compared to my wrath if you try to hurt her again. Understand?" Not until Mace nodded with a very amused expression did Griffon reluctantly release the man.

Mace walked over to Ava and gave her the typical bow. "Accept my apologies for being rough with you lady. I hope I did not cause you injury."

"I'm fine." Ava said clearly upset. Seeing his swollen cheek she took silent pleasure in the thought it might turn into a big black eye.

Mace bowed again and disappeared in the crowd of people. The First Commander called them back to the center of the bailey. And it was an obviously annoyed Ava who spoke up first.

"I hope you aren't under some false pretense that I am from some long lost bloodline." Their silence was more than enough to answer her question. She growled in frustration and rolled her eyes at the lot of them.

The First Commander considered his sons closely. "I honestly don't know the answer to that Ava. The possibility in itself would prove optimistic." He turned to look at her, "What you need to ask yourself—do you have the courage to find out?"

Chapter 18

Ava stormed off more than a little aggravated. She'd arrived here unexpectedly and felt like a puzzle piece finally falling into its place, but the longer she was here it seemed things were getting more and more complicated. Her entire life was spent not knowing what it felt like to really belong, to be comfortable in her own skin. So her arrival had set off an explosion of emotions. She was happy, excited, scared, surprised, and even hopeful. Now she was just annoyed.

Who did these guys think they were? They were tossing her around like sack of potatoes. She'd clearly explained to all of them where she came from but they had it in their heads that she was some long lost Royal. Good grief, all they needed to do was look at her and they would see she wasn't cut from that type of cloth. She was plain Jane Ava and the sooner they all realized it the better.

The more she considered everything, only one aspect about the entire situation really bothered her. If any of what the First Commander told them was true, it could mean that all of these feelings that she had about Falcon and Griffon were merely protective instincts on their behalf and not really heartfelt. She should have known it was too good to be true. They were like the frothy, fluffy, floating goodness on the top of a cappuccino and she was more like the coffee grounds that somehow escaped the filter and settled on the bottom of the cup.

Ava needed time to mull over everything so she headed to the fireplace in the hall. She'd just sat down when Everett and Viktor sidled in. They appeared very concerned about her and since she couldn't understand them she tried to reassure them she was okay. She sat for a long time just staring at the embers. The lack of sleep the night before along with the mentally draining episode in the bailey made her curl up in a ball and close her eyes. The last thing she wished for before she drifted off was to return home. Everett and Viktor retrieved a throw on a nearby bench and draped it over the sleeping girl. Then they perched themselves on the mantle to keep watch.

Griffon sat on his bed tending his busted lip pondering what had just transpired. After Ava had stormed out of the bailey he didn't know what to say or do. The scuffle with Mace had flooded his mind with memories of the many previous fights he'd had within these walls. Most of which had been fought with Falcon at his side. It was strangely comforting to be standing side by side with the same objective, but he honestly baffled at where this strong protective instinct was coming from in regard to Ava. They'd shared several moments on the journey that made him think maybe he'd found someone that would not only understand but also accept him. If the First Commander's notions were correct, then everything could very well have been an illusion. With a groan he lay back on his bed and threw his arm over his face wondering if he would ever be able to face solitude again after the brief time he'd shared with Ava.

Falcon paced in the garden. His emotions a roller coaster—angry, confused, surprised, sad—they repeated over and over. He'd disobeyed a direct order from his First Commander. Something he'd never done before and it was really eating at him. If Ava was a Royal it could mean an end to the unrest in the Kingdom, but at what cost? He'd almost kissed her in the alley. He'd wanted to kiss her. Was any of it real? His jumbled thoughts were getting in the way of reason. He sat down on a bench and put his head in his hands. He ran his long fingers through his hair and tried to clear his mind.

"Bet you weren't expecting any of that."

Falcon looked over to see Slye watching him. "No, that was definitely a surprise."

"Do you believe it's possible? That Ava is a Royal?" Slye questioned.

Falcon considered this carefully. "I guess anything's possible."

"I'd heard about Sentinels, but never thought I would actually see one. It's pretty amazing."

Falcon nodded agreement, "I guess, in a way I'm honored. It's something that would make my father proud-- possibly being able to put an end to the grief of so many."

"You care for Ava." It was a statement more than a question. "Would you pledge to be her Sentinel?"

So many thoughts ran through Falcon's mind. It was as if a herd of wild horses were on the loose and he couldn't think straight for all of the noise so he shrugged.

"I can see you need to be alone. I came to tell you the First Commander has arranged a banquet for tonight. He wants everyone to attend. My guess is he has something up his sleeve. He said not to be late."

Falcon sighed. He did need time to think, but he also knew he respected the First Commander and knew he wouldn't let him down. "Alright, I'll be there."

Slye turned on his heel and left Falcon to his tumultuous thoughts.

It had been over two hours since Slye had woken Ava from her nap to advise her of the evening's plans. She'd soaked in a hot bath and thankfully the pain in her side had finally subsided. She'd almost forgotten about the injury until Mace had manhandled her. When she finished bathing she was surprised to find someone had been in her room and laid a dress out on her bed. There was a white sheer cotton shift and an indigo tunic that layered over top with short sleeves that sat slightly off her shoulders. The ensemble was form fitting and fell luxuriously to her ankles. As she walked, the material swayed back and forth. She brushed out her hair and decided to try to get it off her shoulders in an up do. Several ringlets fell down, but it was the best she could do. She cleaned her slippers and headed downstairs to the hall feeling very feminine.

Ava took her time walking to her destination as her thoughts were a jumbled mess. She'd considered many different alternatives about how to handle this situation but hadn't come up with anything helpful. All she could do now was ride it out. They would discover the truth soon enough.

So engrossed in her thoughts, she certainly hadn't been expecting what she saw as she entered the hall. It had undergone a total transformation in the few hours since she'd left. There were people everywhere. There were minstrels dressed in colorful costumes playing instruments and singing. The tables were overflowing with food and drink. People were laughing and twirling around on the dance floor. It was beautiful mayhem and she laughed out loud. Maybe these festivities could help her relax and forget, even if it was just for a little while.

Ava spied Cricket and Slye sitting across the room and slowly made her way through the throngs of people. Cricket greeted her with a charming smile and motioned for her to sit. She was dressed in a satin dress, black as midnight, with a plunging neckline and a back that draped in layers. She was striking and Ava observed how close the two were sitting and that they were holding hands. The way Slye ogled her was amusing, but it made her feel like an intruder so she was grateful when she saw the First Commander approaching. Not far behind him were Griffon and Falcon, both dressed in elegant clothing and looking illegally handsome. The men joined the trio at the table. Ava felt awkward. After what happened earlier she didn't know exactly how to behave now.

The First Commander surprised them all when he downed a whole cup of ale. He slammed the empty cup down on the table and wiped his mouth with the back of his hand. "Lighten up my friends, this is a celebration. Eat, drink, and enjoy."

Slye didn't need to be told twice. He stood and eagerly pulled Cricket onto the dance floor. They smiled into each other's eyes as they danced away until they were swallowed up by the crowd.

Falcon looked at the First Commander. "I thought you wanted to discuss something important with us tonight."

"I do my boy, but it isn't anything that can't wait a few hours. You've travelled far and deserve an opportunity to relax. Fill your belly and dance with pretty girls. Never know you may get lucky and steal a kiss or two." Just then a woman walked up behind the First Commander and put her hands on his shoulders. She bent down and smacked a big kiss on his cheek. "Do you think you can spare a dance for an old woman?" The First Commander's laughter as he stood and guided the woman, who couldn't have been in her forties, onto the dance floor was a good indicator that talking would have to wait.

That left Ava alone with Griffon and Falcon. Trying her best to ignore them, she concentrated on the assortment of people scattered around the room. It didn't take very long to pick up on a rather interesting pattern. Every other girl from five to thirty five was obviously drooling over the two men sitting at her table. Some were just looking with innocent curiosity while others appeared shy and looked dreamily at the men, most likely wishing they would have the courage to speak to them. It was the older women with their sultry gazes and hungry stares that made her uncomfortable. Their dancing was clearly provocative in an attempt to gain the attention of the two handsome devils. Ava didn't miss the looks of bitter resentment shot her way either.

Just when she'd decided she'd had all she could take, a boy approached her. He was tall and lanky, probably no more than fifteen with red hair and a mile wide-smile. "Hello pretty lady. My name's Jack." He bowed down in front of her until his nose almost touched the floor. Ava had to bite her tongue to keep from laughing at this theatrical display. "Would you do me the great honor of a dance?"

Ava didn't immediately answer. Jack visibly swallowed and looked over his shoulder and turned three shades of red. Ava peered behind him to see several other boys laughing and pointing, clearly making jests at his expense. Well, she would just show them. Putting all of her own insecurities behind her she stood, "I would love to." Jack held out his arm and Ava placed her hand in his elbow and let him escort her onto the dance floor. She took great pleasure in smiling as they walked by the boys who had moments before been laughing at Jack, but were now staring slack- jawed. *Serves them right* she thought.

Griffon sat in stony silence as he watched the young man awkwardly twirl Ava around the dance floor. He hadn't missed what had transpired between the boy and his friends. He knew exactly why Ava agreed to dance with him; she had the most generous heart and in that moment he realized he would somehow have to figure out a way to be worthy enough to earn a place in it for him. He watched the boy clumsily flirt with Ava while she smiled and laughed. Before he knew what was happening he was up out of his seat and heading toward them.

Ava didn't really know how to dance, but it was obvious that Jack didn't either. They basically took turns stepping on each other's toes; every time they did it just made them laugh that much harder and it felt good. Griffon surprised them both when he walked up behind Jack and told him that he would like to cut in. Jack blushed, thanked Ava, and walked away with his chest puffed out and his head held high.

Griffon didn't know what had come over him. Now, here he was on the dance floor with everyone staring at him, including Ava. This was definitely a situation he would normally have avoided under any circumstance. Ava looked up at him with sparkling eyes full of expectation and he reached out his hand. After only a moment of hesitation she placed her hand in his and let him gently pull her closer. As he wrapped his arm around her waist he felt like he was home.

As Griffon began to move Ava noticed an enormous difference. Although it was clumsy, dancing with Jack had been easy and fun, but with Griffon, it was intense. Even though she didn't know the moves he led her through them flawlessly. As they twirled around Ava began to relax. In the first few trips around the floor she caught several women glaring with scornful malice. She looked up at Griffon and saw his attention completely focused on her and they shared a smile as the warm tingling sensation sizzled in their palms. Once she made eye contact with him everything else in the background became nothing more than a colorful blur.

The music ended far too soon; before Griffon could escort Ava back to her seat, there were several men in line asking her to dance. Griffon reluctantly released Ava's hand to an older man with missing teeth; he assumed to be the lesser of the evils and headed back to the table where he and Falcon watched Ava dance the next several dances with a different partner each time.

After about four or five more dances it was clear that no one would give Ava a break, so an annoyed Falcon stalked onto the floor and grabbed her hand before anyone else could secure another dance. He pulled Ava along behind him and walked to a side table where he took a cup of punch and handed it to her. "Drink."

Ava gratefully accepted the cup and emptied it with a huge sigh, "Thank you."

Falcon only nodded. Ava looked over at him and couldn't help admire how handsome he was all cleaned up. She'd come quite accustomed to seeing him with a five o'clock shadow; the stubble gave him a manly aura, made him look older somehow. Now, he was clean shaven, hair all slicked back, vivacious and charismatic all wrapped up into one. He was looking out at the crowd and shook his head back and forth. Strangely enough he looked another direction and shook his head no again.

"What are you *doing*?"

"Since it's so obvious no one wants to dance with you, let's see."

She rolled her eyes at his sarcasm.

"Just trying to deter some of the wet behind the ear, would be suitors trying to get up the courage to ask you to dance."

Oh, the ever chivalrous Falcon. After she drank another cup of punch she'd pretty much caught her breath. Falcon decided the only way to keep the hounds at bay would be to dance with Ava himself so he grabbed her arm and spun her around. The song had a fast tempo and prevented any conversation. They laughed; both completely lost in a moment that ended entirely too quickly. When it was over Falcon escorted Ava back to their table purposefully ignoring the men who approached her.

Ava was confounded that both men were such accomplished dancers. Looks like fighting wasn't the only skill the First Commander taught them. As she sat and absorbed everything that was happening around her the thought crossed her mind that the fall formal couldn't possibly hold a candle to this celebration.

Chapter 19

It was getting fairly late and the festivities were starting to die down. Many people had already departed while others had spent most of the night heavy in their cups had passed out scattered about the hall. The minstrels went from performing high energy music that incited dancing and merriment to playing slower mellow ballads that seemed to blanket the hall into a sedate atmosphere. Slye, Cricket, and the First Commander had finally joined them back at their table. The First Commander relished a cigar while everyone waited with great anticipation to finally discover what he had to say. "

As some of you already know, when Falcon arrived he had a message for me from the commander at the fortress tower of Eden Divide. This is the battlement in the West that is closest to Prime Sovereign Ezekiel's estate and they have their hands full trying to maintain control. Go ahead Falcon and inform everyone else of the message."

"It sounded more like a riddle to me, but the Commander told me 'Hence the next full moon hope will find wings. It is imperative we unite together in order to eliminate the impending threat to our kingdom or we will all fall individually. Whatever you choose, go with grace.' Like I said riddles."

The First Commander took a long draw on his cigar and puffed out smoke in small circles that lazily drifted upward and expanded into larger circles. After several more times of performing this same trick he finally decided it was time to clue everyone in. "What lies ahead will be very dangerous. I want each of you to consider the hazards very carefully before committing."

Ava inwardly groaned at his ominous choice of words. She glanced around the table to gauge the other's reactions and it was obvious that the First Commander was held in high esteem among these individuals and was to be taken very seriously. It didn't bode well.

"In two weeks you will disembark on a journey, a journey of truth. You must venture to the mountains of Burning Ash."

A collective gasp of surprise resonated around the table, but of course Ava was clueless as to why.

"You must access the mountain through a hidden cave. The cave can only be located during the silver moon which is why we will have to wait. Once inside, your objective is to locate the Flame of Consequence."

Falcon huffed, "The Flame of Consequence? I thought that was just a child's fairytale."

"The flame will reveal the truth."

Ava could tell by the mood that this would be no easy venture and knew she needed to arm herself with information. "What is the Flame of Consequence?"

The First Commander proceeded to tell her that it was a source of great power and knowledge, a so-called oracle. If a person not only had an open mind, but also a pure heart then the flame would reveal truth or facts from the past, present, or future.

"So why do I get the feeling there's some sort of catch involved?" Ava started to squirm as suddenly everyone seemed to find the table or the ceiling rather fascinating in order to avoid making eye contact with her. It was Griffon who finally explained.

"The Flame of Consequence is heavily guarded."

"Well, I've seen you all in action, I'm sure it's nothing you can't handle."

"The Reach, Ava, it's guarded by the Reach."

Ava's heart stopped beating and her mouth went dry. Her head started swimming and stars were flashing before her eyes. She was certain she was going to pass out at any moment. It took several minutes for her world to settle so she could regain her composure. She closed her eyes and took deep calming breaths through her nose. When things finally stopped spinning and she could rationalize what they were saying she was baffled. Why should she go to such an ominous place that was riddled with danger?

Then she looked up and saw everyone staring right at her, which was certainly an unordinary experience for her. But there were two pairs of arresting eyes that she just couldn't ignore. Falcon and Griffon, who were both obviously concerned for her welfare, could read her thoughts and yet they were still hopeful. She remembered what she had told them before, that she would help them. One thing she knew for sure, she didn't want to let them down. If she had to go into a spooky mountain to prove who she was, it was the least she could do.

"I made a promise to Falcon and Griffon. I owe them both my life."

The First Commander eyed her speculatively. "Okay, tomorrow morning we begin training. Anyone that will go needs to meet in the bailey at sunrise. We all need to be in our best form so we will be prepared for anything. Let me remind you again that this is going to be risky so please consider carefully before you make your decision."

He bid them all good night and Ava watched as he exited the hall hand in hand with the pretty woman he'd danced with earlier.

All Ava kept thinking was how her life had gone from one extreme to another. Elzbeth had been uneventful and dull. Now she was on an overwhelming thrill ride. Two weeks, that's how much time she had before she would be face to face with the shadows of her nightmares.

While she was deep in thought, everyone left the table except Cricket who was now closely observing Ava. They'd never really spoken to one another. "I never had a chance to thank you for before, the sappacks. You saved me."

Cricket humbly inclined her head and smiled.

"You really don't say much do you? But you don't need to. You are very unusual. It's like you have this commanding presence, but at the same time you blend in so easily. That doesn't make any sense." She groaned and laid her head in her hands. "Nothing makes sense. They are placing all of their hopes on an idea that is so far-fetched, I'm so afraid that I will let them all down. That would just break my heart."

Ava looked up at Cricket. It was strange how she could communicate without ever speaking.

Cricket stood up to leave and as she walked by Ava she reached down and touched her face. She leaned in and whispered, "Your heart is safe." The angelic sound of her voice was almost inaudible, but an immediate sense of calm washed over Ava. She watched Cricket join Slye and they exited the hall together. Ava smiled and headed to bed somehow knowing that tonight her sleep would be dreamless.

Chapter 20

In a dank, dark chamber a man was chained and suspended from the center of the room. His hair as well as his beard was long and scraggly. Dirt and grime covered his entire frame that basically consisted of skin on bone. He was frail and he was hopeless. Even as blood trickled down his arms he no longer noticed the bite of the cuffs as they dug deep into his wrists. He was numb. He'd given up long ago.

A guard entered the cell carrying a bucket of water. He physically held open the man's jaw and forced the water down his throat causing him to choke and sputter. "We can't have you die just yet." The guard told him. "No, no, no, Prime Sovereign Ezekiel has plans for you my friend. He would be none too pleased if you interfered." He patted the man's cheek, "No, he won't even let death interfere." With a vicious laugh the guard left the cell and the man willingly succumbed to dark oblivion.

Everyone gathered in the bailey, all except for Ava, which had the rest of them quite anxious since it was well past sunrise. Falcon paced restlessly and Griffon sat on a bale of hay with his shoulders hunched. They both knew the entire plan revolved around her cooperation. The First Commander was discussing logistics with Slye and Cricket was practicing with her blades. Everett and Viktor were nervously flying back and forth across the bailey—a fiend's method of pacing.

All activity ceased when Ava appeared and approached the First Commander. She was still uncertain about her decision, but she'd spent hours deliberating and came to the conclusion that she'd promised them she would try to help and that's the least she could do. Her greatest fear was causing them heartache later on, but she'd just have to deal with that on her own when the time came.

The First Commander smiled reassuringly at the brave young woman who stood before him. Her willingness to try spoke volumes in regard to her character and he threw up a silent prayer of gratitude.

"I know you have many doubts, Ava, as do we all. The fact of the matter is we have simply run out of options. This may seem like a giant leap of faith, but at this point, it is all the hope we have left."

Ava's heart constricted like it was surrounded by a python. "There's not much I can offer, but I'm willing to try." Ava was rather surprised when he grabbed her and wrapped her in a great big hug.

With a hearty laugh he released her and looked at the others, "Let us begin."

Time flew by. They were up at the crack of dawn and didn't retire until long after the sun went down. Each day was broken into several components; they would strength train by sparring with each other using a variety of weapons. The First Commander continually stressed how important it was to be proficient with all forms of weaponry because there was no guarantee you wouldn't be unarmed at some point. Ava's main struggle was with the heavy battle axes as she just didn't have the upper body strength required to wield them correctly.

The First Commander also instructed them to climb walls and ropes, made them run miles through rough terrain in the woods and around the palace, and swim laps across the nearby river. He even made them catch baby piglets in a muddy pen. He swore it was to work on their dexterity, but as much enjoyment as he seemed to get out of it Ava did have her doubts about his intentions. One thing for certain, he was relentless through it all and pushed them well beyond their limits. He did this because it was his way of giving them better odds for survival.

Certainly unaccustomed to such strenuous activities, the days were grueling for Ava. There wasn't a muscle in her body that didn't protest movement. She woke up in the morning, had breakfast, and tried to endure the rest of the day without making a fool of herself. At night she would stumble to her room and be asleep before her head hit the pillow. One good thing about being so exhausted was the fact her mind was too preoccupied to fret over other matters.

Of course it was impossible to completely forget. Falcon and Griffon were ever present. If they weren't partnered with her they were constantly checking up on her. They would make sure she had plenty of water and that she continued to eat. During their runs if she would fall behind one of them would also conveniently fall behind. If she got tired while swimming one would stop and wait or just offer words of encouragement. It made sense; they obviously felt responsible for her welfare and even though she hated to admit it there were times she could have given up if they'd not been there.

After the eighth day of training the First Commander advised them they would be switching gears the following day. They would still concentrate on strength and endurance during the mornings, but in the afternoons they would concentrate on other areas such as stealth and strategy. Since she was unfamiliar with both Ava went to bed looking forward to rising sun.

She woke up the next morning feeling rested and invigorated. Her muscles were becoming more accustomed to the vigorous demands of the past week. She was still somewhat stiff but it was quickly forgotten once she was up and moving around

After their morning exercises the First Commander paired Ava with Slye to work on some hand-in-hand techniques. Definitely not her forte as her behind hit the ground enough times to jar all of her teeth loose. The worst part about it was the fact she knew he was taking it easy on her. It was impossible to anticipate his next move and it would be futile even if she could. He was exceptionally quick. Since she wasn't quite catching on he decided to tone it down a notch and teach her some simple techniques to free herself if she would get detained.

On the tenth day Ava worked with Cricket for a while on small weapons as well as hand to hand combat. Cricket obviously had the patience of a saint because it took repeated tries for Ava to pick up on the maneuvers she was shown. Then Everett and Viktor demonstrated how to pick locks and set assorted small traps. Ava still couldn't understand their language, but she certainly knew not to underestimate them. They were truly fascinating and it made her wonder what else she might see on this adventure.

Day eleven dawned and brought with it the unavoidable yet somewhat dreaded individual training with Griffon. All of the previous training had been in more of a group setting. Today it would be just the two of them, in the woods, outside of the palace, working on stealth and camouflage. Ava was eager to learn but this would be Griffon's first opportunity to discuss everything that transpired one on one. She knew how much it mattered to him but in a way she just wanted to stick to business and not complicate matters further.

Since the destination that Griffon had decided upon was less than a mile away, they chose to walk. They went empty handed as he informed her that any supplies they needed would be provided by the forest.

Griffon appeared to be somewhat aggravated. He hadn't said two words since they'd left the bailey. She would occasionally glance over to see if his mood had improved, but finally gave up and decided to take in the breathtaking scenery. The first rays of the morning sun were cascading through the trees and illuminating the greenery of the forest floor. A dewy mist was scattered throughout the woods and floated about the flora like the ocean on a breezeless day. Birds flew back and forth chirping their cheerful songs alerting the sleepy woods that it was time to wake. Ava could smell the sweet fragrance of honeysuckle which reminded her of her Aunt and made her homesick for her family.

Griffon finally stopped and glanced at their surroundings. "This will do."

Okay, looks like he's all business. *Isn't that what you wanted?*

"Stealth is the art of illusion and evasion. If you are on the defense, illusion can hide you; if you are on the offense illusion can help you sneak up on opponents. The sole purpose of stealth evasion is to sneak around enemies without confrontation." He slowly stalked in a circle around her. "Both involve patience. If you try to rush, you will most likely blow your cover by making noise that will alert enemies of your whereabouts."

The way he moved about triggered the fight or flight mechanism. Her palms were sweaty and her nerves were on edge.

"Be observant of your environment. Determine what can be used to your advantage. Camouflage for example is very effective. Disguise yourself in shadows or leaves, mud or dirt can be used as cover to help you blend into the surroundings; conceal yourself in rivers or with rocks. The temperature, the weather, and scent must also be taken into consideration."

As he proceeded to educate her on the art of stealth Ava became distracted. When he had to repeat instructions several times he became agitated.

"Why aren't you concentrating? You may not find this very interesting, but it could save your life."

"It's just been a really long couple of weeks, that's all."

Griffon felt bad for reprimanding her, it was so out of character. Her presence was completely voluntary and it would do him good to remember that. "You're right. I'm just worried. I want us all prepared to face what lies ahead."

Ava nodded agreement and the rest of the afternoon flew by. They were both satisfied with what they were able to cover. The next afternoon they stayed in the bailey. Griffon had arranged a test of sorts. He had blind folded men scattered about and her goal was to sneak around them without being detected. They worked for hours and she never made it all the way through once. Her first attempt failed because she made too much noise. Griffon told her it may as well have been a herd of cattle in a stampede. She was breathing too loud on the second round. At least that's what the man said who had risen his hand identifying he'd heard her. When Ava told him it was an impossible feat he demonstrated himself without a hitch. More determined than ever, she made it pretty far on her third attempt, but someone evidently smelled her shampoo. How was she to know that one of them would have such a keen sense of smell? Even though Griffon left her with words of encouragement, she headed to bed sniffing the ends of her hair, frustrated, with no desire to be subjected to whatever Falcon had lined up for her.

When Ava woke, she knew immediately that it was very late. She must have overslept. Throwing covers and grabbing her clothes she dressed as fast as she could and ran down to the hall. When she entered, she saw Falcon sitting in a chair with his feet propped up on the table surrounded by two very attractive females soaking up his attention. As she walked nearer she heard their giggles and the sickening sweet praises they were smothering Falcon with and she couldn't help but roll her eyes.

Falcon noticed her approach and quickly sat up. Did his eyes just light up? The lights were obviously playing tricks on her.

"Good morning, Ava. Did you sleep well?"

The two lady companions who had just been smiling so sweetly at Falcon, deflated when they noted her presence.

"I did." Still a little disoriented from obviously sleeping late she gave him a questioning glance, "Umm, did I oversleep? It seems late?"

"I wanted you to rest. I have a surprise for you. Are you ready?" He couldn't repress his excitement as he grinned from ear to ear.

One of the girls who had been speaking with Falcon cleared her throat to remind him of their presence. He looked over a little surprised. "Oh, ladies, I apologize, but I must excuse myself. We have important matters to attend to." He grabbed Ava's arm and escorted her out of the hall. Whatever it was had him as excited as a school boy. She couldn't resist a look back at the women who stood slack jawed in shock and she felt a little guilty for interrupting.

Chapter 21

Finding Cecil saddled in the bailey was the farthest thing Ava had in mind for a surprise. She was certain the day would entail more hand to hand training or weapon wielding. She quizzically looked at Falcon, "What's this?"

"Today, we take a break. I know I need one. Besides, I think Cecil has been missing you."

Ava had to laugh as she walked up to the giant and smoothed her hand over his nose and muzzle. "I missed you too, Beast." He nudged her with his nose. Falcon came and boosted her in the saddle. After he mounted his own bay stallion, they trotted side by side through the gates and into the brilliant sunshine.

Getting outside of the palace walls for something other than training was exactly what Ava needed. Obviously she'd been much more tense than she had realized. The farther they rode the more relaxed she became and the substantial weight of what lay ahead slowly lifted improving her mood. Falcon gave her pointers on horseback riding so she would be more comfortable in the saddle. They talked and laughed and enjoyed their ride.

They rode up to a wide creek and Falcon stopped. He dismounted and pulled a brown sack off of his saddle. Without a word he walked over to a shady spot under an ancient Sycamore tree and spread out a blanket. Ava looked at him curiously.

"What are you doing?"

He couldn't contain his excitement. "This is part of your surprise a picnic."

This was completely unexpected and incredibly thoughtful! Ava dismounted and left Cecil to graze. She walked over to where Falcon had settled himself on the blanket. He was busy pulling out fresh bread and fruit from the basket. When the heavenly yeasty aroma of the bread wafted up her stomach rumbled loudly in anticipation.

"It's a good thing I brought some food along; it sounds like you're hungry enough to eat one of our horses."

Ava arched her eyebrow at him and shook her head. "I missed breakfast."

"I know."

Falcon handed Ava a thick slice of bread smeared with honey. She devoured it so fast she couldn't remember if she actually even chewed it.

Licking the sticky honey from her fingers she mumbled, "That was delicious." She noticed that Falcon was sitting motionless and looked up at him just as her tongue darted out and licked the palm of her hand. He was staring at her like he wanted to devour her just like she had devoured the sweet bread. His smoldering gaze was extremely intense and it basically consumed all of the oxygen in their general vicinity.

"Ava."

Somehow she managed to whisper, "Yes."

"Do you remember that night in the alley? When you tried to clobber me?"

She swallowed hard. Did she ever remember? It was something she would never forget; just thinking about it made her flush from head to toe. "I do."

"That wasn't the first time I wanted to kiss you," he paused and let out a sigh, "and this isn't the second."

The fact that he was sitting here telling her that on multiple occasions, since they'd first met, he wanted to kiss her made her very, very nervous. Not that the same thought hadn't crossed her mind many times, but it never occurred to her maybe she wasn't the only one contemplating it.

The atmosphere had quickly changed from relaxed to very intense, making Ava nervous and fidgety. The change didn't go unnoticed by Falcon. He'd not intended for the topic of discussion to turn to this, but as he watched her pink tongue dart out to lick her hand he'd simply forgotten everything else. He refused to let the day be spoiled by his ardor so he forcibly doused the candle of desire and started clearing their blanket. He refused to be ashamed of how he felt, he was a man after all, and she was undeniably a temptation.

Ava had walked over to the stream to finish washing the sticky from her fingers. The creek bed was full of blue green shale and dark obsidian stones. The aesthetic magnificence was enhanced with what she considered to be some pretty strange looking fish. They reminded her of a sort of quoi, but they had long whiskers like a catfish only much more attractive. Elegant fins and fan tails of various sizes swam in front of her glowing bright red and orange. It was a sight to behold. She stood up to swing her arms back and forth to help dry her hands. Falcon walked up beside her and picked up a pebble to throw. They both watched as it skipped several times over the translucent surface causing the fish to scatter.

"How did you do that? I've never been able to skip them more than once."

Falcon grinned from ear to ear; thankful he hadn't spoiled their day. "Well, you see there's a trick."

"A trick, huh?"

He skipped another rock. This one went even farther than the first.

"Will you teach me?"

"Can't."

"Can't, or won't?"

"Can't."

"And why not?"

"I'm afraid it's highly classified information."

Ava looked at him in knowing disbelief. "I see. Would it have something to do with wearing the water?"

Falcon looked down quizzically, "What water?"

Too late, he realized his mistake as Ava bent down and splashed water up his shirt and on his face making him sputter at the impact of the cold water.

"Oh you little minx, you're going to pay for that!"

Ava squealed and shot off into the stream barely avoiding his outstretched arms. They took turns splashing and chasing each other completely erasing the earlier tension. When there wasn't a dry thread left on them, they sat on the bank and soaked up the sunshine.

All too soon Falcon stated it was time to head back to the Palace. Ava stood and started working out some of the tangles in her hair. She joined Falcon at the horses. Taking Cecil's reins from Falcon's grasp she let her hand linger. "Thank you. This was so thoughtful."

A slight blush tinged his cheeks. "It was my pleasure."

They mounted their steeds and headed back towards the Palace at a rather leisurely pace wanting to preserve the relaxed atmosphere as long as possible.

Sometime later, when they entered the bailey, they were greeted with an alarming site. Far in the back corner everyone had gathered in a semi-circle staring intently towards the ground. The first thought in Ava's mind was that someone had been injured and her imagination played images of the potential injuries one could receive from the wide array of weaponry: her stomach did a flip flop.

She nearly fell out of the saddle when out of nowhere the spectators threw their hands up in the air and let out a deafening roar. *What on earth are they up to?*

They dismounted and headed toward the assembled group of people. Ava stood on her tiptoes to see what all the commotion was about. Dice. They were playing dice. The First Commander threw the dice up against the wall. Another loud roar erupted making Ava jump. Geesh. The First Commander spotted them, "Falcon, come and take a turn my boy?"

He shook his head and laughed, "Why not." He made his way through the crowd and took the dice.

More cheering ensued as it appeared Falcon had made a good roll. A warm tingling ran up Ava's arm and she looked over to see Griffon standing beside her. "Good grief, are you always so sneaky?"

Griffon only smiled which made Ava chuckle the strong silent type. The game continued for at least another hour. It tickled Ava to see everyone in such good spirits which continued all through dinner. Stories were shared and tall tales of adventure were told. It had been a picture perfect day, one Ava would not soon forget.

The hall eventually cleared and quieted down until all that remained was the inevitable travelers that would depart early the next morning. The silence was broken by the First Commander.

"All preparations have been arranged. We depart at first light. Hopefully we will reach the mountains of Burning Ash within three days. One last time I want to remind everyone that it's not too late to change your mind."

Everyone remained silent.

"Okay then, let's all get some rest."

The dawn brought with it ominous storm clouds and grumbling thunder. A steady sprinkle of rain saturated the landscape and didn't bode well for the days ventures. Although Ava was somewhat excited she would admit only to herself that she was also a little anxious. Sure she'd trained for the last few weeks and was in the best shape she'd ever been in, but she was no warrior. The thought of running into more Krypts made her skin crawl, not to mention the thought of entering a dark cave that was home to the shadows of her nightmares. She would keep these tidbits of information to herself as it would be all that Falcon and Griffon needed in order to call off their journey and she didn't want that.

She was almost too nervous to eat, but made her way to the Great Hall anyway. To her surprise it was empty, so she pocketed a large green apple and took a slice of freshly baked bread that she nibbled as she headed to the bailey, which was now bustling with activity. Ava saw Cecil saddled and ready. He shook his head up and down then whinnied at her in greeting. She walked over to him and rubbed his muzzle. He nudged her chest with his nose and rooted for her apple.

"You rascal well, I suppose," she presented Cecil with the bright green apple from her pocket. While he crunched noisily in obvious enjoyment Ava fiddled with his mane. She didn't have to wait too long before the First Commander arrived and started spouting commands to get everyone organized and prepared to disembark. Ava was amused by how quickly everyone responded to his requests without hesitation; she realized he was well respected and trusted, giving her a renewed sense of courage.

Falcon and Griffon seemed to materialize out of thin air to stand on either side of her. The First Commander saw the trio and headed their way. He stopped in front of them. He looked at Ava and she noticed how his expression softened, "You have the courage of ten men and a heart that's as least as big as the moon." He placed one hand on each of the men's shoulder standing next to her forming somewhat of a circle. "All I ask is that you look out for one another." With that he was gone and they were soon mounted on their horses, ready to depart on a journey to an unfamiliar place, seeking answers to questions Ava believed were quite preposterous. As they left the bailey and rode through the gate it began to sprinkle.

Chapter 22

The flickering flames of the small campfire sizzled with the impact of each plump raindrop. The dismal weather had everyone in a particularly foul mood, none more so than Falcon. He secretly wished the rain was solely to blame for his temperament, but something else had been weighing heavily on his mind. Ever since he'd seen Ava with Griffon in the palace he'd been unable to shake it off. It really irked him that the man had no scruples. Griffon wasn't one to stick around and would eventually end up hurting Ava. The fact she had bonded with both of them didn't sit well either. He could thank the history of the sentinels for that. He'd met her first; didn't that count for something? Real mature *Falcon!*

He looked across the campfire at Ava sitting alone and braving the rain, and then over to Griffon who was watching her like she was the most fascinating thing he'd ever seen.

That's it!

Falcon stalked across the camp. "Griffon, I need to speak with you." He couldn't keep his voice from portraying his obvious frustration. Griffon looked up at him and shook his head but didn't immediately rise. He spared another pining glance toward Ava. Big mistake.

"NOW!" Falcon barked.

That earned him a blistering scowl from Griffon. "Well, since you asked so nicely," but he stood with his bow and followed anyway.

When they reached the tree line Falcon turned and unleashed his wrath. "What exactly do you think you're doing?"

"I dunno. Why don't you clue me in?"

Falcon's voice raised an octave as he barked. "Don't play coy, Griffon, you know damn well I'm talking about Ava."

"What about her?"

"You're messing with her head, leading her to believe she can count on you, and it's going to stop."

"And what makes you think she can't?" "History, Griffon, things get rough and you turn tail and run."

"My history," he ground out a dismissive wave, "has nothing to do with her, why are you even bringing this up?"

Falcon shook his head in disgust, "Let's just say I have a personal interest and I don't want to see her get hurt, not if I can help it.

"Falcon wouldn't bring up the past voluntarily, so what was his motive? Understanding slowly dawned on Griffon. "Ahhh. I see." He leaned on his bow, shook his head and chuckled which did nothing to cool Falcon's ire. "When did the fearless Falcon become afraid of a little competition?"

Falcon clenched his fists and looked down at the ground.

All joking aside Griffon's own temper was on the rise. "Go ahead, tell me I'm wrong."

Falcon's right arm swung of its own volition; with the force of a giant his fist hit Griffon square on the left jaw.

Caught off guard, Griffon stumbled backward with the grace of a drunkard, but it didn't take him long to recover. He knew this spectacle wasn't all about Ava. It was Falcon's way of dealing with his own pent up emotions. The fact of the matter was Falcon wasn't the only one who had been hurt by past events. Filled with a burning rage that consumed his soul Griffon charged forward and slammed into Falcon with such force they both rolled head over heels.

They wrestled around for several minutes taking turns giving and receiving punches. The impact of each blow gradually sapped their rage and replaced it with a mixture of regret and sadness eventually ending their altercation.

Lying on their backs and breathing heavy from their juvenile display it was Falcon's next words that shattered Griffon into a million pieces as if he were a delicate vase falling from the high shelf of a china cabinet.

"You left once Griffon. Have you forgotten I've been on the receiving end of your abandonment? Can't you see it's not only her that will be disappointed?"

If Griffon's resolve were a coffin, then those words brutally drove in the final nail. *What if he was right? What was he even doing here? Those many years ago when he'd walked out of the palace he'd resolved himself to be a loner. If there was even a remote possibility that he would hurt Ava .he would never forgive himself.*

Griffon sat up and roughly wiped the trickle of blood from his nose with his arm. He rose and with his head hung in defeat headed back down the dark path of desolation.

Falcon lay still for several more minutes processing everything that had just happened. Slowly, getting up he headed back towards the camp.

What have I done?

The rain had turned into a steady drizzle that played a rhythmic cadence on the leaves of the trees and soaked everyone as thoroughly as if they had purposefully jumped into a hole of water for sport. There was absolutely not a dry thread on Ava. Rain pooled on her eyelashes and trickled down her cheeks in rivulets. Miserable didn't begin to describe how she felt at this moment.

Looking around the campfire at her fellow companions made her feel like she was part of something so much bigger than herself. This wild adventure, though unexpected, filled her with inspiration and purpose.

Out of the corner of her eye she saw someone enter the camp and even though it was fairly dark and the rain impeded her vision, she could tell that it was Falcon. From his disarray, he'd obviously been in some sort of scuffle. She jumped up and ran over to him. He turned and put his head down avoiding eye contact.

"Are you okay?"

No response.

"Falcon, what happened?"

Still he gave no response. It didn't take long for her to realize Griffon was missing. "Where's Griffon?"

When he finally dared to look at her she didn't need him to answer. She immediately headed in the direction in which he had come.

"Ava." He followed. "Ava, wait."

She ignored him and kept walking. He ran to catch up to her grabbing hold of her arm. She spun around to face him and he could tell by the scowl she wore he was done for.

"Where is he Falcon?"

With a sigh of defeat, "He's gone."

"Why?"

"Let's just say it's was in everyone's best interest."

"Who's everyone? I know I didn't get a vote." She looked him up and down. "Tell me your black eye had nothing to do with it."

He didn't dare look at her and he remained silent because he didn't want to lie.

"You promised me we'd stay together no matter what. We haven't even begun and we're already separated." With a derisive snort she pushed past him and continued on.

Falcon ran to catch her and spun her around to face him. "Ava, you can't fix him. His heart is a void it's empty and you will never fill it." He shook her by the shoulders in the hopes of bringing her to her senses. "I just don't want to see you get hurt."

She wrenched herself free and shoved him back with all of the strength she could muster. "Well then, you'd better hope I can find him."

He watched her figure blend in with the darkness. Protective instinct stronger than his free will urged him to follow, but his intuition told him his presence wasn't wanted so he headed back to camp instead.

Ava's entire frame was shaking she was so furious. If one more person tried to decide what was 'in her best interest' without consulting her she was going to explode. In her angry state of mind, she'd walked a good distance before she realized she had seen no sign of Griffon and it was getting rather dark. The only light was cascaded by the almost full moon. She turned in circles looking at her surroundings trying to get her bearings. She could no longer hear or see the camp; her anger slowly replaced with fear.

"GRIFFON." She shouted. "GRIFFON!" Where are you?"

Tears started to sting her eyes. Now was not the time to cry. She kept walking and calling for him with no response. She wasn't sure how much time had elapsed. Feeling totally exhausted, she sunk to her knees and screamed one last heart wrenching time. "GRIFFON!!"

Defeated, she threw back her head and let the rain wash away her tears. She wiped her face and thought she heard something. She tried to hone in through all the noise of the rain. There it was again. She stood and frantically looked around.

"Ava." Very faint, but she knew it wasn't her imagination.

"GRIFFON?"

She heard her name again. She frantically searched around her as they called several times back and forth. Her pulse raced with anticipation. Finally she heard a branch snap and spun in that direction. Again she heard her name. She ran towards the sound of his voice until finally she could discern a figure making its way down the hill. She waited as he painstakingly trudged the rest of the way down. He hit the flat at a dead run and didn't stop until he was directly in front of her.

"Ava?" His voice strangled with emotion.

She didn't know exactly what possessed her or even if she could explain it if she tried but she was so relieved to have found him she reacted by hurling herself into his arms. Clinging to him she buried her face in his neck and let herself absorb his intoxicating scent. His initial reaction was to tense, but it wasn't long before she felt his long arms slide around behind her and jerk her tightly up against his chest.

No words were necessary to express what they were feeling. Ava loosened her arms from around his neck and ran her hands across his shoulders. She leaned back to look at him, her violet eyes filled with longing. His right hand moved up to cup her cheek and his thumb tenderly stroked her chin; then it moved to her bottom lip. When her lips parted all rational thought vanished.

Griffon's mouth captured Ava's with the fury of a storm. She was sweet nectar and he was the parched hummingbird hungrily drinking his fill. For a few moments the world with all of its problems and disappointments vanished.

This kiss was so much more than physical contact between two people. Electricity flowed between them and rejuvenated their spirits; even as rain streamed down their faces, it in no way dampened the raging fire of their souls. Griffon radiated pure masculinity and Ava was simply swept away. Never in all of her lifetime did she ever expect to experience such a moment of pure and potent intimacy.

All too soon, Griffon pulled back to look at her. She glowed with such a devastating radiance that made him feel as if there were at least a hundred drummers beating on his chest with their sticks; her eyes were not only filled with passion but with unwavering faith. Amethyst pools that swallowed him whole to see his reflection, well, you could say it in no way compared to the image he had of himself. He closed his eyes and silently cursed.

Ava was perfectly content where she was at the moment but she could tell by the change in Griffon's composure that it wouldn't last much longer as his entire frame had went rigid and he pulled away. She looked at his face, but he still had his eyes closed and the lips that had just ravished her own went from plump and inviting to a thin white line.

"What's wrong?" She whispered.

He slowly extricated himself and turned around to collect his thoughts. It was very difficult to concentrate in such close proximity this girl, let alone form a rational thought.

"Griffon?"

She could tell he was waging some sort of internal struggle and gave him a minute, but when he was still silent she decided to say something. "It's okay; you don't have to say anything. We can talk later back at camp, or maybe in the morning."

"I'm not going back, Ava." His monotone admission wasn't expected. Now it was her turn to be silent. Had she misheard him?

She was quiet for so long Griffon turned to look at her just to reassure himself that she was in fact there with him and he hadn't concocted their whole encounter in his imagination. Her bottom lip quivered and even though they were concealed by the rain he also knew tears were present.

"I'm sorry, Ava," he reached for her but she stepped back, "don't cry. It's going to be ok."

"Why," an almost whisper, "why are you leaving?"

"I simply must."

"Nothing is ever simple. Is it because of me? Or Falcon?" She couldn't prevent the desperate sob that escaped her lips.

He was broken. When he'd left the Palace so long ago he imagined that he could never feel worse. He'd been mistaken. Was this to be his fate from now on? To leave the ones he loved in order to prevent heartache and yet leaving caused more heartache: a conundrum with no solution.

"You'll be better off in the long run without me, Ava. I promise."

There they were again, those meaningless words. She looked up at him and somehow managed to muster enough will to find her voice, "Keep your empty promises." She turned and ran away. For the first time in as long as she could remember she actually ran toward oblivion instead of away from it.

Chapter 23

Rumbling thunder resonated across the dark overcast sky. The ominous weather paralleled Ava's mood. Tears of sorrow as well as sickening heartache had caused sleep to elude her. Exhausted didn't even begin to describe how she felt. Like a gas gauge on empty she was emotionally drained. She lay still and listened to the surrounding woods as the buzz of activity animated them with life and wondered if she had the will to continue. At least the rain had stopped.

She covered her eyes with her hands and thought about everything she had to face. Griffon was gone. Each time she thought about it she felt ill. And then there was Falcon. She needed to speak with him; she'd been so enraged the night before she'd let her anger do all of the talking. Through the night she rationalized that Falcon had done nothing but try and protect her from the moment they'd met. It was completely unfair to treat him the way she had because in her heart she realized it was his own insecurities that had made him react the way he did; he was trying to protect himself as well. Oh, the irony of reflection. Ava stood and shook out her blankets, time to face the day.

Falcon closely watched Ava all morning and the sight was heartbreaking--the blame was solely his. Last night, he'd paced holes in the ground until she'd returned in tears; he was unsure whether they were caused by finding Griffon or the fact that she had returned alone. He couldn't muster the courage to ask. The only thought that repeatedly ran through his mind was he gave a whole new definition to the word bastard.

That very moment Ava looked up at him with a reserved smile that caused his throat to squeeze. He had to mend whatever he'd broken. Somehow he'd make this up to her. Just then he saw Mace approach her. They spoke momentarily and then the burly soldier headed his way.

"First Commander would like to have a word with you immediately; said it's a matter of great urgency and not to keep him waiting."

Falcon nodded. "Where is he?"

"You'll find him at the front of the camp making preparations to leave.

"Okay, thanks," Falcon said as he continued packing up his supplies.

Like a statue, Mace didn't move.

"Is there something else?" Falcon asked a little bewildered.

"No, just wondering what part of 'immediately' or 'urgent' you may have misunderstood."

"Are you always this uptight?

Mace just grunted.

Falcon closed his bag and hefted it on his shoulder. Putting his hands up in the air he told Mace, "I'm going. I'm going. Don't get all bent out of shape."

As Falcon walked closer to the front of the camp, Viktor and Everett decided to make a rare appearance. Since they'd left the Palace he'd barely seen them. They swarmed around him. "Where have you miscreants been?"

Giving him no response, they flew off in the same direction he was headed. As Falcon neared the front of the camp he could hear the First Commander's booming voice giving various orders in preparations for their departure. As he rounded the last tent being dismantled, he saw the First Commander sitting on one of several logs that had been drug around the camp fire to serve as makeshift benches along with Slye, Cricket, Ava and now the fiends.

"Nice of you to finally join us," the Commander told him slapping him on the back. Although he didn't say anything he hadn't failed to notice Falcon's eye. "It looks like we are just waiting for Griffon.

Falcon looked at Ava, who appeared to have found something suddenly very interesting about her shoe.

"Has anyone seen him?" The Commander asked looking around the assembled group.

"Not since last night." Slye interjected.

The silence seemed to stretch endlessly on.

"Can someone go look for him?"

Since Falcon and Ava were the only two present that knew what had transpired the previous night. He felt responsible to do damage control. "He's gone."

"Gone? Where?"

"I'm not sure." Falcon didn't dare look at Ava. He didn't think he could handle the disappointment he already clearly imagined written on her face.

Being very intuitive, the First Commander detected the strained atmosphere and knew something had occurred. "The business that has triggered his departure must be of crucial importance. We'll continue on with the certainty that our paths will inevitably cross again."

Clearing his throat he stood and started pacing back and forth between them. "Within two days we will arrive at the mountains of Burning Ash where you must embark on an epic mission, to locate the Flame of Consequence." He deliberately made eye contact with each of them. "When we arrive, only three will be allowed entrance into the cave. It was to be Ava, Griffon, and Falcon, but now there will be only two—unless someone wants to volunteer."

"I'll do it."

Everyone turned around in surprise, none more so than Ava, to see Mace leaning on his huge axe and obviously listening to their conversation.

"Are you sure, Mace?" The First Commander shared a knowing look of understanding that expressed more than words possibly could between two battle worn soldiers.

"I'm sure." With that he joined their circle and kneeled down to listen to the rest of the First Commander's instructions.

"The Flame of Consequence is said to be an oracle that will hopefully enlighten us with an explanation of all that has happened. No one can enter unless accompanied by a Royal and a Royal unaccompanied by a Sentinel isn't guaranteed to exit alive."

A collective gasp of shock echoed around the circle.

"What do you mean not guaranteed to make it out alive?" Falcon asked as calmly as he could manage.

"I'm just telling you what I know from history. The only ones allowed entrance are Royals. In my lifetime, no Royal ever visited the Flame of Consequence. Even in times of great need, the Deacon and Deaconess avoided the Flame saying that such power would ultimately come with a high price."

"Then it's too dangerous, there must be another way."

Ava's head jerked up. "No! I said that I would do this and no one is going to stop me."

Falcon looked over at her and all further protests died on his tongue. Deflated, he hung his head and listened as the First Commander continued.

"I don't know how accurate the rest of my information is since it was passed down generation to generation through stories. It was said that there was one sole purpose for the Reach and that was to protect the Flame and its power. They themselves are mysterious creatures typically represented in shadow form. Some people believe that the man who saved your ancestors so long ago was actually the Reach taken to human form and if that is accurate, then they are where your powers originated.

The special relationship between Royals and their Sentinels is the sole reason you have the ability to enter the cave. The Reach will inevitably test your endurance to determine if you are worthy of the knowledge the Flame holds--the same way your ancestors proved themselves in battle so long ago. If they deem you worthy, there shouldn't be any problems, but if they deem you unworthy then there will most likely be conflict. If a Royal has Sentinels present then it can be assumed that they are held in high regard to be gifted with the pledge. It could be a deterrent."

The First Commander could see information overload written all over their faces.

Mace was the first to speak, "Deterrent to what exactly?"

"That's a very good question that I don't have the answer to. It may be physical, mental, emotional trial; or it could possibly be all three. So little is known about what could happen that we are basically going in blind. Regardless, I would prefer to see it all avoided and take no chances. If Ava goes in without Sentinels, the chances are very slim that she won't encounter the demons of her nightmares. I fear she won't escape unscathed."

Falcon looked at Ava sitting across from him. Her defiant gaze was piercing. She was just waiting for him to make another protest. She would be disappointed.

"This pledge you keep talking about, what is it exactly?"

"It is the oath given by a pledgling to a Royal."

"What oath? Is it some kind of ritual?"

The First Commander scratched his jaw, "Well, that's another matter entirely."

"You don't know. Do you?" It was Slye who spoke up this time with wry amusement.

"Not exactly. We were all very close. Gideon, Manford, and I, but I was never a Sentinel. In the grand scheme of things, no ritual was performed. One morning they left the hall as pledglings and later when they returned, they were Sentinels. I asked once how it happened. They told me it was essentially very personal and emotive. So, of course I asked why they did it and they said, 'Intuition.'

Falcon stood and started pacing in agitation. "Let me see if I understand. Basically, we will enter this cave to find the Flame, very likely encounter the Reach, may or may not even obtain the information we seek, and are at the mercy of some ancient bond that supposedly binds Royals to pledglings?"

The First Commander nodded, "That pretty much sums it up."

Falcon walked away from the group angrily shaking his head.

Ava watched as he stopped a few yards away. She could almost hear his internal deliberations. He looked up at the sky momentarily then looked down at the ground shaking his head. He turned and walked back to stand with them once again.

Falcon looked at Ava, "This exceeds every aspect of what we originally asked of you. You are not obligated in any way, so I honestly need to know now after you've heard about all of the imminent danger if you are certain that you want to go through with this?"

"Yes, I need to do this."

Falcon conceded with a nod. "Okay then, let's get moving."

Everyone started bustling to finish preparations. Falcon remained and stared at the ground. He wasn't surprised when the First Commander approached him.

"You worry for the girl."

Falcon looked into the eyes of the only father he'd ever known. He didn't have to reply.

"Of course you do. Now is the time for action. Are you willing to sacrifice your free will and become a Sentinel?" He paused to let Falcon absorb the full weight of that question. "If so you need to be around her as much as possible. If any of this information is valid, hopefully being in close proximity will enlighten you to what needs to be done."

"I fear being around me is not high on her list of priorities right now."

"It doesn't matter, Falcon." The urgent clipped tone surprised Falcon. "Being a Sentinel is more than feelings. You must be willing to lay down your life for this person whether you love them or hate them. Life happens and emotions can overwhelm you as they change in the blink of an eye. The one true constant must be the willingness to understand the duty. Nothing can get in the way of that duty. Do you understand?"

Falcon pinched the bridge of his nose and closed his eyes. Releasing a big sigh he nodded. He reached down to pick up his pack and slung it over his shoulder. As he walked by the First Commander he muttered, "I understand." Then he went off in search of Ava.

No one had seemed to notice that sometime during their discussion, Everett and Viktor, had hastily departed toward the tree line with a covert purpose and still had not returned.

Chapter 24

Falcon didn't catch Ava before the First Commander ordered their departure. As they rode out he saw her riding with Cricket and Slye. He was a little disgusted with this turn of events. He'd had no idea what they were getting themselves into. If he had, he never would have considered dragging Ava into it. If only he could quell the uneasy feeling that caused pin pricks all over his skin.

They rode on for several hours. The forest path they travelled slowly opened up and the trees became fewer and far between. The terrain was rockier and Falcon could see the mountains looming in the distance. The rain had stopped but the sky was still cloaked in dark shrouds of gray. Their progress was hindered by a thin veil of fog that covered the road. The weather impeding their travel was going to make progress slow.

After a while though, they finally caught an unexpected break; the sky lightened considerably and the fog mostly dissipated. When they reached the halfway point the First Commander called halt for a brief respite before travelling on to the base of the mountain where he intended to camp for the night.

Falcon knew this would be his opportunity to approach Ava and try to make amends, if it were even possible. He walked around the sparse area looking for someplace that offered even an ounce of privacy. His efforts were rewarded when he spotted three gigantic stones off to his right. They were easily twice as tall as him and formed a makeshift barricade. That would suffice nicely.

As luck would have it, he spotted Ava headed in the direction of the rocks. Now or never, he headed after her.

"Ava."

She turned at the sound of her name. The sadness reflected in his eyes tortured her.

"Can we talk?"

She shook her head and let him lead her towards the rocks she was already headed for in the hopes of obtaining a moment of solitude.

Once they were obscured from the view of their companions, Falcon started his customary pacing. Ava couldn't prevent a smile at his nervous antics.

Falcon didn't know how to begin to apologize. He was a nervous wreck. If he said the wrong thing it could possibly make matters worse.

"I'm sorry, Falcon." That stopped him dead in his tracks. He spun to look at Ava just to see if he were hearing things. "What?"

"For the other night, I'm sorry. I was upset and the way I spoke to you was out of line."

"Stop, Ava!" Agitated, he ran his hand roughly through his hair. "You have nothing to apologize for. I was the one out of line. I purposefully instigated that fight with Griffon. I knew exactly how to push the right buttons to make him leave." He resumed his pacing.

Ava shoved her hands in her pockets to keep them from shaking as she watched him pace. It wasn't long before he stopped and kicked at the ground with the toe of his shoe.

"Falcon, look at me." She waited until he finally turned to face her. "Griffon is a grown man. He left because he wanted to. Yes, you may have pointed things out to him that you feel guilty about, but in the short time I've known him I don't believe anyone could force him to do anything he didn't want to. Wouldn't you agree?"

It amazed Falcon how much wisdom this girl possessed at her age. It was uncanny how she was able to throw a whole new perspective on things to ease his mind. That very moment he realized she was too good for all of them.

Just then the sun broke through the clouds behind Ava. The brilliant rays of amber bathed her in a radiant glow. Falcon stared at the magnificent sight before him and he felt a searing heat that centered in his very core and eventually inched its way out to his skin. It took his breath away and he gasped for air. His knees buckled and he hit the ground clutching his torso with his arms. White lights swam before his eyes and he was certain he was going to lose consciousness. The blistering pain gradually reduced to a warm ember that brought with it a whole new enlightenment.

Ava knelt down beside Falcon. "What's wrong? Are you okay?" She rubbed his back and smoothed his hair from his forehead. The tormented look on his face was torture. When the episode passed, Falcon looked up into her dewy amethyst eyes. It reminded her of when they first met and the look of complete understanding they had shared. Even though he had been a stranger, the depths of his copper eyes were like a doorway that allowed her to peek into his soul and know she could trust him.

Never breaking eye contact, he reached over and enfolded her slender hands in his own. His markings began to radiate a translucent glow and when he spoke it was in a gruff whisper:

"Ava," he swallowed hard, "By the sweat of my brow, until my last breath my blood, is your blood my life, is your life. I willingly forsake all others. On my honor, I Falcon Reed, pledge my fealty and therefore forfeit my freedom to become protector to you descendant of the royal bloodline."

By the time he finished Ava's hands were also bathed in the luminous glow. Speechless was the only word to describe her at the moment. The heartfelt words he spoke were beyond anything she ever expected to hear from anyone. The conviction and sincerity this man had simply amazed her. Ava wrapped her arms around his neck and hugged him. She felt safe and even though she knew he would be disappointed once he realized she wasn't a Royal, she would let herself savor this moment of adulation. Right now, it was just Ava and Falcon, kneeling on the ground, embracing one another. Everything else would just have to wait.

Two minutes could have passed or two hours for all she knew. This precious moment was suspended in time. When Ava swiped away tears with her left hand something unexpected caught her eye. She gently tugged her sleeve up and there on the inside of her left wrist was what appeared to be a tattoo in the shape of a wing.

She leaned back and rubbed it with her thumb, but it didn't smudge. She licked her thumb and tried again. Still the wing remained.

"What is it?"

With arched brows she looked at him; her mouth opened and then closed. Not knowing how to respond, instead she showed him. With surprise clearly written on his face and regardless of the fact that she herself had just tried to wipe it off, he too rubbed at the mark trying to erase it.

"What does this mean? It has to mean something." The way he spoke quietly to himself worried Ava.

"Falcon," she paused to contemplate the best way to relate her feelings, "what you just promised is by far the most genuine and precious gift," she couldn't contain her exasperation, "but I need you to remember that this is all just theory. Please tell me you understand that."

The genuine pleading in her eyes spoke volumes, but Falcon would not be swayed. Beyond the shadow of a doubt he recognized a miracle when he saw one. He also understood the pressure that Ava was under with so many people certain she was someone she herself didn't even believe.

"Okay, Ava." He couldn't resist rubbing the wing with his thumb in the barest caress. Standing up he offered his outstretched hand to assist her up. She pulled her sleeve back down and while she proceeded to dust off her pants they heard someone calling for them.

Extending his arm, Falcon asked, "Shall we?"

Ava nodded and slipped her arm through his. Arm in arm they made their way back to their group of companions. What could have been an uncomfortable conversation had surprisingly turned into an occasion that they would both remember with heartfelt tenderness.

They rode hard for several more hours, maneuvering through some incredibly tight spots including a couple of treacherous ravines. Ava was very thankful when they exited the last one. The setting sun filled the ravine with spooky shadows that gave the landscape eerie lifelike characteristics. It was almost like the walls were moving and reminded her of her past nightmares.

Not long after exiting the ravine the party came to a halt at the base of a very large and intimidating mountain. This must be it, the Mountains of Burning Ash. Ava craned her neck to examine the craggy gray mountain more closely. The ominous way it loomed over her reminded her of how her seventh period science teacher stared at her over his spectacles. Both were intimidating. It would be no simple task to navigate up the rugged terrain. It was clear the mountain radiated "do not disturb" just great. So, this is where they would proceed into a cave that supposedly contained some sort of oracle that would enlighten them to past, present or future truth; a simple fact that filled Ava with dread and made her feel hollow. This could possibly be the end to the adventure of her life. Disappointment would be rampant once everyone realized she wasn't who they believed her to be...or more like who they hoped her to be.

The weary travelers erected several tents around a single fire. The earlier abundance of rain produced heavy dew and everyone sat close to the fire trying to keep warm and dry.

Food and drink were eventually passed around and with full stomachs they all settled in to get what rest they could.

Through the tent flaps Ava could see how the enormous silver moon cast a luminous glow on the mountain. Tomorrow it would be full and they would be able to locate the entrance that would take them to the Flame of Consequence. She shivered, but it wasn't because of the weather, it was the thought of entering the cave and the possibilities of what they may encounter. Needless to say sleep was elusive as she tossed and turned most of the night. Exhaustion eventually won and she drifted off into a fitful slumber.

Random flashes of three different men plagued her dreams. One was older with long scraggly hair and a scruffy gray beard. He was shackled at the wrists in a dark room. He was too thin; she could see the contour of his rib cage skin on bone. And there were marks all over his body scars? Had he been beaten? Tortured, maybe? He was limp in his chains with his head hung and his face was obscured by shadow.

The second man was much more vivid and clear, like he was standing right in front of her dark complexion, arresting green eyes, and hair dark as coal peppered with gray. This man was more intense. One minute he was staring straight ahead and she felt as if his gaze devoured her. The next minute he appeared to be in some sort of rage. His temper obviously flaring he flung his arms, yelled at someone or something she was unable to see or hear what he was saying, and proceeded to demolish any object within his reach.

The last man was younger. He was clean cut. He had dirty blonde hair and wore some sort of robe or cape. Every time his face appeared she thought she recognized him. Something about him was eerily familiar.

Flash after flash, man after man, it all mixed into a swirling spiral until she was unable to differentiate them. The flashes stopped and everything went dark. Now she could hear something. Loud, chaotic, and menacing then more flashes.

This time she saw Krypts, lots of them. The noise was coming from them. The filthy beings had her completely surrounded and they were cheering in victory. Terror seized her and she choked on the scream she was unable to voice.

Ever so slowly the Krypts started closing in on her. With each step forward she felt like she was in a vice that squeezed the life breath right out of her. They were so close now she could smell their foul stench. There were reaching out for her with grinning snarls of certain victory.

Chapter 25

"Wake up Ava."

She jerked awake, wide eyed with fear. Grabbing her chest and gasping to fill her deprived lungs with oxygen. Kneeling before her was the First Commander wearing a look of genuine concern. In this moment she truly missed her Aunt and Uncle.

"It's okay love, it was just a dream."

A shiver of fear tiptoed over her body and she covered her face with her hands taking a minute to get her frazzled nerves under control.

"Come and sit with me by the fire." The Commander instructed soothingly.

With one last shaky sigh to get her emotions in check, Ava tossed her blanket to the side and slipped on her boots. As she left the tent and headed to the fire she could tell the temperature had dropped significantly. Once seated, the First Commander wrapped a blanket around her shoulders and seated himself on her right. She stared into the flames of orange and gold and watched as the embers floated upward. Cricket appeared with a mug of steaming liquid. She wrapped both of Ava's hands around the mug. Ava looked into her honest eyes and a sense of calm washed over her.

Cricket returned to the other side of the fire and resumed her place by Slye. He lifted his blanket and she snuggled up against him. The sight of two people so genuinely devoted to one another made her feel hollow. Would she ever know what that felt like?

Ava sipped the amber liquid from her mug and savored the warmth as she swallowed. Again she looked at the two sleeping figures across from her. She knew when she'd first met them that there was something special about them, but she was just beginning to see. Cricket had some sort of ability to calm or soothe others. She'd first seen it with Guntha at the inn. She hadn't really understood what happened, but now as she'd been the receiver twice she was beginning to understand. In practicing with Slye she had noticed he moved quick as lightning. It was almost inhuman. She wondered if he had any other tricks up his sleeve.

The First Commander had been sipping from his own mug that was now empty. He stood to get himself a refill and asked Ava if she'd like another as well. She politely declined. He sat back down beside her but still didn't say anything.

Ava emptied her mug and sat it at her feet. She wrapped herself more tightly in her blanket. "This time it wasn't the shadows. There were three men," she paused to remember, "one was old and gray he appeared to be a prisoner and the other man was maybe your age. He seemed dark and so angry."

"Do you remember what he looked like?"

"His hair was black as a crow's feathers, scattered with gray, bronze skin. His eyes I know it was a dream, but it felt like he was looking right at me. Like all I had to do was reach out my hand to touch him." She sighed and leaned her head over on the Commander's massive shoulder. "I've never seen someone with eyes that color green."

"Sounds like you've had your first glimpse of Prime Sovereign Ezekiel. He's got the strangest eyes I've ever seen, almost unearthly. It's quite interesting that you pictured him so clearly when you've never met him. And the third man?"

"You might think I'm crazy, but he looked very familiar. I haven't been able to wrap my head around it; I know I've seen him before. There were Krypts too, lots of them. I was surrounded."

It was quiet except for the occasional snore coming from the tents. Sitting by the fire with the First Commander gave Ava a sense of comfort and she was grateful.

"I need to ask you something Ava and I hope you don't think me too forward. I was riding with Falcon this afternoon and he told me what happened between the two of you. It was very interesting to hear, but I'm more interested in the mark that appeared on your wrist. May I see it?"

She released the blanket and pulled up her sleeve to expose the delicate wing on her left wrist. She extended her arm out so he could see it.

He rubbed the wing with his forefinger. His perplexed expression made her chuckle.

"I must admit that is very unusual indeed. This happened after he pledged himself?"

She shrugged her shoulders. "Honestly, I don't know. Falcon seems to think so." He released her wrist and she wrapped herself back up in her blanket.

"I understand you are still doubtful; hopefully, tomorrow will enlighten us all." T

The next time Ava woke she was still sitting by the fire that had burned to mere coals. The First Commander was nowhere in sight, but the others were up and about. Off in the distance she could see Cricket and Slye with Falcon huddled together in conversation. Mace and two other soldiers were taking down tents. Ava stood and dusted out her blanket. Today was the inevitable day that her companions would have to accept the truth. It saddened her some, but it also would be a relief.

She freshened up the best she could and went in search of the First Commander to find out when they would start up the mountain. She heard a strange sound and followed the noise. She discovered it was the First Commander sharpening his blade.

"Good morning."

"Good morning, love."

She stopped beside him, "When do we head out to find the cave?"

He stopped his stroke on the blade and lifted it to inspect his work. "Within the hour, enough time for everyone to pack up. Falcon, Mace, and I will be the only ones to accompany you up the mountain. The others will be waiting here prepared to depart as soon as we get back. We are very close to our defensive line of control. We could run into Krypts anytime and I would prefer to avoid that at all costs."

Ava swallowed hard, "You and me both."

The First Commander resumed his work and Ava wandered off to find something to eat. Her mind was preoccupied and she didn't see Falcon walking towards her until he was almost directly in front of her. He was carrying a mug and a slice of bread which he offered her when he reached her. She accepted it gratefully.

"Will we be taking the horses?"

"No, we go on foot from here. Due to the terrain, trying to take our mounts any further would be cumbersome."

Although the bread was delicious, she found she'd suddenly lost her appetite. This was it; today the truth would be revealed. She could only hope it wasn't detrimental to the treasured relationships she'd formed with her friends.

The First Commander was giving the order to leave much sooner than Ava expected. She hugged Cricket and Slye and gave Cecil an apple she had saved for him. She mused over the fact she'd become such good friends with the great beast considering her initial reaction when she'd first set eyes on him. She'd been undeniably terrified. It was hard to fathom that reaction now; he was like a big teddy bear. With a final caress on his soft nose she followed the men toward the path that led up the mountain. A feeling of unease settled in her gut that she just couldn't shake; it wasn't right. Although she still wasn't convinced she was a Royal, deep down, she knew she had to find out the truth. As they trekked, she couldn't help but feel this journey was incomplete without Griffon.

The air was still cool and Ava could see their breath as they zigzagged up the mountainside. The rocky path was littered with small pebbles that rolled under her feet and occasionally caused her to lose her footing. On one such occasion, she was sure she would have tumbled back down the mountain if Mace hadn't been there to steady her. So, she started watching the ground in front of her instead of marveling at the majesty of the mountain.

There was no conversation. What was there to say? Everyone was so uncertain about the outcome of this venture. When they topped the second ridge of the enormous mountain Ava nearly ran smack dab into the back of the First Commander, who had unexpectedly stopped his ascent. Ava peered around the man's massive torso to see what was in their path. She blinked just to make sure her eyes weren't playing tricks on her. No it wasn't an illusion. She was transfixed by the billowy mist that surrounded the silhouette of a man standing there at the edge of the cliff; it was Griffon.

Ava swallowed the lump in her throat; an emotion she couldn't label threatened to overwhelm her. She was uncertain if she was nervous or relieved. The First Commander turned to look at her, the question in his eyes was clear. Was this ok with her? She placed her hand on his arm and walked around him. Next was Falcon, who had been leading them up the mountain. She stopped in front of him and took his hand in hers. This unexpected gesture made his head shoot up in surprise to look at her.

"Don't worry." She squeezed his hand and turned to walk towards the mysterious man who left her a conflicted mess of emotions. His face was a blank slate. When she finally stood beside him she felt awkward. Why was he here? Why had he returned? What had changed? The minute of silence seemed to stretch for an eternity. Griffon shifted from one foot to the other. Finally mustering enough courage, he turned to face her.

"I never made it very far." He shook his head from side to side. "Everything seemed upside down. It felt like my body was going in one direction but my stubborn soul stayed behind felt like I was being ripped apart."

Ava absorbed his statement and decided she wouldn't dissect it; what good would it do, "How did you find us?"

He looked towards Falcon and Ava followed his line of sight. Everett and Viktor were with him sharing their own version of the story. "Falcon's fiends found me. Very persistent pests of his, I didn't understand half of what they were trying to tell me, but they made it abundantly clear how dangerous it is for you to attempt this, without me, that is."

Vain much? What could she say that wouldn't destroy his oversized ego? "We were all well aware of the dangers when we started. Besides, Mace has volunteered and we all know that he is more than capable of getting the job done. So, there's nothing for you to worry about. You're off the hook."

He nodded his head in agreement but the look in his eye conveyed an entirely different message.

"Listen very carefully to what I'm about to say," he took a step forward that brought him incredibly close, "I realize apologizing isn't nearly enough to compensate for the hurt I've caused you. It's haunted me since that moment and I would give anything to reverse time, but rest assured I will not make that same mistake again." He moved his hand up to cup her cheek.

At first she kept her gaze averted to his chest but he waited with abundant patience. Giving her time to reign in her jumbled emotions she mustered enough nerve to look up at him and was surprised by what she saw. His face was pale and his lips were clenched together tightly. His eyes were shut and his body clearly tensed up in pain.

"Griffon? What's wrong? Are you alright?"

He didn't respond, but did manage a small nod. To see him in such pain was heartbreaking and it surprised her that he still managed to cup her face with such gentleness. Eventually the moment passed and when Griffon was able to open his eyes and look at her she was flooded with relief. In the brilliant sapphire depths, vibrant life sparkled. He released a huge sigh and the grim set of his lips was replaced with a quirky smile.

"Ava, there's something I need to tell you." He kneeled down on one knee before her and took hold of her hands. Once he was situated he looked up at her and she knew what was about to happen. "Upon the sweat of my brow and until my dying breath, my blood is now your blood my life is now your life. I, Griffon Gray, give my oath to you above all others; I sacrifice my freedom to become Sentinel and protector to you, Ava, descendant of the royal bloodline." With his final words he looked down to see their hands bathed in a radiant blue haze. After it slowly faded Griffon stood, but couldn't bring himself to release her hands just yet.

Ava couldn't believe her ears let alone her eyes. She looked down and turned her right wrist up which low and behold was now adorned with a wing. Nothing made sense, Griffon's brow arched as he quizzically looked down at her wrist. She couldn't resist rubbing her fingers across it just to see if it wiped away. Worth a try anyway, but of course the wing remained. Griffon lifted her wrist and gently placed a kiss on the feather.

"I am sorry. I hope one day you can forgive me." The last thing he expected her to do was rush into his chest and hug him, which is exactly what she did. He reached around and encircled her in his embrace laying his cheek on her head. "I'll take this as a good sign."

Ava smiled and couldn't help but laugh. She whispered thank you into his chest. Several moments passed and then someone cleared their throat breaking the momentary trance Ava was in and reminding her they weren't alone. The two stepped away from each other and turned toward the other men.

The First Commander approached Griffon and gave him a hearty slap on the back. "Now that's my boy." He took Ava's right hand in his and turned it over to inspect the wing. "I've never witnessed the like." He released her hand and headed up the trail.

Mace was next, but he merely grunted as he walked past, which left only Falcon. Tension was thick and clearly neither man knew how to react. Ava didn't know whether to stay or leave. They couldn't stand here forever. Numerous emotions bombarded Falcon at once. Relief that Griffon had returned unharmed, regret that he had returned, jealousy that he too pledged fealty to Ava, and guilt for feeling the latter two. One thing he knew for certain, he couldn't disappoint Ava again; so he would do whatever he had to in order to keep her safe and happy.

When Falcon approached Griffon, Ava held her breath. Relief flooded her when Falcon reached out his arm, "It's good to see you." Perplexed by this reaction it took Griffon a moment to respond by grasping Falcon's arm, "You too, brother." The fact Falcon didn't contradict this statement surprised Griffon. Falcon released his arm and held out his hand to Ava, "Shall we go?"

Ava gifted him with the sweetest smile and Falcon knew in his hear that he'd made the right decision. She took his hand and let him lead her up the trail. They didn't go far before she turned around to look at Griffon. "Coming?" Griffon nodded and grabbing his bow which he had left leaning against a boulder, he jogged after them, wondering for the millionth time why he'd left in the first place.

Chapter 26

The boulder Ava sat on was hard and cold. She nervously rubbed at the wings on her wrists and contemplated how they came to be or what they meant. They magically appeared, but she didn't believe in magic. Did she? Of course a few weeks ago she hadn't believed in fiends either, yet there they were. It was dusk now and the companions had stopped on the next to highest ridge. When the full moon rose they would be able to locate the entrance to the cave. Ava didn't know what to believe. Her mind kept pondering the disappointment she would cause when people realized she was just Ava no one else, no one special. With each passing minute her heart ached more. Just when she didn't think she could stand it anymore the First Commander called for them.

She anxiously stood and walked over to the men. The First Commander pointed at the moon. "Just a minute more and the moon will align with the Earth and the Sun. According to legend, that is when we should be able to see the cave entrance. We need to be prepared since I'm not exactly sure what we are looking for. Time is of the essence, so be ready."

From where they stood on the mountain the oversize moon cast a soft hue of light that gave a romantic glow. It was almost like she could reach out and touch it. Her thoughts were interrupted when the First Commander told them "Now, look now."

She turned frantically and saw the others had already dispersed. She took several steps back and craned her neck to look at the mountain side. Even with the light of the moon, it was difficult to discern shadow from what could potentially be an opening. There was a place on the right upper side that could be a circular entrance, but it didn't look big enough for a body to pass through. She took another step back; not paying attention to where she was there was nothing for her heel to hit but air. The next few seconds seemed to take an eternity to pass. She started flailing her arms to regain her balance but her backward momentum was too great. With eyes as wide as saucers, she looked back and knew without a doubt she was about to fall down a mountain that had taken them all day to climb.

Just when she closed her eyes accepting fate and the fact there was nothing she could do her right foot slipped and propelled her forward. Instead of flying backwards she slid straight down. Somehow she managed to grab hold of a protruding root with her left hand which kept her from tumbling all the way down, but it hurt. She could feel the burn in her biceps. She looked down and could see a plateau. If she let go she would survive the fall, but it wouldn't be without injury. She looked up at the root that she had grabbed. It wouldn't hold her weight much longer, but it was all there was. She placed her feet on the slick rock and pushed up with all her strength and managed to grab the root with her right hand. The jerk caused the root to give and she squealed.

Even though she was dangling in the air she tried to stay calm. She looked down towards the plateau to examine it more carefully. Sharp rocks protruded everywhere. Something in her peripheral vision drew her attention. *It can't be.*

She heard someone shout her name.

"Here, I'm down here."

"Ava?" Falcon looked over the edge and saw her. He lay on his stomach and reached down for her. "Take my hand."

She'd been hanging there so long that her muscles felt weak. She didn't know if she could reach up. "I don't know if I can." As soon as the words escaped her lips her hands grip on the muddy root slipped and produced a shocked gasp from Ava.

When that happened, Falcon's markings began to glow; he managed to reach down and grab the root with his right hand. With pure brute strength he somehow managed to raise the root up enough for her to reach his hand. She released the root and wrapped her other hand around his wrist. The mud on her palms made their grip precarious. He took his right hand and grabbed her forearm. Once he had a good hold he gradually pulled her to safety. He helped her to her feet and squeezed her tightly against his chest; he was going to have to be more vigilant.

She looked up at him with a shaky breath, "That was close." She put her forehead on his chest for a minute more. Again she looked up at him, this time noting how concerned he was. "I'm usually not so graceful," she shakily tried to joke. He chuckled and pulled her tighter against his chest and placed a kiss on her forehead. "I believe I saw the opening to the cave. There's a plateau just below."

"Then we'd best have a closer look." He yelled for the rest of the party to join them. "Ava thinks she may have found the opening."

"Where is it?" The First Commander asked. Falcon walked over to the edge and pointed downward. Griffon walked over to the edge and looked down. He didn't say anything, but Ava knew he didn't need to ask by the way he assessed the mud on her clothes. "Mace, we're gonna need some rope."

It took only a few minutes for the rope to be secured on a tree. Griffon insisted on going first. He propelled down with fluid grace. Ava could hear him scuffle around and then it got very quiet. Just when she was starting to get worried she saw light and heard him call out that it was in fact the entrance. In turns they each climbed down the rope toward the opening, which unfortunately didn't take quite long enough to reach as far as Ava was concerned. In what seemed like a matter of minutes they were standing before the cave that she'd had such terrible nightmares about. Fear took root in her gut and she wasn't sure if she could make her feet move. Falcon and Griffon stood with her, one on each side.

The First Commander stood before them giving final instructions. Most of which she missed. He shook the men's hands and told them to be brave and trust their instincts. Then he stepped in front of her. She was surprised when he embraced her. In a barely audible whisper he told her to keep her heart and mind open. Be brave and trust the men who stood beside her. She managed a nod. Then the men started forward toward the entrance. She couldn't immediately follow; it was as if her feet were planted firmly to the ground by the terror knotted in her chest and she felt the urge to vomit. She clutched her hands to her abdomen and took several deep breaths. Be rational. Be logical. You aren't who they think, so nothing here can hurt you.

Looking up at the men who were now waiting for her she somehow mustered enough courage to put one foot in front of the other. When they had first spotted the entrance, she thought it would be very narrow, but now that they were here it was much wider at the base than she'd expected. The way it was laid within the mountain made sense as to why you could only see it during a full moon. Already in the time it had taken them to climb there, the top of the bolt had already disappeared. It reminded her of the illusion of water on a paved road. Sort of like a mirage.

They stopped momentarily to light two torches. Griffon would lead, followed by Ava and Falcon. As they crossed the threshold, Ava suddenly stopped. Griffon turned to look at her and she turned to look at Falcon. "Look at you, it's amazing." The two men looked at each other. Both of them radiating a soft glow from their markings–Griffon's a cerulean blue and Falcon's a pale gold. Now, they had all witnessed a faint glow when they'd been in previous altercations, but this was the first time all of their markings were ignited when there was no imminent danger. It was truly a sight to behold.

The cave opened up into a large room with an arched ceiling littered with stalactites sparkling like icicles. The air was chilly and damp. The light from the torches skipped across the angular crevices of the rock walls. Ava couldn't decide if it was her eyes playing tricks on her or if the walls were moving. She decided to focus her attention on Griffon's back. The gentle slopes of the floor bed reminded her of a roller coaster. The deeper they went the more stalagmites she noticed, some taller than her. This being her first time in a cave, she tried to soak the many unfamiliar wonders she saw and write them into her memory.

Griffon stopped and Falcon stepped forward to see what was happening. Apparently the tunnel narrowed and forked. As the two debated which route to take, Ava made the mistake of looking back. Not sure what she was expecting to see, it caught her off guard to see nothing except pitch black and endless darkness that left her with a hollow empty feeling. She started to shiver from the cold or her fear, more than likely a combination of both.

The men decided to take the left fork. As far as they could see it appeared to be the easier tunnel to maneuver. As the walls closed in and they were forced to go single file it took everything she had to fight the claustrophobic mentality. The surface of the rock was wet and slick. The dampness gave off the dingy smell of mildew.

A solid hour passed in the narrow tunnel. Just when she thought it would never end the entry way opened up and they were right back where they had started.

"Damn it." Griffon slung down his pack. "It must have looped and led us right back to where we started." Falcon said as he dug through his own pack. He pulled out a bar of soap and put an x at the entrance to that tunnel and the trio headed down the right hand fork which was much more difficult to navigate. It didn't take long before the passageway became so narrow that they had to walk sideways in order to squeeze through several tight spots.

The prickly hair on the back of Ava's neck was on high alert. Unable to shake the feeling that something was watching them she tried to think about anything else. She tried to remember her bedroom and exactly how everything was arranged; the attic and how the paint was cracked in one corner because the ceiling had a leak; her Aunt and Uncle. Nothing could shake the creepy feeling that there were eyes on her.

They encountered several more passages that looped around. If it hadn't been for the marks Falcon placed on the stone they could have endlessly walked in circles. It wasn't until they had eliminated all of the wrong paths that they finally found the correct one. Literally running into a wall they thought was a dead end until Falcon looked up.

"Up we go," he said.

It took a while to maneuver up through the vertical crevice. While some spots were tight, others were wide and forced them to make a sort of human chain to continue their climb. Years of erosion did provide the surface with pitted crevices that served as hand-holds; Mother Nature at her best.

Exhausted from the effort, they decided to take a break at the top of the passageway. Ava could see there was only one tunnel to travel. No more wasted time trying to find the right way to go. It was slanted downhill and had a stream of water running through its center.

A canteen was passed around and once they all caught their breath they headed down the tunnel. The deeper they seemed to go, the cooler the temperature. Ava could almost see her breath and nervously surveyed their surroundings. "What did you say?" She asked her escorts.

"I never said anything." Falcon, who was leading the way advised.

"Me either." Griffon said from behind.

Ava nervously glanced around again. "I swear I heard someone mumbling. It wasn't me was it?"

That earned her a few snickers. "Glad I could amuse you given the circumstances." More snickers.

Maneuvering the tunnel became more difficult. The steep down grade continued and the water was now up to their knees. The current pushed them relentlessly causing a constant battle to stay upright. The roar of the water made it almost impossible to hear one another. Needless to say progress was slow.

Falcon struggled to keep his footing; the rock bed below must have been covered in some form of algae. He felt like he was trying to walk on ice. The pressure of the current hit him in the back of the knees and didn't help the situation. He would lift one foot and almost topple over. They hugged the wall of the tunnel and tried to keep an arm on one another to provide balance.

It seemed the further they went the deeper the water level. Falcon couldn't feel his legs. The water was now waist high. He stopped and looked back at Ava and Griffon. They were both pale and shivering also. "I think we should go back." He yelled so they could hear him over the rushing water. "We don't know how far this goes and the water is getting too deep."

"No, we can't go back. There's no other way." Ava protested.

Griffon, who still had a hold of her right elbow, said, "He's right Ava. We need to go back, we'll find another way."

If she hadn't been so cold she would have protested more, but the way her teeth chattered she couldn't vocalize anything. Falcon moved to turn the rest of the way around. In doing so, he dislodged Ava's footing; the water's swift current drug her under. Griffon tried to pull her back up, but his balance teetered with her full weight. Since he wasn't about to let go, he went under with her.

Falcon watched in horror as the hungry current swallowed his companions. He made a desperate dive to grab them which was a mistake the water swept him away as well. They bobbed along for several minutes; even though the water was waist high Ava still struggled to keep her head above the surface. It was frightening being under the dark water and each time she emerged she frantically tried to catch a glimpse of the reassuring glow from Falcon or Griffon.

Gradually the water level started to recede, the current became less strong and they were able to regain their footing and stand up. Eventually it tapered off altogether.

They were drenched from the water slide; not to mention frigid. They tried to wring some of the water out of their clothes. The torches were doused and if it wasn't for the remarkable glow coming from the men they would be in the dark.

Commme to uuusss!!!

The words echoed off of the stone walls. Ava's head darted in all directions as did her companions. "Did you hear that?" She asked through chattering teeth.

"Yes, but where did it come from?" Falcon pulled the dagger out of his boot. He and Griffon sandwiched Ava between them. Their physical discomfort from the wet clothes and cold air temporarily forgotten.

"Over there." Griffon pointed toward their left.

They made their way towards whatever or whoever it was they heard. They found a tunnel opening. As far as Ava was concerned it was more like a crawl space.

Waaiit!! Don't go Staaaay with us!

This time it sounded like it originated behind them and they all turned. Instead of a singular voice it was more like many voices speaking at once; almost like static feedback. Trying to adjust their vision to the distant darkness, they squinted; what they saw next was surreal. The darkness seemed to be moving forward, reaching out to them with shadowy tentacles.

"My dream "Ava whispered.

Falcon looked at her and back at the shadowy apparition that was undoubtedly headed straight for them.

"Come on Ava, we have to go through." Griffon grabbed her arm and pulled her towards the passageway.

Ava was a statue terrified by the reality of her dream. She could only watch as the darkness weaved its way toward her; all the while whispering for her.

Falcon could see she was transfixed so he placed himself in front of her obscuring the terror behind him. He grabbed her shoulders and looked her in the eye. "Ava, we have to go. Now."

Falcon's expression and urgent tone finally broke the spell and she moved forward. Griffon squatted and started making his way through the passage first. When he was a few feet in Ava followed him. Falcon took one last look behind them just to see if this was some figment of their imagination. Seeing the shadow still weaving closer answered his question and he quickly followed suite behind Ava.

The passage took them at least a half mile deeper into the cave. Every time they would slow down the voices would get louder and they would hastily continue on their way. Ava's hands and knees suffered several scuffs and bruises along the way. She was beginning to believe the tunnel never ended and they would be stuck underground forever. But eventually it did open up and they were able to stand. They all stretched to relieve the strain of their aching back and neck muscles.

"Look there." Ava pointed down the corridor. There was light coming from something. "What do you think it is?"

Falcon shrugged his shoulders. "I don't know, but it can't be worse than what is behind us."

Griffon didn't have a good feeling about this. But then again he hadn't had a good feeling since before they entered the cave. As far as he was concerned they couldn't find the Flame of Consequence soon enough.

He proceeded forward. The tunnel took a bend to the right and then gradually opened wide. He stopped in his tracks.

Ava came to stand beside him and was immediately mesmerized. Soft white light filled the room illuminating a subterranean lake. The peacock blue water was crystal clear and the walls glittered with sparkly white marble all around. The trio stared at the portrait of untouched pure beauty.

Relief washed over them. They were out of the dark and away from the shadows. Falcon and Griffon's glow faded back to their original faint marks and they all began to relax. Ava walked forward to the edge of the water. Kneeling down she looked at her reflection. She stuck the tips of her fingers in the water and watched as the ripples distorted her appearance. "Ouch."

"What is it?" Griffon asked from behind her.

She looked at the tip of her index finger which now had a single drop of blood on it. Then she looked back at the water. There appeared to be some sharp coral where she had stuck her hand. "Nothing, I just pricked my finger. Hmmm, I didn't even see it." As she stood up to turn around, the single drop of blood dripped down into the water and dissolved. Once she turned around she froze. She couldn't muster a scream but the fear in her eyes did more than enough to communicate something was very wrong. They had a pretty good idea what it was too.

Falcon swirled around and Griffon dived and rolled to the side. Neither attempt was successful. Long smoky arms slithered up from the water around them; pinning their arms and legs. Falcon was pivoted up against the wall completely immobilized. The more he struggled the tighter the smoky apparition squeezed.

Griffon was caught by his right ankle. He still struggled to get free but the shadow ruthlessly slung him against the ground like a sack of feed. The sickening sound of impact jarred him from head to toe and rattled his teeth. The smoke swirled around his shoulders and ankles and he was pinned to the ground.

Falcon yelled for her to run, but a shadow quickly wrapped around his neck and squeezed until he was quiet. His face red, he uselessly clawed at the darkness around his neck so he could return the supply of oxygen.

Ava watched in disbelief. In less than a minute, her shadowy nightmares had incapacitated two men she knew to be skilled warriors. What could she possibly do? She didn't have to wonder very long as she was now the primary focus of the smoky shadows that slithered their way toward her.

Chapter 27

She couldn't run; she refused to leave Falcon and Griffon behind so her fear transformed into anger.

"STOP! Let them go!" She shouted, frantically glancing in all directions for help that wasn't there. The shadow specters now had her surrounded. "What do you want?" She turned in circles to try and find the source, but all of the shadows looked the same. She glanced down to see the circle getting smaller, but right before the smoke could touch her someone roared a single command that echoed off the walls and vibrated the entire room.

"Cease!"

Ava spun around to see who had spoken. But there was no one to be seen. She heard a strange sound like wood splitting and tremors shook the ground. When she looked over at the lake the water directly in the center of the lake was churning and starting to bubble. At first the bubbles were fat and lazy, but it wasn't long before it turned into a rapid boil. Water vapor rose above the lake and spread out like a blanket. All of a sudden, the tremors stopped and the bubbling ceased.

Ava spared a glance at her two imprisoned companions. Their eyes were fixated on the lake. She looked back and through the haze was able to see something moving in the water. With deliberate leisure the figure made its way to the shore. Ava's chin fell and she stared star struck at the sight before her. Exiting the water was a reptilian head and as it continued forward water sluiced down its body. No friggin' way!

"A dragon?" Griffon croaked. He looked at Falcon who couldn't respond because of the death grip the shadow still had on his neck.

Exquisite scales in a myriad of blue and green hues covered the beast. It had almost been transparent while it was in the water. Silver horns boldly protruded from its head. Similar yet smaller spikes paraded down its back all the way to its spiked tail. Webbed wings were tucked neatly to each side. Their bat like structure was also tipped in silver. Aquamarine eyes examined them with intense regard; as if to determine the order in which they would be consumed: appetizer, dinner, and dessert. Gills were positioned just below the ears. Something you wouldn't expect to see on a dragon, but since this was her first dragon encounter, who was she to say what was to be expected?

With each breath, a steamy smoke emitted from its nostrils. Ava had no desire to find the source of that smoke.

"The blood, was it yours girl?"

Ava provided no response.

"Stubborn or foolish?" He scrutinized Ava until she started squirming. "Answer my question."

"Release my friends." The bold remark surprised even her. The dragon snorted and blue sparks shot from its mouth.

"Foolish." His attention moved from Ava to Griffon, who was still pinned on the ground. A new shadow wrapped around his midsection several times and started to squeeze. Ava could hear the air escape his lungs and saw the alarm in his eyes. She went to take a step toward him but the shadows violently pushed her back.

"STOP! You're going to kill him. Stop." Still the shadow continued to squeeze the life breath from Griffon like he was a rag doll. "Okay. Yes, I cut my finger in the water, it was my blood."

The shadow stopped squeezing and Griffon coughed and gagged with the effort to fill his lungs. The magnificent creature moved forward with a smooth grace and stopped before Ava whose rage had been fueled by his malicious display. Mustering all of her courage, she stared him dead in the eye, "We've come seeking the Flame of Consequence. We desperately need to find it."

"*As protector of the flame, I know your purpose.*" He lowered his head until their eyes were inches apart. Ava could see her reflection in the dragon's pupils. "*Only those deemed worthy are granted access to its secrets; therefore, you must first pass a test.*"

"A test?"

"*There is purity in your heart, but doubt in your mind.*" He circled around Ava as he continued to speak, drawing a circle with his tail. "*Your companions believe you are of royal blood. I can see in their hearts that they are truly convinced. If it is the Flame of Consequence you desire, then you too must be convinced.*"

"I don't understand." Was she supposed to figure out some sort of riddle? If that was the case then they were all in deep trouble. The dragon inhaled deeply, his massive sides expanding causing a rainbow of reflection from his scales; when he exhaled, a blazing fire burst forth. Unlike normal flames, the fire was like crystalline ice which licked at the circle and ignited the ring. The unusual flames shot up over Ava's head; reflexively she threw up her arms to protect her face from the scorching heat. Falcon and Griffon futilely struggled to free themselves, their bodies bathed in light over Ava's current predicament.

"**My fire will bring no harm to a Royal. Your test,**" he said as he circled around her, "**is to simply exit the circle.**"

"Are you crazy? And if I'm not a Royal?"

"**Then you will burn. Ashes to ashes.**"

Panic seized Ava. What was she going to do? How were they going to get out of this mess?

"**Immobilized by fear, a compromise perhaps?**"

Good grief, why didn't he say that to begin with?

"**Sacrifice,**" he nodded towards her two companions, "**trade their lives for your own.**"

"Never," Ava gasped in disbelief. The dragon approached the circle and stuck its head through the flames. Obviously the fire had no effect on him.

"**You die, they die, or you all die. It matters not.**" The slits of his eyes narrowed as he closely scrutinized her. "**This is the consequence for refusing or failing the test. This is the price that must be paid.**"

For one more moment he stared deeply into her eyes to convey that the choice was hers to make and then removed his head from the circle. Ava closed her eyes, overwhelmed by this strange turn of events, she thought about her Aunt and Uncle. If only they were here now they would know what to do. She tried to form a picture in her mind of the last time she'd seen them. She wanted to remember them happy.

She opened her eyes and took a moment to look at Falcon who was vigorously shaking his head in protest, still unable to speak due to the shadow's death grip on his neck. Griffon was lying with his face pressed against the ground; his pleading eyes begging her not to listen to the beast. Even if they were convinced of her identity, they still didn't want her to take any risks. These two brave men had saved her life so many times since she'd arrived. Now it was her turn to return the favor. She'd made her choice. With steely resolve she ignored their pleas and took a small step forward.

The acrid smell of smoke was like acid in her throat. Fear was foremost in her mind; fear of the pain that would consume her once she entered the flame. It couldn't last long as the emanating heat was too intense. At least there was that. Another step forward, Ava closed her eyes. She heard Griffon's scratchy scream and closed her eyes. Think happy thoughts.

One more step. She felt her hair lift and the sting of the flame like frost bite sear over her skin; incinerating her. Another step, the sweltering, oppressive heat completely consumed her now. There was no oxygen, she couldn't breathe. Won't be long now. One final step, fresh air blasted in her face with the force of a wrecking ball. She had exited the flame. Her eyes flew open and she looked down at her body in disbelief. She whipped her head around to look back at the circle she had just exited in time to see the last flicker of flame extinguish.

"**Congratulations, girl, you have passed.**" And with that the beastly dragon waded back into the lake and disappeared under the water.

Ava looked at Falcon and Griffon who were now regarding her with looks of awe. The shadows still had them pinned.

"**This way Ava.**"

Being addressed by her first name caught her off guard. "How do you know my name?"

"**J am ancient, J am wise.**"

The center of the lake was not only bubbling again but also glowing. Blinding lights spewed up like a geyser and formed a sphere. The sound it made reminded her of a downed electric line snapping and cracking.

"**The Flame will now grant you the knowledge that you seek.**"

This had been their purpose from the start. To lose her resolve now would only deprive them of what they needed most. She had literally just walked through fire so she was certain she could handle whatever came next. With hesitant steps she progressed forward to the water's edge.

Just when she was about to set her foot in the water, lights shot out from the Flame and encircled her in a cocoon. Lifting her off of her feet, the light transported her into the sphere where she floated like a fishing bobber. The beams of light picked up speed and the humming sound rose to a fever pitch. It didn't take long for everything outside of the sphere to become a blur. She could feel electric pulses tingling all over her body. When the noise was so loud she could no longer resist the urge to cover her ears the light exploded and wave after wave shot through her.

Falcon was helpless. All he could do was watch Ava's limp body in the sphere as the light crisscrossed through her. Some Sentinel he turned out to be. He looked down at Griffon and saw the same pain reflected in his eyes, but that didn't provide any consolation.

Each beam of light that shot through Ava brought with it a vision or a memory. She wasn't exactly quite sure. She saw people she didn't recognize; it was all very confusing. There was a couple dressed in regal attire seated in a garden. They were gazing at each other with such intense love that Ava could feel it wrap around her. Next, she saw them in a carriage travelling down a road. They were being escorted by several soldiers. Something terrible happened. The carriage sped up. They were running from something. Krypts. They were everywhere. All of a sudden the carriage crashed onto its side. A different man barreled up on his horse and pulled the couple from the carriage and placed them side by side; they were injured. From out of nowhere a Krypt came and killed the man who had just rescued the couple. A bird's eye view granted Ava a momentary look at the carnage left on the field.

The light beams momentarily stopped and Ava sucked in a breath. She could feel the tears on her cheeks, but she couldn't wipe them away. She felt drained. What had she just seen? Again the beams relentlessly weaved their way through her body. This time she saw two figures standing at the edge of the battle field. Once the battle had ended, one of the figures, a man, moved forward toward the slain couple. He knelt down by the woman and placed his hands on her stomach. Ava could hear him chanting but the words were unfamiliar to her. He gently moved his hands down her stomach; the lower he went the louder his chant became. Now Ava could see the woman was clearly very pregnant. Clover green light spread from the man's hands across the woman's stomach. He continued to slowly move downward and out of nowhere Ava heard the most unexpected sound a baby cry.

The man picked up the infant, wrapped it in his cape, and headed back towards the figure that had remained at the edge of the tree line. Once there he handed the infant to his companion. Like a microscope zooming in on a glass slide, Ava could see the man embrace his companion. When they backed away from one another Ava couldn't believe her eyes. They looked so familiar their appearance reminded her of a younger version of her Aunt and Uncle. They smiled at one another and he protectively placed his arm around the woman and they disappeared into the forest.

Again the beams stopped and Ava had a moment to catch her breath. She felt like these were all pieces to a puzzle that she was expected to put together and she had no clue what the final picture looked like.

More beams started, this time much faster. Ava saw her home. She saw images of her childhood. Different ages, things that she was too young to remember. Time spent with her Aunt and Uncle, but the people she kept seeing were the same two from the battlefield. She could feel their love. It couldn't have been any more evident even if they had been right there with her, holding her and telling her how much they cared. She felt happy and safe, but this wasn't making any sense.

All at once, the angry man from her nightmares appeared, the one the First Commander had called Prime Sovereign Ezekiel. Speeding down a road on horseback, he charged onto the field in which the battle had occurred. He found the slain couple and realized the baby was gone. Clearly furious, he mounted his horse and left. She sees him again opening a door and there shackled in the center of the room is the other man from her dreams. He shouts at the man repeatedly, "Where is the child?" Asking questions, but receiving no answers, the man grabbed a fistful of the prisoner's hair and roughly yanked his head backwards, "Hold your tongue, Manford, it will give me great pleasure wringing the truth from you."

Feeling weak as a kitten, Ava was unsure how much more of this she could handle, but the beams relentlessly continued. Once again she saw the woman who had carried the baby into the forest. This time she looked like she had been beaten. Her face was swollen and bloody. She was kneeling on some sort of platform that a crowd had gathered round. Prime Sovereign Ezekiel circled around her like a buzzard. He kneeled down before her, "Where is he? Is he out there now?"

The woman ignored him, so he stood and shouted to the crowd, "Are you willing to sacrifice your wife?" He throws his arm up in the air and the woman's body violently jerked upward until she was suspended in the air. Ezekiel closed his fist and the woman writhed in pain. He scanned the crowd hoping for some reaction, hoping that this display would get him what he wanted, but the crowd remained silent.

Clearly perturbed Prime Sovereign Ezekiel looked at the woman who was gritting her teeth against the pain. "No matter, rest assured I will find her." Taking one more moment to enjoy the woman's misery he sneered, "One way or another." Lifting his arm higher, he swiftly closed his fist. The woman's back arched and she started to convulse. Red streaks of light shot through her body and disappeared. Just when she thought it was over, the red light exploded out of the woman's body and she fell limp and lifeless to the platform. Grief like Ava had never known enveloped her heart.

Overwhelming truth assaulted Ava's mind. The baby it was her. It was her parents who had died on that battlefield. The light gently floated her back towards the lake's edge and placed her on the cool ground. She was completely limp. Her mind was spinning, information overload. She could hear Griffon and Falcon calling for her but it sounded like they were on opposite ends of a tunnel. All she could manage to do was stare at the shiny ceiling above her. The pull of oblivion that she typically ran away from was tempting her and she had no strength left to fight it. Her only choice was to succumb and so she did.

Chapter 28

As soon as the shadowy scepters released Griffon he was up off the ground and at Ava's side in an instant. She was so pale and her breathing was shallow. He called her name repeatedly and softly patted her cheeks, but it evoked no response. He moved behind her and pulled her head and back up against his chest. Falcon soon joined him and vigorously rubbed her cold hands and pleaded for her to wake up. He exchanged a helpless look with Griffon.

Griffon's trained his eyes on the lake. He stroked her hair and placed his cheek on the top of her head. Closing his eyes he silently pleaded to the Heavens above. A few miserable minutes passed before Ava finally moaned. Both heads shot up and looked at her. Through squinted eyelids she saw several men sway above her, but she logically knew there should be only two. She blinked numerous times trying to bring their faces back into focus. She could hear them asking her questions. Was she okay? Was she hurt? What could they do to help? All legitimate questions, but right at the moment she couldn't provide answers to any of them.

So much information in such a short amount of time; it was a lot to process. As far as she was concerned, she should be dead. No one can walk through fire; it's impossible. Yet here she was. She gradually tried to sit up. She felt like she'd been hit by a train. Finally, able to see clearly, she recognized the concern written on the faces of her companions. Any other time she would have tried to say something to ease their minds; to assure them she was alright, but the truth was she really didn't know.

And then it hit her, "I saw them!" She looked at Falcon who was still kneeled by her side, "I saw my parents. They didn't leave me. Everything I have believed my entire life," a half hiccup, half sob escaped her lips, "was a lie." A tear escaped the corner of her eye.

On unsteady legs, she stood up with the help of both men until she regained her equilibrium. Seeing that she was stable on her feet Falcon released her arm. "What now?"

Ava looked at Griffon. "Your father."

"My father?"
"Manford Gray–he's a prisoner." She watched him closely in order to gauge his reaction. Other than a twitch on his left jaw, as if he gritted his teeth, he somehow managed to keep his composure.

"Where?" Bitterness, long ago buried, simmered to the surface and threatened to boil over with that single word.

"I'm not sure, a cell somewhere. I didn't see anything other than the room he was shackled in." Maybe that hadn't been the best choice of words. She watched as his muscles tensed and his hands clenched into fists. Like a rubber band stretched to the limit he was ready to snap any second.

"Who has him shackled?" The question seemed painful for him.

"According to a description that I gave the First Commander from one of my nightmares, I believe, Ezekiel is the man I saw with him."

Falcon couldn't believe his ears,

"Do you realize what this means? You can prove his innocence. You can stop all of these malicious rumors." He was cut of mid-sentence when Griffon held up his hand. "Just stop! That's not our purpose."

"But Griffon, don't you see?"

"I said drop it." Falcon knew it was a touchy subject so he would let it go for now, but after all of the suffering that he witnessed, he wouldn't forget.

"Was there anything else Ava?"

"Yes, I saw other things, other people. Some I didn't recognize." Ava spared a look at Griffon and could see that he was starting to relax now that they weren't focused on him.

The last thing any of them expected was for the dragon to rocket up from the center of the lake. They whirled around in disbelief. Ava was thrust between Griffon and Falcon. They protectively held one arm out in front of her and they each had a dagger in the other. With each pump of the dragon's massive wings, gusts of air sprinkled them with water. It hovered there momentarily before it finally spoke.

"Such loyalty is rare. Either of these men would willingly sacrifice themselves for you. Am I wrong?"

Neither man disagreed.

"Honorable indeed. Your journey requires great courage. Evil is rampant. Just as you are willing to sacrifice for a noble cause, others are willing to do the same for greed."

He tucked his wings around like a cocoon and started to spin like a top. All of a sudden the spinning stopped and he exploded like a firework into a brilliant smoke that hovered over the lake.

Falcon and Griffon relaxed their stance. Ava stared in awe. There wasn't even time to blink when the smoke burst forward and weaved its way into Ava's chest. Surrounded by light she heard the dragon's voice one last time.

"For a soul so pure, a gift."

She could feel herself falling backwards. Strong arms caught her before she hit the ground. *What was that?* She noticed a soft glow and looked down at her hands. The light was coming from her wrists. She turned them over and stared in disbelief as the marks momentarily fluttered. Distracted by this bizarre occurrence she didn't notice what happened to her companions. Their markings surged, like a light bulb right before it blows.

"Did you feel that?" Falcon looked over at Griffon.

"Yes."

"What was it?"

Shrugging his shoulders and shaking his head, Falcon said "I'm not sure."

Ava held up her wrists to reveal the phenomenon to them. "What do you think this means?" The glow faded and the wings returned to normal.

Griffon held out his hand to help her to her feet. "Let's just get out of here before we encounter any other surprises."

Obviously unable to return the way they came they searched for an alternate route out of the cave. They ended up exiting the cave a plateau higher than the cave entrance, which is where they had originally started before Ava had slipped. Luckily the rope was still tied around the tree and they worked their way back down to the entrance. The First Commander was very surprised to see them come down the rope. He'd assumed they would exit the same way they entered.

Ava could see he was biting at the bit to ask all sorts of questions, but he refrained. Probably had something to do with their bedraggled appearance; he was taking pity on them. He ushered them back down the mountain where camp had been set up and everyone was now gathered around a large fire. Seeing the flames reminded Ava of just how cold she really was.

The First Commander ordered them to get out of their wet clothes and get dried off. He and Mace created a make-shift privacy screen with a couple of blankets and some rope. Ava went first and when she had finished, Cricket handed her a blanket which she wrapped around herself and made her way to the fire. When she was situated Cricket wrapped another blanket around her shoulders. She grasped the ends tightly together and watched as Cricket spread her clothes out to dry.

After a few minutes of staring at the fire she looked over her shoulder and the bottom fell out of her stomach. Griffon was spreading his wet clothes out to dry. He had a blanket wrapped around his waist leaving his entire torso bare. When he was finished he turned and made his way towards the fire. Ava was bewitched; she couldn't take her eyes off of him. He had such a smooth grace, the way his muscles contracted with each movement, the way the blanket drooped precariously low on his hips, the contrast of his tan body against his long pale feet peeping out with each step, but most of all the way his heated gaze bore into her. Her mouth actually watered.

Ava's reaction did not go unnoticed by Griffon. Tension filled the space between them and vibrated with their physical awareness of one another. As he walked toward her he could almost read her thoughts. The way her eyes roamed down his body gave him goose bumps; the potent reaction was the same as if she had physically reached out with her hands and touched him.

The way she made him feel was unlike anything he had ever experienced. He didn't know how much of it had to do with his pledge to be her Sentinel, but right now he didn't care. With deliberate leisure he sauntered towards her wanting her to soak him in as he was soaking her in. Her long wet hair cascaded down her back, her soft, pale skin exposed; a temptation even for a monk. But more than anything it was her eyes that had his attention; they spoke volumes.

When he finally made it over to the fire he sat down beside her. Neither one spoke a word; they just continued to gaze at each other. Their reverie was interrupted when Cricket brought bowls of stew to them. When Ava took her bowl her stomach growled and she smiled sheepishly. Savoring each bite, Ava took her time chewing. No words were spoken between them, but the chemistry was palpable. Griffon left to refill his bowl while Ava was still working on her first. Just as she stuck a plump piece of potato in her mouth and started to chew someone sat down next to her. Figuring Griffon had returned, she continued to eat.

"Must be good." Falcon said. "It might surprise you that Mace fixed this stew. It's an old family recipe."

Ava looked over at Falcon and cursed the water in the cave for making them take their clothes off. He too was wrapped indecently in a blanket; sitting beside her all handsome with his rippling muscles and freshly combed hair; masculinity radiated off of him like micro waves. This was just too much.

"You okay?" he asked. Ava blinked at him. "Ava?"

Finding her tongue she managed to squeak, "The food is good." *The food is good. What is wrong with you?*

Falcon finished with his bowl and sat it down. He looked over at Ava a little worried; after everything that happened in the cave she was acting strange. He watched her take a bite of food and chew it. When she swallowed it drew his attention to her long neck. It was very graceful. As he looked at her neck he noticed that her blanket had slipped off her shoulder. So he stared at the delicate bones and the creamy skin. When his gaze moved to the center of her chest where the blanket was secured he quickly looked away.

Ava knew she couldn't eat another bite. She could feel Falcon's gaze on her. Each place that his eyes lingered felt like hot coals on her skin. She felt him look away and clear his throat. Standing up he walked in front of her. His belly button directly in her line of vision; is it possible to have a beautiful belly button?

Kneeling down in front of her he grabbed the blanket and pulled it back up over her shoulder; the whole time never breaking eye contact. No words were necessary to convey what he was feeling. She could see how much he cared for her. He tucked her hair behind her ear and took both of their bowls.

"Goodnight, Ava, get some rest." She watched him go to the other side of the fire and admired the view the whole way.

Only when Cricket retrieved the bowls from him and he sprawled out on his blanket to try and get some rest was she able to stop staring. Ava spread another blanket on the ground and lay down. She stared at the flames and watched the shadows created by the fire frolic to and fro. Before long she heard low snoring from some of her companions. Even though she was exhausted, she couldn't seem to drift off.

She'd faced the shadows of her nightmares, encountered a dragon, found the Flame of Consequence, walked through fire, and realized she was in fact a descendant of Royal blood. What exactly did that mean anyway? This land was in chaos. It was evident someone wanted the bloodline to be extinct, so she wasn't safe. Would she ever be able to return home? Did she really consider it home now? Technically this is where she was born. What about her Aunt and Uncle? Thinking about her parents filled her with sadness.

When she contemplated the meaning of all she saw in the Flame she felt like she was in an identity crisis. So many things weighed heavily on her mind. Maybe she was over-stimulated. She flopped over on her side. Guilt ate at her conscious; with everything that had occurred she couldn't erase the images of two half naked men from memory. Maybe those sights were permanently branded in her brain.

There was no denying she was attracted to both men, which she found surprising since they were so different. Both men were tall, but where Griffon was sinewy, Falcon was solid and stout. Griffon was more reserved and believed actions spoke louder than words; that would explain all of his pent up emotions. Falcon was carefree and sometimes talked too much. He was a gentleman and tended to carry his military training over into everyday life. Although extremely disciplined he was easy to get along with. He was more of an open book where Griffon tended to be more of a mystery.

She'd shared an electrifying kiss with Griffon. One he clearly hadn't forgotten given his cocky display earlier. Falcon admitted that he had a deep desire to kiss her, but hadn't acted on the impulse. In the back of her mind she couldn't help but wonder about their feelings. Were they genuine? Or did the Sentinel business have them all confused? She'd only been kissed once before. It happened when she was eleven and it didn't last but a split second. So the kiss between her and Griffon had been a whole new shocking experience; it made her toes curl. Would it be the same to kiss Falcon?

What is wrong with you? How can you even be contemplating this right now? Oh yeah, the half-naked exhibition earlier, that's why. Desire is a fickle thing. With that she rolled over turning her back on the confusing temptations lying across from her on the other side of the fire.

Chapter 29

A good night of rest was just what the doctor ordered. Ava woke up feeling rejuvenated; the awkward and uncomfortable situation of the prior evening was temporarily forgotten. By the time she'd made her way over to join the others for breakfast, the First Commander had been brought up to speed on everything that transpired in the cave. He was animated with excitement over their dragon encounter; like a kid at Christmas.

Ava seated herself by Cricket who handed her a piece of bread. The bread was a little chewy but given their circumstance she was grateful to have anything. As she swallowed, a mug appeared in front of her. She wrapped her hand around the handle and looked up to see Falcon's smiling face, so handsome and clean shaven. She stared a little longer than necessary but couldn't help herself. He was truly a sight to behold. Somehow she managed to mutter her thanks. She watched him walk away with Everett and Viktor trailing behind him. She envied him; she could only imagine what it would be like to have such devoted and loyal friends as them.

The First Commander asked several questions about what she had seen in the flame, but no matter how important it may be, Ava couldn't bring herself to divulge the details of what she'd seen concerning her Aunt. Maybe she was in denial or maybe she just hoped she could alter that vision. But the First Commander was a very wise man and could tell she was withholding details. She squirmed under his scrutiny, but she somehow managed to keep her lips sealed. With a grunt he stood and gave the order to break camp and prepare to depart.

Ava made her way over to Cecil who was being saddled by Griffon. How strange to think she was actually glad to be reunited with her giant horse. She ran her hand up and down his neck; a ritual that seemed to calm them both. She'd come to appreciate his unique scent; a mixture of sweet grass and hay. It had a soothing effect on her frayed nerves. Closing her eyes she pictured herself galloping through a field with Cecil. She would give him free reign and let him run as hard and fast as he wanted. Absorbed in her daydream she missed the first shouts of alarm, but when Cecil whinnied and stamped his foot she became aware that something was amiss.

The First Commander was shouting orders left and right. Mace was already armed with a blade in one hand and an axe in the other. The ferocious look on his face was truly frightening. Cricket and Slye were also prepared and armed. Falcon and Griffon were beside her before she'd even comprehended what was happening.

Griffon reached behind him to tuck Ava more securely behind them. Glancing over his shoulder, "No matter what happens, do not separate from us." Falcon looked at him with his mouth set in a grim line. The two were becoming so much easier to read. This particular look was a common understanding that no matter what transpired, they would both die before anything happened to her.

The racket was louder and Ava peeped between the shoulders of the united wall in front of her. A queasy feeling settled in her stomach as she looked at the horde of Krypts headed towards them. There were too many to count. Most were on foot although there were several on animals that looked similar to the Sappacks that had attacked them, only much, much larger.

The First Commander had ordered them into a semi-circle back to back with her somewhat cocooned in the middle. She assumed he was trying to prevent their separation. It seemed the Krypts approached in slow motion, but Ava knew it was just the anticipation of the impending conflict. Both Falcon and Griffon crouched into a fighting stance and although she'd already seen it several times, when their markings ignited she was mesmerized. She felt a nudge on her hand and looked down to see that Falcon had his knife in hand and was reaching it to her; the same knife she had held during their first encounter with the Krypts. With a combination of dread and fear she wrapped her fingers around the metal handle. Even though she'd trained for weeks, she felt inept with the blade in her hands. Could she really kill someone? She didn't think so. But she could protect herself and escape an attacker if necessary.

Watching them approach was like watching the countdown before a race; five, four, three, two, one, and like a bullet everyone rushes forward; in this case more Krypts than she could count in all of their grotesque glory; the noise so loud now she could barely differentiate who it was coming from.

Mace was the first to encounter the monsters. He was a giant of a man and one would think his size would make him slow and clumsy, but that wasn't the case at all. The extraordinary way he wielded his weapons with swift and precise aim was graceful and smooth. He instinctively knew when to dodge and when to advance. He dispatched at least six Krypts before her attention was drawn to the First Commander. He too wore the mask of a fierce warrior and it was obvious he could handle his own. It wasn't a surprise to her that Slye and Cricket stayed close to one another. She was armed with her Shuriken blades and moved with the speed of a rocket, she almost seemed to blur. This was the first time that Ava witnessed Slye's rather unusual talent. Fire exploded in quick bursts all around him. Where exactly was that coming from? The source didn't matter as much as the result. Most of the Krypts riding towards them were forced to dismount the skittish animals that were retreating from the flames.

Within a matter of seconds some of the assailants smashed through the initial line of defense and headed directly toward them. The Krypts had an evident eagerness for bloodshed and Ava knew they were about to have their hands full. Her brave Sentinels never broke form; they remained diligent and immobile in front of her as a force field to shield her from harm. She was overwhelmed by what they were willing to sacrifice on her behalf. She cringed at the sound of clashing metal that broke her trance. Both Sentinels were now engaged in combat with the Krypts. Griffon was up against two while Falcon fended off three; with their adept skills it didn't take long for them to eliminate this initial onslaught. Their numbers were so vast that more were breaking through continually keeping them occupied. The scene before her could have been directly taken from a horror movie.

Ava heard the First Commander shouting orders for everyone to move back. She swerved to her left as the sound of a blood hurdling cry was rent above all of the other noise to the sight off a single Krypt that had flanked them. He was barreling towards her armed with a dirty dagger. She had only a moment to prepare herself; the dagger was in his right hand so she prepared to block. When he was before her he swung his right arm down. Ava threw her left arm up to the side and blocked the blow, but his momentum was so great the force caused her to lose her balance. She tumbled sideways and attempted to roll away. The Krypt grabbed her ankle and roughly jerked her back. She kicked like a bucking bronco hoping that her foot would land a solid blow that would disengage the monster's hold on her leg, but it only seemed to amuse him. He reached down to grab her collar and jerk her upright. That's when it occurred to her she still held the dagger. The ogre towered above her once she was on her feet and the putrid smell of his foul breath encircled her she plunged the blade forward; the sensation of the blade piercing the skin and muscle instantly made her queasy. The Krypt let out an enraged cry of pain and in a fury slung her away. Unable to break her fall, she landed hard on her backside.

Falcon who still had his hands full glanced back to check on Ava just in time to see her fly through the air. Fury unlike any he had ever known consumed him. He immediately headed towards her but the advancing Krypts had other ideas. As they encircled him they laughed knowing that they were about to accomplish their mission. The golden illumination of his marks became blinding, but he knew he wouldn't reach her in time. He looked to his right to see Griffon slice open one Krypt and dismember another. He would only have a moment before more Krypts were on him.

GRIFFON!" he bellowed so he would be heard over the noise.

Griffon's head jerked up as he recognized the pleading in the call for help. He saw Falcon and the intensity of his glow made him squint, but he was able to see that he was pointing at something with his sword. Griffon's line of sight followed the sword to the Krypt advancing on Ava, who was lying on the ground. He would never make it to her in time.

Ava scrambled backwards. The Krypt grabbed the handle of the dagger and slowly removed the blade from his thigh. And she thought she'd been queasy before. He held the dagger, now covered with scarlet, in his hand. Pure rage filled his eyes as he approached her. She attempted to roll onto her hands and knees so she could stand up and run, but with a vicious kick to her shoulder he forced her back over. When she tried to move again he stomped down hard on her midsection knocking the breath from her; black dots swirled before her eyes.

Pinned by his leg she was unable to move her torso so she struck out with her fists trying to land a blow to his injury. Her vain attempt was unsuccessful and only caused him to apply more pressure on her chest. She wouldn't be able to escape. Black dots became more numerous and obscured her vision so she closed her eyes.

Panic seized Griffon as he watched the scene play out before him. He unsheathed his bow and readied an arrow. His aim must be precise; he wouldn't get a second chance, of that much he was certain. He centered himself and pulled back the string. Fatigued from wielding his sword made his biceps burn and his arm wavered; the mere thought of failing Ava was more powerful than any physical weakness. Dipping down into the deepest depths of his reserve, he mustered the will to steady his arm. His vision travelled down the arrow and pinpointed the Krypt. The many distractions coming from the busy hum of their surroundings became obscured. Filled with a renewed confidence, Griffon closed his eyes and released the arrow, with complete faith that it would find its mark.

The crushing weight on Ava's chest abruptly subsided and she sucked in the precious air her lungs had been deprived of; the burn as the oxygen filled her lungs caused her to cough. She felt sharp pain in her torso and hoped she didn't have a broken rib. She was slightly alarmed when strong hands grabbed her arm and jerked her up, but when she saw that it was Falcon who had a hold of her she relaxed. She looked over at the Krypt sprawled on the ground with an arrow protruding through his left eye and knew who to thank later.

Somehow they had managed to hold their own against the Krypts. She looked ahead to see their companions running towards them. Confused by this she looked beyond them and saw the army on the horizon that was headed their way. What could they do against so many?

Griffon rushed up to them. "We have to go, now. There's just too many."

Ava nodded and they turned and started back the way they had come. Every step jarred her sore ribs; the pain was excruciating. The First Commander eventually caught up to them as they were mounting their horses.

"We have to make it around the pass. There is a short cut through the mountain. It will buy us some time at least."

As they headed back in the direction they came Ava saw a figure perched on the cliff above them. She reined Cecil in and he stamped impatiently. He was very eager to outrun the impending danger he sensed behind them. Griffon also pulled back when he saw Ava slow down.

"What's wrong?" She pointed up the mountain. Griffon looked up. The figure raised his arms high in the air straight above his head. He started bringing them down in an arc. The ground under their feet started shaking and Ava looked at Griffon alarmed.

"They're going to bring the mountain down on us."

Griffon slapped Cecil on the rear and kicked his own mount into action. Looking up he saw the figure repeat the gesture of raising his arms and bringing them down in an arc. A strange disturbance in the air between his arms was visible, but he didn't slow down to try and figure out what it was. The third time the figure brought his arms down, rocks started tumbling down the side of the mountain. This wasn't good.

Ava held her breath as they rushed forward. The motion from riding Cecil was more than she could bear; it took all of her strength just to remain seated. She and Griffon had fallen somewhat behind the others when they had briefly stopped. It appeared they had cleared the figure causing the rockslide and were now out of harm's way. It was just the two of them, now riding directly underneath the figure. She glanced back to see that there were several Krypts very close to them. Turning back, Ava swallowed hard as she saw a large boulder rolling down the mountain. What was behind them didn't matter, they would be crushed.

Before the boulder could fall it somehow suspended in mid-air. Ava looked up at the figure to see that one of his arms was now stretched out before him, palm up, and he appeared to be preventing the boulder from falling. As soon as she and Griffon had passed, he slammed his arm down and the boulder smashed into the pass taking with it their pursuers. Rocks and debris continued to fall and pile up completely blocking the road. They were safe for now.

Everyone met on the other side of the mountain to regroup and form a plan. They had managed to escape with minimal injuries; Mace had a nasty gash on his side and Slye took a blow to the head. She could overhear them discussing the identity of the stranger on the mountain.

The First Commander assessed Ava's ribs. "Nothings broken, but I suspect you'll be a little sore." He noticed her nervously rubbing at the blood stains on her sleeve and took her hand in his. "You did well today."

She looked up at him in surprise. "No, I didn't. All of that training and I still couldn't hold my own."

"Now, that's not true. You didn't panic, you kept your wits and you reacted. In just a few weeks of training you remembered the basics and it most likely saved your life." Seeing she wasn't convinced he squeezed her hand and continued, "What you need to realize is that it takes years to hone battle skills, to build up the strength and endurance it takes to fight like a warrior. No one expected you to single handedly take down an opponent; all we hoped for was you to gain the ability to defend yourself. And that's exactly what you did." With a fatherly pat on her hand he left her to her thoughts.

Thank the stars; they had somehow managed to survive to contemplate their next move. The unexpected attack had them all rather frazzled. Ava stood by Cecil as she listened to the First Commander when an odd sensation tingled along her spine. Ever so slowly she turned around. Standing several yards behind her was the unidentified stranger from the mountain. Uncertain on how to react, she stayed immobile, but as if sensing her unease Griffon appeared at her side; seeing the stranger he placed his hand on the hilt of his sword.

Holding his hands up with outstretched arms the figure approached her, "I mean you no harm."

The strange voice got everyone's attention and they all gathered around Ava. He took a couple more steps before he was halted by the First Commander.

Ava was amazed to be looking into the eyes of one of the familiar strangers from her dreams. Part of her was aware that it was indeed a younger version of someone she cherished, but reason made her doubt. *How is this possible?*

"Oh my little dove, I was afraid I wouldn't find you."

The words of endearment only her Uncle Ignacious would use broke down her reserve and she knew that regardless of how illogical it may seem, it was in fact her uncle standing before her; just much different than the last time she had seen him. They simultaneously closed the space between them and embraced each other.

Stepping back she looked up at him. Taking her fingers she outlined the wrinkles just starting to form on his forehead. "How?" "

This is how I looked the day your Aunt and I left this world."

"Where is Aunt Irene?"

Unfortunately, he couldn't hide the look of concern that crossed his features. "There is much for us to discuss."

"Tell me." Ava couldn't disguise the quiver in her voice. She was sure she already knew the answer, but refused to believe it to be true until he confirmed her fears.

With a great sigh he looked off into the distance, clearly avoiding her question; she noticed how he fidgeted with the button on his sleeve. Finally he spoke the words she dreaded to hear. "I'm afraid she's been captured."

The world was spinning around Ava. She knew all too well what this meant. In a rushed panic she started gathering her things.

Ignacious watched as Ava struggled with her belongings. "What is it Ava? What's wrong?"

She paused to look up into the beseeching eyes of the Uncle she could never lie to. She grabbed his arm and led him out of earshot of her companions. "He's going to kill her." Her Uncle's face, like a kaleidoscope, changed through numerous emotions. "Did you hear what I said?"

In a gravelly whisper, "I heard." He swallowed the lump in his throat. "But there's nothing we can do."

Mouth agape she stared at him, "What do you mean there's nothing we can do. We're going to go get her right now."

"We can't Ava. I promised her that I would do everything in my power to keep you safe, out of harm's way."

"Well, I didn't promise and I am going with or without you."

Griffon and Falcon who had been silent bystanders during their exchange shifted uncomfortably. It was Falcon who tried to be the voice of reason. "Ava, you should listen to him. Maybe we can figure something out, have someone else go for your Aunt while you stay here."

She glared at the three men standing before her and shook her head in disbelief. "We're wasting time." She stood and threw her pack over her shoulder. Looking at Griffon she asked, "And what about you?"

Besides one eyebrow slightly lifting his expression didn't change as he simply stated, "I go where you go."

Surprised, but mostly relieved at his response she nodded and headed off to find her horse. In reality she had no idea what she would have done if someone hadn't agreed to accompany her. She had no clue how to find her way or what she would do if she encountered the psychopath who not only had Griffon's father, but now also had her Aunt. Nor did she have a plan on how to rescue them; talk about counting your chickens before they hatch. Ava didn't make it to the horses before her Uncle caught up to her.

"Ava, be reasonable and listen to me. There's so much more you need to know." Aggravated with him she chose to ignore him. He reached to grab her elbow in order to spin her around, but his hand only grasped at air as someone spun him around; in a flash Griffon had his elbow and dagger up against the man's throat.

In his eyes Ava saw a glimpse of utter protectiveness and she had no doubt that he wouldn't hesitate to use his blade on her behalf. She laid her hand on his shoulder yet he didn't break eye contact with her Uncle.

"Griffon, it's okay." Still, he held the blade tightly against her Uncle's neck and in a tone befitting his mood he advised, "Hands off. Understand?"

Uncle Ignacious wanted to smile, but knew it wouldn't be prudent at this exact moment, so he only shook his head in acknowledgement. It appeared Ava had managed to find herself some devoted protectors. Griffon lowered his blade and stepped back so Ava could look at her Uncle.

"So, tell me everything."

Chapter 30

"I am Prime Sovereign Ezekiel's brother."

The sheer force of the flip flop in Ava's stomach staggered her as her Uncle continued his explanation.

"Irene really is your Aunt by blood. She was the sister of the Deaconess. I met Irene one day while she was gathering plants in the forest for medicine. I was immediately smitten. At first she didn't know who I was, but it wasn't long before she recognized me. I thought for sure she would flee and I would never see her again, but what she did surprised me even more. She sat down and talked with me for hours. I didn't exactly have a good reputation. I did many things that I regret and wish I could take back. My brother can be very persuasive." He paused and swallowed hard as if he were trying to endure those bad memories. "The more time I spent with her it was easier to see the error of my ways and change the path I was on. She saved me. So, when I heard of Ezekiel's plan to kill the Royals, I informed her immediately.

We were unable to save your parents, but we were able to save you. Ezekiel is relentless and we knew he would never stop looking for you once he realized you survived. We used a spell to take us through a vortex out of this world to a safe place he wouldn't be able to find you."

"So why am I here now? Why did I come back?"

"I was suspicious when you started having your dreams and described them to me. The magic we used to transport us had only one purpose and that was to preserve the Royal bloodline. So, I sent word back to Wystan, commander at

Eden Divide, a most trusted, comrade to give him the message. We didn't know where you'd be or who you'd encounter. We had to make sure our trusted comrades were forewarned in hopes of keeping you safe."

He wrapped her hand in both of his as he continued, "Your name is Avaline Hope and you are the descendant to the royal bloodline. It was my message that Falcon carried, *'Hence the next full moon hope will find wings.'* You are the only one who can reunite the kingdom against my brother. You are our last hope. If we are unsuccessful, all will be lost."

That certainly wasn't what she expected to hear; nothing like the fate of a kingdom resting on your shoulders to make you feel responsible.

"How could you possibly know this was going to happen?"

He graced her with an all too familiar smile, "It was destined to happen little dove. We just didn't know exactly when. So you see, my brother either wants to use you for something or he wants you dead. Either way he must not succeed. Your Aunt insisted that you be kept out of his reach."

"How was she captured?" Her Uncle cringed at this question and it took him a moment to find his voice.

"It was when we first returned. The vortex deposited us in the middle of a Krypt camp. There were Krypts everywhere. We never could have anticipated there would be so many already. She sacrificed herself so that I could escape; knowing that if my brother got his hands on me he would be able to manipulate me into using my abilities on his behalf."

He exhaled in a deep sigh of defeat. "And that would not be good for anyone concerned."

"We have to save her. Don't you see that? I can't leave her there." Ava released his hand and paced several feet away. Looking at the ground she mumbled, "It's my fault, all of it, and I can't live with that." Not looking back she continued on her way and didn't stop until she was situated on Cecil's back. She turned to Griffon, "Which way?"

With a nod, he gently kicked his mount, "Follow me." They hadn't rode ten feet when Falcon blocked their path with his horse. Ava looked at him but couldn't gauge his mood. The last thing she wanted or needed was a confrontation. Falcon looked at Griffon, "I hope you have a plan." And with that he turned his stallion and headed down the road. Out of the corner of her eye Ava saw the corner of Griffon's mouth curve into a smile; well, there may be hope after all.

It wasn't long before the rest of the horses caught up to them. Uncle Ignacious pulled his horse up alongside Ava's. "I couldn't let you go alone. If your Aunt found out about that I'd be in even more trouble."

Ava gave him a nervous smile, one that didn't reach her heart. All she could see was the flashes of Ezekiel and her Aunt. How he ruthlessly massacred her with no remorse. He was cold and calculated which made him very, very dangerous. She was the only one who knew that her Aunt's life hung in the balance and if they didn't hurry they weren't going to make it in time to save her.

The party stopped on the outskirts of Songston Proper. The First Commander thought it best for the majority of them to stay at the edge of town in case they needed to make a fast getaway. Mace would accompany Ava into town along with her Sentinels. Mace would scout and then find a safe place to serve as lookout in order to alert them to any impending threats.

Falcon and Griffon would stay with Ava and search for her Aunt. Before the three hooded figures entered the streets of Songston Proper they had decided to head for the inn that Falcon's sister owned. Since it was a hub of gossip, he hoped she would be able to alert them to any new faces that had arrived in the last couple of days. If she didn't already know, he was certain she would be able to find out.

The sun had made its descent casting shadows over the streets and adding camouflage for the travelers. They hoped to keep their identities a secret for the time being; no one knew for sure how far Ezekiel would go to get to Ava. It was clear he was motivated and they thought he could possibly even have gone as far as to hire assassins. They could not afford to let their guard down.

Since he was most familiar with the area, Falcon led the way through the various alleys. They didn't run into any of Ezekiel's soldiers or spot any for that matter. He was in Songston Proper of that much they were certain. So why was he keeping such a low profile? Finally reaching the inn they entered through the back entrance that led to the kitchen.

Falcon had just removed his hood when a little girl in a red dress with blonde ringlets bounced into the room singing a merry tune. At first she didn't notice the room's occupants as she skipped to a cupboard and on her tiptoes reached as far as she could toward a candy jar just out of reach. Ava watched the warm smile of familiarity dawn on Falcon's face.

"Does your mother know what you're up to?" Falcon queried.

The little girl gasped and whirled around with a mixed look of surprise and shock on her face for being caught in the act. That was until she saw who had spoken.

"Unca Fawkin" She ran across the room and catapulted into her Uncle's arms. He picked her up and twirled her around laughing at her excitement. She clung to his neck and giggled with delight. Releasing her hold she leaned back in his arms and took his cheeks in her chubby little hands. "Can you stay wif us?"

Falcon set the girl on her feet and kneeled down before her. "For just a little while." They heard footsteps in the hallway a moment before the door swung open.

"Gracie you'd better not be in that candy" The woman's words cut off mid-sentence when she saw who was with her daughter. "Falcon." She rushed toward him and he barely had time to stand before she too threw herself at him.

It gave Ava a warm fuzzy feeling to see how much love this family shared. As the siblings reunited, Ava looked at the kitchen. It was clearly lived in, but also gave a cozy, comfortable vibe. The furniture was roughly made, but had been painted neutral tones that gave it a certain feminine appeal. There walls were adorned with several paintings and the thought crossed Ava's mind that Falcon's sister may have painted them. Finally being released from the bear hug, Falcon motioned toward his companions.

"Penley, you remember Griffon. And this is Ava." With a warm smile and open arms she greeted them, "It's so nice to see you again Griffon. And Ava, it's very nice to meet you. What's mine is yours, that is," Turning back to her brother she grabbed his hand, "can you stay?"

"That's something we should probably discuss without such little ears around."

Familiar with her brother, Penley was able to easily read between the lines. Kneeling down before her daughter she smiled, "Gracie, I need you to go find your father and tell him that I need him in the kitchen. Don't tell him that Uncle Falcon is here, okay. It's a surprise. Can you do that?"

"Yes, Mommy." "Thank you, Gracie. That will earn you a sugar stick."

Walking over to the cupboard she opened the jar and pulled out one of the candy sticks and handed it to her daughter whose eyes were as big as saucers as she took the candy and plopped it in her mouth; happily slurping she exited the kitchen through the squeaky door.

"Please, sit." Penley motioned toward the table in the center of the room. Griffon helped Ava remove her cape and went to hang it on a hook. Ava walked toward the table and Falcon pulled a chair out for her to be seated. Penley retrieved mugs and a pitcher to pour them all drinks and then joined them. Griffon stood with his hip propped against the counter. "How have you been? Please tell me you aren't in some sort of trouble."

Falcon had to chuckle. "Not exactly." He got a funny look on his face. "Why would you think that?"

"Let's just say that you are rather predictable. You visit us three times a year—spring, fall, and winter. You were just here a couple of months ago, so this visit is unexpected."

"I'm not predictable " The raised eyebrow, you know I'm right, there's no need to argue with me look that Penley bestowed on Falcon told him it would be of no use to argue so he chose to ignore it, "We are here looking for someone— Ava's Aunt. Her name is Irene and we have it on good authority that Prime Sovereign Ezekiel has her prisoner somewhere here in Songston Proper. We're hoping you may have some information or heard rumors."

Penley nodded and frowned. "There has been unusual soldier activity in town, but I haven't heard that Ezekiel has been here. Whatever they are up to has been kept hush, hush. But you may find what you need to know tomorrow. They've declared a meeting at town square tomorrow at noon."

Ava turned a pasty white. She knew what would happen at town square. Falcon jumped out of his chair and kneeled before her,

"Ava, what is it?" Griffon joined him. Their obvious concern gave her courage, so she put on her best poker face to divulge the secret she'd kept from them.

"There's something I didn't tell you." But before she could finish the kitchen door swung open and a large man filled the doorway. He briefly paused; surprised to see they had guests. Falcon stood and turned. Walking over to his brother in law he extended his hand, "Hello, Owen." They shook hands and Owen pulled him into an embrace. Soundly thumping Falcon on the back Owen released him. "It's good to see you stranger. Your sister has been worried about you."

Falcon introduced Owen to Griffon and Ava and filled him in on the purpose of their unexpected arrival. Owen stood behind his wife with a hand protectively on her shoulder. "I haven't heard any of the customers talking about Ezekiel. If he's here, he's keeping it under wraps."

Griffon remained vigilant at Ava's side. He was worried about her. He realized that somewhere along the way he had honed in on her expressions and emotions. Oddly, it made him feel even more connected to her.

Ava knew she needed to divulge her vision sooner than later, but keeping it to herself made her feel as if she had some control over it. She sat listlessly and half listened to the conversation taking place. She knew that Owen was gracious enough to do some investigation on their behalf. He would try to obtain information by asking their loyal patrons and other townsfolk that he knew could be trusted.

Once he departed, Penley fixed them a bite to eat and their ears were filled with tall tales from Gracie who was very excited to have visitors. Although Griffon didn't say much, it was impossible to prevent the smiles brought forth by the little girl's antics. Once the plates were cleared Gracie hopped on Falcon's lap and asked him to tell her a story; he of course complied. He told her a familiar tale of adventure that sounded much like a happy version of their cave escapade.

Griffon excused himself and headed outside. Ava sat with her head propped in her hand and watched as the little girl got sleepy in Falcon's arms. It wasn't long before she drifted off and Falcon departed with Penley through the squeaky kitchen door to carry her to bed.

Falcon gently laid Gracie down and placed a kiss on the top of her head. He smoothed her hair back and relished her angelic beauty. Penley looked at her brother and crossed her arms. "Now tell me the rest of the story."

Falcon shook his head. He should have known his sister would know there was more to it. It's as if motherhood turns on some sixth sense. With a sigh he started with how he discovered Ava in the meadow and continued to their appearance at her doorstep. "So you see why it's so important that we find her Aunt. Ava is of Royal blood and I have pledged my life to her. She has the ability to put an end to Ezekiel and all of the evil that has plagued this land. She must succeed, no matter the consequence."

Penley walked forward and hugged her brother. She was older than Falcon and remembered their father well. He had been a Sentinel to the Royals and she knew the sacrifices that entailed. Sixty seconds after she walked into the kitchen she knew that her brother had some sort of attachment to Ava. But she also knew Falcon well and knew that his attachment went much deeper than a pledge of loyalty.

Ava was absorbed in her own worries so she didn't notice that Penley had reentered the kitchen.

"Even under these circumstances, you are still the first girl my brother has ever brought home."

Ava jerked at the sound of Penley's voice beside her. "I'm sorry, what did you say?"

"Falcon, you're the first girl he's ever brought here."

"Oh, it's not like that. He just brought me here to help find my Aunt."

"No doubt my brother is chivalrous, but I know him well and it is clear he has tender feelings for you."

Ava swallowed. She didn't know how much Falcon wanted his sister to know, but she also didn't want her to be misled. She shifted uncomfortably in her chair. "I'm not sure what Falcon has told you."

"About finding you in the middle of nowhere, eternally pledging his loyalty to be your Sentinel, placing all of his hope and faith in a girl he's just met to put an end to Prime Sovereign Ezekiel. Am I missing anything?"

Ava stared agape. "So he filled you in. That's good. Secrets aren't...good." Ava mentally kicked herself because apparently she was the only one withholding information. "Evidently this pledge can intensify feelings, kind of blows things out of proportion."

Penley cocked her head and squinted. "I like you Ava, but I love my brother, so please be conscious of his feelings. I don't want him to get hurt." Ava's blank expression made it obvious she didn't understand, so Penley continued, "I'm talking about Griffon—the man practically consumes you with his eyes."

Ava swallowed. "It's just the pledge."

Penley snickered. "Maybe some of it, but as a fellow woman I can assure you that Griffon is smitten and has been for some time."

They were interrupted by the back door opening. Griffon entered and closed the door behind him. He removed his hood immediately scanning the room to locate Ava. Once their eyes locked the unbearable pressure in his chest subsided. It took all of his willpower to quell the overwhelming urge to stalk across the room and pull her into his embrace so he could kiss her senseless.

Penley stood and leaned down to whisper in Ava's ear, "Consumes you with his eyes."

That remark made Ava blink and break eye contact with Griffon. Penley went to the stove and put on some water to boil.

Falcon entered the kitchen that was now so quiet you could hear a pin drop. "Did I miss something?" Griffon shook his head no and walked over to the sink, rolling up his sleeves he started doing the dishes. Falcon pitched in and they soon had a rhythm.

Ava watched mesmerized until she felt a tug on her sleeve. She looked down to find Gracie's cherub face staring up at her.

"Hello, Gracie. Aren't you supposed to be in bed?" Before Ava could say anything else the little girl climbed into her lap. She stroked Ava's cheek and laid her head on her shoulder. Ava smiled at the simple gesture.

Then Gracie sat up and looked at Ava. "Will you save us Ava?" Her confused expression prompted Gracie to continue, "I's supposed to be sleeping, but I heard Unca Fawkin tell Mommy that you were the one who could save us and stop the mean man." When Ava didn't immediately respond the little girl impatiently asked, "So, will you?"

Ava sighed and tapped the little girl on the nose. "For you Gracie I would try anything." That seemed to be the right answer as Gracie threw her arms around Ava's neck and squeezed, finally releasing her she snuggled back into her lap.

"Ava"

"Yes, Gracie"

"Aren't they beaufal?"

Ava looked at the two men that Gracie referenced and couldn't disagree. "Yes, they certainly are."

Then Penley appeared with her hands on her hips. "Gracie, you are supposed to be in bed young lady."

"I know Mommy. I had to ask Ava if she would save us like you said." Falcon dropped the plate he was washing, splashing water on his shirt.

"I thought you were sleeping."

"Mommy, I pwetended so I could hear Unca Fawkin's story."

Penley shook her finger at her daughter, "That's not nice Gracie. Now, up to bed little one." Gracie gave Ava one last hug and hopped down.

"Night Unca Fawkin, Night Gwiffon." They echoed her goodnight and watched her head back upstairs with her mother.

Chapter 31

Several hours went by before Owen finally returned. Ava anxiously awaited him to get settled and fill them in on any news he may have obtained.

"I'm afraid it's not good news. Prime Sovereign Ezekiel is here. I couldn't find out exactly where. He does have a prisoner—a woman. From what I can tell he wants to use her to draw someone out and I assume that's you Ava. You see, it's a trap."

Ava wasn't surprised to hear this news as the Flame of Consequence had already granted her the knowledge. Falcon sat down beside her. "Ava, you don't seem surprised." She swallowed hard and could barely speak above a whisper, "The Flame of Consequence showed me my Aunt's death. I'm here to prevent that from happening."

"We have to get you out of here Ava. This is a trap, it isn't safe for you." The pleading tone in his voice was heart wrenching.

"I can't leave, I have to try and save her."

Falcon jumped up and stalked across the room. "You stubborn fool, don't you see it's inevitable to happen or the Flame wouldn't have showed it to you. There's nothing you can do. We're leaving." Falcon started gathering their cloaks and bags, but Ava remained seated. He was oblivious to this until he opened the door and turned to see that no one had budged. Evident anger seethed just below the surface ready to explode. "Ava, we're leaving."

Ava realized that this was the angriest she had ever seen Falcon; he was nitro glycerin and the slightest movement could set him off. She nervously squirmed in her chair and somehow managed to squeak, "I can't."

His face contorted with rage as he slammed his fist into the door jam. Turning around his gaze rested on Griffon. "Are you going to let her do this? Let her put herself in harm's way for something that is destined to be?"

Griffon waged his own internal battle, but knew he would stand by Ava, no matter what. "What if it was your family, Falcon? No matter how the odds were stacked against you, you would try and save them."

Like a balloon, Falcon's anger slowly deflated. Griffon was right, if it was his family he would try regardless of the circumstances. He hung up their cloaks and without saying another word walked outside.

Owen and Penley left the kitchen leaving Griffon alone with Ava. She stood with her arms crossed and nervously paced back and forth. She had made several passes when she turned to find Griffon standing directly in her path. She looked up at his face, into the azure blue eyes that did exactly as Penley said consumed her.

"You should have told us, Ava about your Aunt." More than anything she wanted to look away, but his close proximity, the familiar masculine smell that belonged solely to Griffon, the inviting heat that radiated from his chest like a beacon, glued her to the spot.

"I wanted to." She whispered.

"I was afraid that you both would react the way Falcon did and try to keep me from coming."

He nodded his understanding and reached up to place his hands on her shoulders; like a bee to honey she was drawn into his embrace. He rubbed soothing circles on her back and placed his lips against her forehead. The heat of his lips against her skin was searing. Ava's breathing accelerated in sync with Griffon's. She dared to remove her head from his chest and look at him. Desire stared back at her with a force she'd never known. His lips were slightly parted and he ravaged her with his hungry eyes. One hand moved up to cup her face while his other arm possessively tightened around her waist to bring their lips a mere whisper away from one another. Remembering the potency of their first kiss Ava's eyes started to blink closed.

The hinges on the kitchen door squeaked and Griffon hastily separated himself from Ava. The unexpected separation made her balance teeter. Confused she looked up to see Penley had entered the kitchen. Somehow Griffon had positioned himself at the counter tinkering with a towel. Nothing would have seemed amiss if it wasn't for Ava. She wasn't able to recover from such an intimate situation as quickly. The blush that highlighted her cheeks as well as her guilty appearance gave her away.

Ava knew by Penley's expression that she was well aware of what had just transpired, but she never made any remarks. She walked over to pour a glass of water. Griffon mumbled that he was going to find Falcon and went outside. Penley poured her water and left a confused Ava alone in the kitchen. Griffon found Falcon outside in the stable leaning against a pole. He propped himself up on the other side and silently stood with him.

Falcon sighed, "I lost my temper." Griffon smiled and scuffed the ground with his boot. "Is Ava okay? I didn't mean to yell at her."

Griffon cleared his throat and tried to clear his mind of the intimate embrace he'd just shared with Ava. "She's fine. She just wanted to try, you know."

Falcon swallowed hard. "I know." He swallowed again. "Griffon, you know me. This isn't like me to get so emotional. But when Ava's involved, I feel like a volcano. I never know when I'm going to erupt." He held out the hand he'd just punched the wall with to flex it open. His knuckles were red and starting to swell.

Griffon understood all too well. "I know it doesn't make sense, but this is normal. The First Commander did warn us to be prepared for heightened emotions, a stronger connection mentally and physically to the person you pledge to."

"Could it be more acute because we pledged ourselves to a woman?" Falcon didn't know if he should continue, but who else could he discuss this with? No one but Griffon was in the same boat as him. I'm not sure if it's just me, but I have developed an intense attraction to Ava. And the problem is I can't recall whether it started before or after my pledge."

Griffon hated to hear that Falcon was attracted to Ava as well, but he'd already assumed as much. Hearing it out loud just authenticated it. He wouldn't lie to Falcon. "I do have strong feelings for Ava that I believe go beyond protective instinct." The two men silently absorbed the other's admission.

Falcon didn't want this to put them at odds. "So, what do we do?"

Griffon tapped the ground with the toe of his boot. "I honestly have no clue. We're confused, she's confused..." His thoughts trailed off.

Falcon turned to face Griffon. "What I do know is that it is very difficult to decipher which emotions are genuine from the ones generated by our oath and the last thing in the world that I want is for one of us to get hurt."

"I agree, but where does that leave us?" "In a predicament I think it would be best if we took our time trying to figure this out. Let's not make any hasty decisions." Griffon shook his head because it was the logical thing to do but he wasn't sure he would be able to keep his hands to himself.

Ava tip-toed into the kitchen and slumped down at the table. Worried, she'd left to locate her Sentinels and found them in the barn. Listening to them discuss the emotional confusion their oath affected them caused a numbing pain to settle over her. She was like a thirsty dog lapping up their attention and they weren't even sure their feelings were authentic. *Ava, you are such an idiot.*

She rolled her head in her hands, exhausted. They needed time and space to consider their feelings; she needed it to recover from the heartache she now felt. It dawned on her exactly what she needed to do. Time was her only foe. She grabbed her cloak and quietly left the kitchen. She knew that her Aunt would be at the town square at noon. All she had to do was find a way to stop the maniacal mad man who intended to kill her.

The Sentinels were furious when they'd returned to the house to find Ava had left on her own. They had no idea where she was but they certainly had an idea on what she intended to do. Neither put it beyond her to sacrifice herself for her Aunt. Griffon paced back and forth while Falcon got his affairs with his family situated.

"Owen, you have to leave the inn. Take Gracie and Penley to the Palace, you will be safe there. What Ezekiel is trying with Ava's aunt, to draw her out, he could try it with our family if he finds out we have pledged ourselves to her. He will stop at nothing to get what he wants so we need to take precautions."

"Don't worry; I'll get them there safely. You just be careful. From what I hear there are soldiers everywhere. Some of them are disguised." Owen shook his hand and moved out of the way so Penley could crush him in a hug.

"You be careful, Falcon. Do you understand? Don't do something stupid. I know you care about this girl, and I know that your oath says you will forfeit your life for her, but I don't want you to. Do what you have to get everyone out safe. Okay." She stood back and wiped a tear from her cheek.

"I'll do my best." Falcon looked down at Gracie who stood with her head down. He kneeled in front of her and lifted her chin with his finger. "What's the matter Gracie?"

She sniffed loudly, "Ava weft. She said she would save us from the bad man."

Falcon hugged the little girl up tightly. "She left to protect you, Gracie. She gave her word that she would try and stop the bad man and she will keep her promise. My Ava, she's a fighter." He rubbed a curly ringlet between his fingers. "Now, you are going to take a trip with your mother and father to the Palace. So, run along and get your things."

Gracie reluctantly let go and walked over to Griffon. She grabbed his finger in her chubby little hand. "Bye, bye Gwiffon." He squeezed her hand and then she was gone.

Falcon donned his cape and he and Griffon put up their hoods. With one last look at his family, Falcon closed the door and walked outside to search for the stubborn girl who had him torn up inside and out. He didn't know which he would do to her first when he found her, strangle her or kiss her. He only hoped he had an opportunity to find out.

Chapter 32

From where Ava stood she could see the town square below. Just like her vision there was some sort of stage erected in the center. She'd considered every possibility, but couldn't come up with a viable solution to save her Aunt. All she had was a dagger. She would have to be very close to inflict any damage.

The way the stage was set up, it would be completely surrounded by guards leaving no way to easily get through them, which was probably Ezekiel's intention all along. She'd briefly practiced with Cricket at throwing blades, but she hadn't had much success. She primarily missed her target and inadvertently hit something behind it. She couldn't risk throwing the blade and hitting her Aunt by mistake. Maybe she could cause some sort of commotion that would distract the majority of the guards and then find a way to free her Aunt.

By the scurry of activity and people gathering she knew it must be getting close to noon. Oh, how she wished someone was there to help her decide. She heard shouting below. There was a large group of people heading up one of the alley's toward the make shift stage. Most of them were dressed identical in burnt orange uniforms. She assumed she was getting her first glimpse of Ezekiel's minions. As they got closer she could see that the orange color stretched as far as her eye could see and a lump formed in her throat. She didn't stand a chance. The soldiers formed a barricade around the stage.

It seemed like it took an eternity for the parade to stop. Just when it reached the point of ridiculous, the sea of orange parted and the man from her dreams appeared before her in the flesh. It was surreal to be looking down at someone she'd never met before in her life but his face was not that of a stranger. He was appropriately attired in all black and strutted onto the stage with an air of authority. His smooth, aristocratic voice soon filled the square

"You're all probably wondering why I called you here today." He meticulously scanned the crowd with his dark eyes. "Maybe you have heard that there is a traitor in our midst." A collective gasp of shock echoed from the crowd. "I am here to do you all a great service; fish out this traitorous rat and dispose of him."

An orange garbed minion walked up on the stage with a prisoner in tow and roughly shoved her onto the platform. She hit her knees and hung her head. Ava swallowed the bile in her throat and covered her mouth in her hand to prevent herself from calling out. It was her Aunt, just like the vision. Ezekiel placed his arms behind his back and paced around the woman. Once he was in front of her, he kneeled down. "Where is my brother?" he asked coldly.

She looked up at him, her face bloody and swollen. Even in her current predicament she tried her best to keep her back straight and her chin up in defiance. With a weak laugh she told him, "Ignacious will never come back to you. He belongs with me."

This statement spiraled his anger out of control. He stood and shouted toward the crowd, "Are you willing to sacrifice your wife?" He threw his arm up in the air and the woman's body jerked violently upward, suspended in mid-air. Ezekiel slowly started to close his fist and the woman writhed in pain. He manically scanned the crowd hoping to see someone have a reaction, hoping this display would get him what he wanted, but the crowd remained silent. Ava knew she was out of time. She had to do something.

The moment she went to hurl herself into motion, someone grabbed her from behind and she found herself struggling. Frantically she fought the vice like grip. "Stop, Ava, it's me." Hearing Griffon's voice momentarily soothed her and she ceased her struggle. Spinning her around she could see how concerned he was. "What were you thinking taking off on your own? Do you have any idea how worried we were?"

She didn't have time to deal with this right now. "I have to stop him." Again she tried to run toward the stage, but Griffon wrestled her back against his chest.

"No, Ava, don't you see that's exactly what he wants. You'll play right into his hands."

"He wants my Uncle, not me." She frantically twisted against his hold.

"He wants your Uncle in order to find the Royal baby that escaped him before. You run up there and you hand him exactly what he wants on a silver platter."

Ava could hear Ezekiel shouting other comments in the background, but all of her attention was focused on the battered face of her Aunt. It terrified her to think of what she'd been through. Ava was weak and helpless; completely useless to her Aunt. She pleaded and prayed for someone to help her Aunt; to stop the scene that transpired before her. She watched a furious Ezekiel approach her Aunt and closely examine the woman who gritted her teeth against the pain. "No matter, rest assured I will find him." Taking one more moment to enjoy the woman's misery he sneered, "One way or another"

Lifting his arm higher, he swiftly closed his fist. The woman's back arched and she started to convulse. Red streaks of light shot through her body and disappeared. Just when she thought it was over, the red light exploded out of the woman's body and she evaporated in thin air. All that was left of her beloved Aunt were the ashes that rained down on the platform.

Ava screamed just as the crowd erupted in outrage which somehow managed to drown out her cry of agony. She stared at the ashes of her Aunt on the platform, the only mother she'd ever known. Her heart splintered into tiny shards and she was certain she would never be whole again. Griffon spun her around and wrapped her up in his strong embrace, but even the safe haven of his arms could not console her. He whispered comforting words in her ear, told her that it would be okay, promised that she would never be alone, and apologized at least ten times for not being able to stop what had just transpired.

The utter despair she was feeling vibrated through him, directly piercing his core; his soul quaked with her turbulent grief. It was as if he'd just lost his family too. When Griffon smoothed his hand down her back, he could see that Ezekiel's gaze rested on them. He knew the man was suspicious. Guiding Ava by the shoulder he started shoving their way back through the angry crowd.

It was time for them to find Falcon and Mace and leave Songston Proper. There was nothing left there for any of them. He'd navigated them through several alleys when Falcon suddenly appeared at their side. "I was hoping you'd find us soon. I wasn't sure how to get out of here." Falcon had witnessed the death of Ava's Aunt from across the square. He'd seen Griffon struggling with Ava and knew there was nothing they could do. He was so attuned to her he felt her scream of anguish like she had shouted it directly in his ear. She stood so motionless that it worried him.

He reached out for her hand, taking hold of her cold her fingers, "Ava." She looked up at him, the hollow look in her eyes literally caused him physical pain; his gut twisted into a knot. Heartbreak emanated from her; to see the silent tears as they spilled down her pale cheeks, the quiver of her bottom lip, and the slight slump of her shoulders. The vibrant woman whose very existence animated the world around her and brought forth the very best in others through untarnished innocence was now destroyed. Her spirit was broken. More than any battle he'd ever fought, any adversary he'd ever faced, this by far frightened him the most.

Relief flooded Falcon when he saw Mace; the giant of a man was standing with all of their horses saddled and ready to depart. As far as he was concerned they couldn't get away from Songston Proper soon enough. The town was plagued with Ezekiel's men like an infestation. He wanted to get Ava away from this place that he knew would torment her memories for a long time to come. More than anything he wanted to repair what was broken. He knew that it wouldn't happen overnight; although, he would will it to heal if he could.

When they reached the horses Falcon helped Ava mount Cecil and they rode out as quickly and quietly as possible, trying to go unnoticed. When they were past the gates, the horses were nudged to a much quicker pace in order to reach their camp and the rest of their companions.

Grasping Cecil's reins with all of the strength she could muster, Ava tried to concentrate on the task at hand and maintain her seat. She really wasn't a very accomplished rider and it was especially tricky when they were riding so fast. She tried to absorb the horse's warmth and take comfort from him; as if he could sense her unease he whinnied and shook his head.

Their ride back to reunite with the others seemed to take forever. How could she face her Uncle? She had failed and her Aunt was the one who had to pay the price. Why did she even think she had a chance of stopping him? It was all of the Royal mumbo jumbo that everyone was chattering about. She'd actually believed if she was a descendent of some Royal bloodline that she would be able to thwart Ezekiel with some super human power. She'd been a fool. She was plain old inconsequential Ava, just in a different place. Swallowing her self-pity as it were an unpleasant cold medicine Ava dismounted Cecil. Everyone was anxiously awaiting their arrival.

Her Uncle approached, "I was so terrified; you'd been in there entirely too long. I told them we needed to come find you, but..." His sentence trailed off as he scanned the other people who had just arrived, everyone except his wife. Reality slowly sank in the light in his eyes dimmed and he pulled Ava into his embrace.

She was well aware that it was very difficult for him to keep his composure. "I couldn't stop it."

Uncle Ignacious shushed her before she could finish her sentence. In a strangled voice he said, "Oh, my little dove, although I hoped, there was nothing you could possibly do."

She felt his sharp intake of breath that held so much sorrow. She couldn't contain her own agony much longer so she moved a step back.

"Ava, look at me."

Ava looked up into the tear rimmed eyes of her Uncle and she choked back a sob. She covered her mouth with her hand and darted away from everyone. After a few near stumbles she gained her footing and sprinted into the woods with her cape trailing behind her. Tears were blurring her vision and her chest heaved with the exertion of running while crying so hard.

The men watched as she darted away. Her Uncle futilely reached for her hand. Falcon stood in momentary shock and in that single moment of pause, Griffon rushed after her, and he cursed his own hesitation.

Griffon ran after Ava and realized it wouldn't be an easy task to catch up to her. She was running as if the devil himself were chasing after her. She wound her way through the brush in the woods. He refrained from calling out to her. In her current state of mind she wouldn't be happy if she knew he was in pursuit. With his last energy reserve he pushed forward and ran up beside her. He could see she was an emotional mess and didn't immediately notice him. Just a little bit more and he passed her. Spinning around sideways he grabbed her around the waist as she ran by. The startled look on her face was the last thing he saw before they both tumbled backwards. He managed to adjust himself just in time to take the brunt of the fall.

It took Ava a moment to process what had just happened. She placed her hands on the chest below her and pushed up. Sapphire blue eyes filled with compassion were staring at her. She could see her reflection in his pupils and knew she was a snotty, wet mess, but that didn't matter. She sat back on her knees and Griffon pushed himself into a sitting position. Sitting face to face, their chests heaving with the exertion of running so hard, Griffon didn't say a word. He reached up to tuck a strand of wayward hair behind her ear and that was all it took for her composure to crumble. She grabbed her hands to her chest and leaned forward in a heart wrenching sob. Griffon scooted forward and pulled her against his chest. He wrapped his arms around her tightly and squeezed. Grabbing his shirt in a death like grip, she laid her head on his chest and wept. He silently prayed to whoever was listening to ease her pain. He bargained to the Heavens to let him absorb her heartache and endure the suffering in her stead.

Eventually, Ava's grip on his shirt loosened and she scooted closer toward him to wrap her arms around his neck. He ran one hand up her back and tenderly cupped the back of her head. For what seemed like an eternity she whimpered in his neck. She had cried until there were no tears left for her to shed and with each breath trembles racked her body.

Griffon was grateful when exhaustion finally brought sleep to the woman he held in his arms. He stroked her hair and placed a kiss on her forehead. His left leg had fallen asleep, but somehow he managed to stand with Ava cradled in his arms. Looking at her face, now splotchy with puffy eyes, he realized just how vulnerable she was. In that moment he mourned for her lost innocence. The sting of tears pierced his eyes and threatened to spill over as he made his way back toward their camp, where he was certain there were many concerned people waiting impatiently for them.

Chapter 33

The sparkling rays of the morning sun shining through the trees blinded Ava. She blinked several times to focus. There was a slight breeze that rustled the leaves and the shimmering rays were breathtaking as they peeked through. Nature, in all its splendor, was a sight to behold. All was right with the world until the events of the prior day crashed down and brought with it an empty, hollow feeling. She lay immobile and continued to stare at the leaves. Her Aunt was gone forever and she felt responsible.

Could she deal with that? She didn't have a choice. She was certain about one thing; Prime Sovereign Ezekiel would stop at nothing to obtain what he wanted. Killing was as natural to him as talking and came just as easy. She'd thought she'd seen evil in Elzbeth when she'd met Olivia for the first time, but she knew now she'd been very wrong. Evil oozed out of Ezekiel like a volcano after it erupted. What could they do now? She continued to watch the leaves and squinted when they started to look fuzzy.

Out of nowhere a face appeared; simultaneously she was swathed in an invisible veil of solace that seemed to ebb the painful bite of death. Her anguish was still there, she could feel it poking and prodding in a vain attempt to conquer her resolve. In that moment Ava realized her life indeed had a greater purpose; she could make a difference. Not all was lost, after all.

The First Commander was pacing back and forth. Mace sat on a stump sharpening his axe. Griffon leaned up against a tree in deep conversation with Falcon; they both looked very concerned. Everett and Viktor impatiently circled around them. Uncle Ignacious sat talking with Slye and Cricket. Ava slowed her pace as she approached to not only appreciate, but to give thanks for each one of her companions. She'd grown very close to each of them in a very short amount of time. She felt more at home here, more like herself. Although she may not be exactly what they expected or even what they needed, she refused to give up. She would sacrifice everything to help them.

With a sigh she walked forward to join them. As soon as they heard her footsteps they were all on their feet staring at her. She approached her Uncle and gave him a quick hug. When she let go he looked down at her. "Little dove, it's good to see you." He gave a smile, albeit a sad one, but a smile nonetheless.

Falcon appeared beside her with a steaming mug of cider. As he handed it to her he placed his hand over hers and squeezed. There was no masking his emotion. He had genuine concern written all over his face. She thanked him and took a drink of the hot liquid. It burned all of the way down and for once in her life she was grateful for her singed tongue. A reminder that she was very much alive and there was lots of work to be done. Before she looked, she knew Griffon stood on her other side. She glanced over at him and realized she had no idea how she'd made it back to the camp last night. Had he carried her all that way? She wasn't sure why he'd followed her. For a split second, she had been angry when she'd seen him. But it was as if he knew exactly what she needed. Without him, she could have easily given up. Being held in his strong embrace, his warmth seeping into her and penetrating her broken heart had somehow kept her whole.

Everyone was now gathered in a circle looking at her expectantly. It was the First Commander who asked the question that was on everyone's mind. "What do you want to do now?"

Ava was amused by their stunned expressions when she blurted, "We're going to rescue Manford Gray." But none more so than Griffon whose brow arched inquisitively.

The First Commander stammered as he tried to produce a coherent sentence. "What..but..that's impossible."

Ava looked at him a little amused that he seemed flustered by the idea. "Nothing's impossible."

Uncle Ignacious stepped in front of her. "Ava, I cannot allow you to do this."

"I wasn't asking for permission, Uncle. This is part of my destiny." She could see he was visibly upset so she took his hand. "I wasn't able to save Aunt Irene. The Flame of Consequence foretold this; I just didn't want to accept it as truth. But, the Flame also showed me Manford was still alive and being held captive. He's been a prisoner far too long and it is time he had his freedom."

Griffon leaned in towards her ear, "Can I talk to you for a minute?" Ava nodded and the pair walked several feet away from the circle. Griffon took her hands in his. "Ava, you have a big heart, but you don't owe my father anything."

She looked down at their joined hands and opened her fingers to link them through his. She loved the buzz of warmth created when they touched. What could she say to convince this man? "Yesterday, when I was running, I was emotionally lost, but you wouldn't let that happen. Griffon, you followed me and consoled me, even when I didn't think that's what I needed or wanted for that matter."

Griffon didn't like where this was going. He tried his best to stay rational. "Ava, I pledged to protect you. It's not just a job to me. I don't believe I was ever in any danger, unless it was drowning in your tears. What you are suggesting is dangerous. There's a big difference. You saw how many men Ezekiel had at Songston Proper. I guarantee there's at least quadruple at his fortress."

Ava squeezed his hands. "I know the risks. I've seen first-hand what he is capable of. And whether you choose to believe it or not, I am emotionally invested in this." She released his hands and motioned toward their companions. "These people, they are my family. This place is now my home. But it's not just something we need to do, it is my duty to do what is in the best interest of this kingdom whether it is needed or wanted."

Griffon couldn't believe she had the nerve to play the royalty card. They'd spent weeks now trying to convince her she was a Royal. All the while she denied her birthright. Conveniently, she chose to remember it now and use it as persuasion.

Ava looked at Griffon. "This is something we need to do. So..." She looked at him expectantly.

What else could he say but, "I go where you go."

Ava nodded and they rejoined the circle. She looked at Falcon who was standing with his hands behind his back. His face was expressionless, but she needed to be sure he had the opportunity to voice his opinion. "Falcon, is there anything you want to say?"

Falcon considered this for a minute. He shook his head and smirked, "If I had only known Manford was being held captive, I would have tried to free him years ago, even if I had to do it myself or die trying."

It was just like Falcon to be hard on his self for something he wasn't even aware of.

"Well, that settles it. Let's go back to the Palace and figure this out." Ava announced.

As she walked by her Uncle he stopped her. "Little dove, don't do this, its suicide. My brother is just too powerful. Your Aunt wouldn't want you to do this."

Ava nodded. "I know Uncle. I agree with everything you just said, but we have to try." He sighed and she watched his shoulders slump in defeat.

So, it was decided. They mounted their horses and headed back toward the Palace to plan the impossible. Ava was well aware of the challenges that lie ahead of them and knew that the odds were not in their favor. But she could not ignore the burning ember of faith in her core that radiated warmth and pulsated with life. It was a conveyor belt of confidence, continually reassuring her she was on the right path; the path that destiny had laid out before her like a red carpet.

What she needed now more than anything was to find the inner courage to make her brave enough to embrace that destiny with arms wide open.

Epilogue

Manford Gray leaned against the cold wall of his cell with his head hung staring at what was left of the disgusting rag that covered his body; a body that he no longer recognized. Firm muscles once strong and healthy had vanished. He could see the contour of his ribs over a concave stomach. Skin that was once firm and tan had lost elasticity. He was a shell of his former self and the one thing that he wondered was why he couldn't close his eyes and enter oblivion. He no longer had the will to live. He'd wished and prayed for death more times than he would ever care to admit. How he survived the torture of Ezekiel for as long as he had was nothing short of a miracle. It made him wonder if he didn't yet have a higher purpose to serve.

He had long ago become accustomed to the murky, musty hole that had been his prison for so long he'd lost track of time; when he'd acknowledged the fact that the desolate place would be his grave. He'd spent years stripping every detail of his capture to its bare bone; contemplating on whether or not he could have done anything to prevent what had happened. He had mourned the loss of the Royals. Prime Sovereign Ezekiel had relished in providing details of their untimely demise during his many sessions of punishment. But he took even greater pleasure in providing details about his son, Griffon. Years he tormented him with false stories about his son's death. Elaborate detailed stories of an agonizing prolonged death.

He had no tears left to shed by the time he'd caught on. It was Ezekiel's mistake to devise a story about Griffon being captured and now being held a prisoner in the very same dungeon. The explicit details of torment that filled Manford's ears regarding the brutal treatment of his son was sickening.

He had begged for mercy on behalf of his son. He offered to sacrifice himself to replace his son; willing to accept punishment for both of them.

Then one day there was a new guard. He wasn't like the others. There was kindness in his eyes. He tried to bring food that wasn't covered in bugs or filth; water that was clean and didn't smell of urine. On the days Prime Sovereign Ezekiel took it upon himself to pay Manford a visit and teach him a lesson this guard would take pity. He would sneak a soothing balm to cover the lacerations on his beaten body. He was a spark; a spark of light in the darkest chasm; a sprig of hope.

The guard did something that no one dared attempt. He found out the truth. He informed Manford that Griffon was not and had never been a prisoner. He had been raised by the First Commander. When he was older, things had gotten rough because of rumors about his father's betrayal. He eventually left the Palace in search of answers and no one had seen him since.

Manford had been flooded with relief. For the next few weeks, no matter what happened to him he couldn't help but smile. This of course infuriated Ezekiel who of course found a way to put a stop to it. One day when they brought Manford out of his cell for a routine beating, he was shocked to see that the guard was shackled in his place. Manford tried to pretend that he had no connection to the man. But when Ezekiel ordered two of his henchmen to start beating him, Manford couldn't contain his emotion. He yelled at them to stop, to take him instead. But that wasn't Prime Sovereign Ezekiel's style. Instead, he forced Manford to observe as a helpless witness as they beat the guard. Each time that he closed his eyes or looked away they would cease and force him to look.

If he refused, they prolonged the torture. It could have went on for days, but time was lost to him in this place.

It ended with a plea. The guard was beyond saving. He was dying an agonizingly slow death, but he somehow managed to gasp through the pain, "Please...please."

So, Manford did the only thing he could. He looked into the eyes of the only man to show him kindness in over a decade. He watched as the two burly men kicked and stomped him until the spark of life was extinguished. He never even knew his name.

Manford's reverie was interrupted by angry voices storming down the corridor. The voices grew louder and it was only a matter of moments before the door to his cell crashed open with great force. Ezekiel filled the doorway with evident rage. He stalked across the cell and grabbed Manford's neck with almost enough force to break it. Raising his face mere inches from his, spittle reigned across Manford's face as Ezekiel spoke, "Something very interesting transpired today old friend." His eyes filled with disgust as he examined the shell of a man before him. Sniffing the air, Ezekiel crinkled his nose and shoved Manford back down. He then started to pace back and forth in the dim light of the cell.

"Something happened today at my little demonstration. You know the one I told you about?" He stopped pacing to look at Manford, well aware he would not receive a response. "All those years ago, my bastard brother betrayed me over the wiles of a woman, Irene, the sister of the Deaconess. Much to my surprise, they have returned. They were almost unrecognizable—they haven't aged, but luck was not in their favor as I managed to capture his precious love. I do fear the rumors about the Royal bloodline not being extinct may be true."

He resumed his pacing. "My error was underestimating his devotion. He is well aware of my methods of obtaining information form my prisoners. I figured it would only be a matter of hours before he was breaking down my door. So when he didn't show, I began to question Irene. Nothing I did to her would change her story. She just repeated over and over that Ignacious would not show as they had made a vow to one another."

Manford shift his position on the floor. He'd grown quite tired of the present company. "Your point?"

Ezekiel spun and backhanded Manford. He somehow managed to keep himself from hitting the ground. He shook his head to stop the room from spinning and spit out a mouthful of blood.

Ezekiel kneeled down beside him, "My point is that no one saved Irene today. But when I struck the final blow that ended her miserable existence, I noticed a face in the crowd. One I hadn't seen in years." He leaned in closer. "It was your son Manford. It was Griffon."

Manford couldn't prevent the look of surprise and shock that crossed his face. By his present state of annoyance, Manford knew Ezekiel wasn't pulling his leg this time.

Ezekiel stood, "Yes, I thought the news would please you." A cynical smile bloomed as he slowly whispered, "There's only one problem you see. I believe he has what I want."

Manford swallowed hard. "We both know I always get what I want, no matter who gets in the way."

Where he mustered the strength was beyond him, but Manford somehow managed to lunge at Ezekiel. He grabbed a fistful of his collar, "You leave my son alone!"

Two guards were there before he could say anything else and wrestled him loose. Ezekiel straightened his collar and smoothed back his hair. With swift grace he proceeded to use Manford as a punching bag. When Ezekiel's rage was spent, the guards released his arms and he slumped to the floor in a heap. Ezekiel dusted his hands together and turned to leave. "You and your son are already dead; I just haven't killed you yet." The cell door slammed with a loud bang as the exited into the hallway.

Manford rolled over onto his back. Despite the beating he'd just endured, he couldn't suppress the smile that played at the corner of his mouth. Ezekiel was unaware that his news had done the opposite of what he expected. He'd hoped to break his resolve, but instead he reignited his will. Griffon was alive. There was hope after all.

The story of Ava and her Sentinels will continue.

Look for

Caged Hope.

Coming soon…

ISBN-13: 978-0615777665

ISBN-10: 061577766X

June 1, 2013

www.ingramcontent.com/pod-product-compliance
Lightning Source LLC
Chambersburg PA
CBHW061545170626
46811CB00001B/87